THE MAN
IN THE
MICROWAVE
OVEN

ALSO BY SUSAN COX

The Man on the Washing Machine

THE MAN
IN THE
MICROWAVE
OVEN

Susan Cox

MINOTAUR
BOOKS

New York

First published in the United States by Minotaur Books,
an imprint of St. Martin's Publishing Group

THE MAN IN THE MICROWAVE OVEN. Copyright © 2020 by Susan
Cox. All rights reserved. Printed in the United States of
America. For information, address St. Martin's
Publishing Group, 120 Broadway, New York, NY 10271.

www.minotaurbooks.com

Library of Congress Cataloging-in-Publication Data

Names: Cox, Susan (Susan Rosemary), author.
Title: The man in the microwave oven / Susan Cox.
Description: First edition. | New York : Minotaur Books,
    2020. | Series: Theo Bogart mysteries ; 2
Identifiers: LCCN 2020033951 | ISBN 9781250116208
    (hardcover) | ISBN 9781250116215 (ebook)
Subjects: GSAFD: Mystery fiction.
Classification: LCC PS3603.O927 M34 2020 | DDC
    813/.6—dc23
LC record available at https://lccn.loc.gov/2020033951

Our books may be purchased in bulk for promotional,
educational, or business use. Please contact your local
bookseller or the Macmillan Corporate and Premium
Sales Department at 1-800-221-7945, extension 5442, or
by email at MacmillanSpecialMarkets@macmillan.com.

First Edition: 2020

10 9 8 7 6 5 4 3 2 1

THE MAN
IN THE
MICROWAVE
OVEN

CHAPTER ONE

I saw Katrina Dermody alive for the last time before dawn on a dismal San Francisco morning, when she was heading north and I was heading south on Polk Street, near where we both lived. Her new Tesla was supposed to be housed in the garage she was having renovated for it, but the work wasn't finished and she had to park her bright blue baby on the street. I was surprised no one had keyed it or slashed its tires, honestly. One of Katrina's clients was trying to push through planning permission for a fifteen-story condo in our neighborhood of two- and three-story apartment buildings built around a small, private park on the nicer end of Polk. We were usually a friendly little community, but life for the past few months had been enlivened by sign-yielding protests, raucous meetings with the city, and general havoc, most of it Katrina's doing. With her talent for reducing people to white-faced terror or murderous rage, often in the space of a single conversation, Katrina played what my American lover, Ben, called hardball.

Matthew, a homeless, semipermanent resident of our sidewalk, was cowering and mumbling in the corner of a doorway, trying to hide under his duvet, so presumably Katrina had given him both barrels, and not for the first time. When she wasn't happy she applied a scorched earth policy, and everyone in her path got burned. The only way to deal with her was to stand your ground and fight back. Matthew, who could barely put together a lucid sentence or pull on a pair of jeans, wasn't a fighter.

All the same, one of the odd things about Katrina, and there were several, was the occasional flash of generosity that seemed to overtake her, almost like a nervous tic. She shared her apartment—which admittedly would comfortably house the Trapp Family Singers—with an impecunious cousin who was trying to make his way as a freelance journalist, and I'd once seen her handing Matthew some folded-up bills. Another time she'd dropped a blanket on him. There'd been no gentleness—she'd dropped the folded blanket on him as he slept, and he'd jumped awake like a startled deer with the blanket teetering on his head like an ungainly hat. Because of those occasional, clumsy efforts, and because my grandfather once told me that kindness can be learned, I tried, I really did, to stifle my first impulse when I saw her that morning, which was to bare my teeth.

She was about fifty, with expensively streaked blonde hair and a wardrobe of custom-tailored suits. With her phone awkwardly tucked between her ear and her shoulder, she was raging at whoever was on the other end of the call, which was pretty much her default. Even from twenty feet away I heard her snarl, "You'll regret it, you son of a bitch!" I'd heard she shouted similar things at her harried staff, usually when they were working overtime at the weekends, which probably explained why she was always looking for a new paralegal.

I raised a hand to acknowledge her, which she ignored, choosing to add into her phone, "It's criminal fraud, you prick. And the models will be hearing from the FBI. You have til tomorrow to fix it!"

Huh. That sounded like a Fashion Week crisis, but what could be fraudulent there? A padded sock? Knockoff Gucci knickers? As far as I was concerned, five in the morning was too early for that level of intensity. Maybe that was her strategy—get them while they're still half asleep and vulnerable. I yawned and blinked a few times and tried not to listen as she continued to sandblast the poor bastard on the other end of the call, relieved it wasn't me.

She'd built up a hefty enemies list in her thirty years as an attorney, and I had, sadly, added myself to that number by being the public face of the group of residents opposing her client's condo. The other neighborhood association officers managed to keep their heads down more often than not, but I'd spoken out publicly and as the neighborhood association secretary I'd signed many letters to her, to the developer, and to the city. I tried not to think about whether my signature, a falsehood like almost everything about me, was even legal.

Her response had been to serve me with a payback lawsuit. Her live-in cousin had tripped in the doorway of my bath and body shop when he was so drunk he could barely stand, and apparently it was my fault. I was certain she'd bought him the tequila and aimed him in my direction like a poisoned arrow.

She would have been disappointed to know that the lawsuit barely moved the needle on the gauge of my anxieties. Until Katrina dropped hints that morning about exposing me I thought I didn't have the bandwidth to worry about one more thing. I had bigger worries. For one thing, Ben had been in harm's way somewhere overseas for several very long weeks. I'd thought I was getting involved with a social worker, which was true. But he was also a lawyer with a military background, and he was still in the Individual Ready Reserve, which I'd been surprised to learn meant he could be recalled to duty at any time. Things were still new with us, and the time apart wasn't helping. We didn't know a lot about each other, and I'd even suspected him of murder when we met, largely because of the secrets he was keeping. What he didn't know—because I hadn't told him—was that I was living my own secret life in the West Coast home of Out and Proud. The irony wasn't lost on me.

I desperately needed a cup of tea.

My friend, Nat, who was about to reopen the defunct coffee shop down the block, was waiting for me in his doorway, sipping from a paper cup and watching me approach with his usual casual ease. The lettering on the green canvas awning above him used to read *Helga's Coffee and Bakery*, and now it just said *The Coffee*, with the letter "o" fashioned into a coffee bean. I told Nat it showed a sad lack of originality. I'd suggested Shaky Grounds, but he'd just rolled his eyes. But that's cute for a San Francisco coffee shop, right? He didn't agree, so The Coffee it was. The official opening was still a week away, but for the past few mornings he'd had the doors open by six for what our hacker friend Haruto called early adopters. I'd been helping him out for an hour or two, since my own shop didn't open until ten. As a dedicated tea drinker, I was immune to the scent of brewing coffee wafting down the street, but it was a heady lure to a surprising number of our neighbors. Even though we're not an early-rising town on the whole, having coffee ready for the zombie hordes at dawn had already earned Nat promises of eternal devotion and repeat custom. He and his former partner had recently dissolved their high-end jewelry business, and the partner had decamped to New York. I thought it was good riddance, but Nat was still a little bit tender from the breakup.

I took my usual few seconds to admire him. He was tall and slim, with skin the color of milky cocoa and almond-shaped eyes that were usually alight with humor or curiosity, and sometimes both. He'd been my dearest friend even before he made a hobby of saving my life and I thought he was the best-looking man in San Francisco. He was going to pull customers into his coffee shop from up and down the Kinsey Scale like catnip.

("Don't say 'pull,'" he'd said when I teased him. "Why not?" "Never mind; forget I said anythin'.")

Nat was from Texas, and gay, and both subcultures had their hidden vocabs. Even after nearly a year in America, I still had a lot to learn about both, so I didn't always understand what he was talking about. I just tried to internalize the casual lessons he tossed my way, without asking too many questions. In the meantime, he kept sending me lists of old movies to watch so I could improve my American slang. ("These films are all in black and white," I complained. "Yeah, but the slang is still good." "'Java' is current slang for 'coffee'?" "Betcha ass.") I had my doubts, but the movies were good anyway, and I especially liked the ones filmed locally. I even caught a glimpse of my building in one of them, circa 1945, pre–parking meters, when the street was all residential. At first I envied the men in their suits and fedora hats and the women in wide-shouldered suits and lace-up high heels, because I thought life must have been simpler back then, but a world war had just ended, so perhaps not.

Nat tilted his head in Katrina's direction and winked at me, inviting me to join in his fascination with whatever nastiness she was brewing. I was usually his willing coconspirator, but Katrina chose that moment to glance at him. She caught the wink and flushed. He looked back at her innocently and took another sip of his coffee.

Her cheeks slightly pink from left-over anger, she tossed her phone into her car and turned to me, her mouth twisted into a sneer. "Theophania Bogart, or whatever your name is, you know about criminal fraud, am I right?"

I thought I kept control of my expression, but she looked satisfied with the result of the barb. One more sentence could have brought my life here to an end, but she was content to let me flop around with the hook in my mouth, rather than going for the humane kill. She enjoyed seeing her victims squirm. As elegant and composed as ever, she threw her overstuffed briefcase into her car and folded herself into the driver's seat. Nat and I exchanged a glance, his full of curiosity and mine full of guilt, and then Katrina was gone, tires squealing, toward another drama-filled, fourteen-hour workday.

The words "criminal fraud" stayed with me for hours, like a particularly insidious earworm.

CHAPTER TWO

Knowing how she operated, I half expected to hear from Katrina later that day with further details of what she'd discovered about my life and what I'd have to do to prevent her from exposing me. I spent a good deal of the day trying to decide how I'd deal with the threat—tell her to publish and be damned? Make a preemptive strike and tell my friends the truth? I even briefly considered murder—not personally, but in a Henry II sort of way, wishing someone else would murder Thomas à Becket for me.

But I didn't hear from her and nothing had changed by the next morning, even the weather, which was again raw and damp and dripping with fog. All summer, while tourists shiver in their shorts, hastily buying sweatshirts with *Property of Alcatraz* printed on the front, natives pull on their gloves and wooly hats and wait smugly for the sunny days of September and October. I'd lived here long enough to be unsurprised by the weather and, being English, I was accustomed to cold. I just pulled my hoodie closed and yawned as I drew close to home.

When Ben was away I'd taken to wandering the city instead of lying in bed staring at the ceiling. Unlike New York, which we're told never sleeps, most of San Francisco dozed away the late night and early morning hours, and

I'd found the streets had a special charm when they were quiet and empty of traffic. The foghorn on the Golden Gate Bridge moaned on foggy nights, like a watchman chanting "All's well," while the city slept. The occasional person I met on my walks gave me a sharp, city dweller's once-over before returning to whatever business they were conducting at four a.m. Someone might trot briskly down a set of outdoor steps, clang the security gate closed, and hustle away into the shadows, or a streetwalker would give me a sisterly chin lift, but by and large I felt as if had the city to myself.

By five a.m. I'd been out for a couple of hours and was heading back down Polk Street to help Nat get coffee brewing and scones baked in time to open The Coffee. I raised a hand in greeting when I saw Katrina's car at the curb with its headlights on, partly because I was trying to be a grown-up and partly because I could hear my grandfather's advice in my head: "Courtesy costs nothing, Theophania, and often pays dividends." He'd disapproved of most of my life choices since I was seventeen, but he loved me and I loved him back, even if neither of us was very verbal about it. He'd even transplanted himself here, unasked, when I couldn't bear my grim notoriety in England for one more day.

Katrina ignored me, which, after the previous day's snarl-fest, was almost a relief, but I dipped down to look into her car, so she couldn't pretend she hadn't seen me. Thanks to the streetlight above us, I could see a reddish splatter covering much of the side window. What remained of her head was resting against the headrest as if she were napping, except her pale blue eyes stared at me, wide and unblinking, from the other side of the glass. I almost fell over in my haste to back away, and hit my head on the streetlight pole.

Still holding my head, I looked frantically up and down the street. As I expected, no lights showed in The Coffee or in the other street-level storefronts in both directions. A shopping cart half filled with cans and bottles and a grubby duvet was parked in a nearby doorway, but there was no sign of Matthew, who usually spent three or four nights a week there. Only a couple of distant upper windows were showing lights, and none was within shouting range. I was alone, which meant there was no one to share, or take over, what was obviously going to be a grisly duty.

It took me a few ineffective tugs to understand that the driver's door was locked, to run around the car, pull open the passenger door, and scramble inside onto my knees. Of course she was dead—half her head was missing—but I ridiculously felt for a pulse in her neck anyway. Her skin was cold. I swallowed the bile in my mouth when she fell stiffly against the window with a horrible little squelch.

The car was so quiet I wasn't sure it was turned on, but its headlights were still blazing, so power had to be coming from somewhere. Katrina had explained to everyone who would listen that the car turned itself on when she sat in the driver's seat. I didn't know if it had an override switch or where to find it, anyway, so I moved cautiously, afraid it might throw itself into gear—or whatever electric cars do—and run off with us. I looked around on the floor and between the seats, in a confused effort to understand what had happened. Her briefcase was open and tipped over on the back seat, its papers scattered there and spilling onto the floor, but I couldn't see a gun, and in fairness it was hard to imagine Katrina taking her own life. It was murder, then, and I was probably obliterating clues by the dozen squirming around on the passenger seat. Somehow resisting a strong urge to just walk away and leave this nightmare for someone else to deal with, I climbed out of the car and pulled out my phone.

Katrina was unpleasant and bellicose and she bore a mean grudge, and instead of feeling sympathy for her unpleasant end, I was struggling with a complicated brew of horror, resentment, and relief. As it turned out, I wasn't alone. Some of us were just surprised it hadn't happened sooner.

CHAPTER THREE

Good morning Ms. . . . Bogart."

I managed not to groan aloud as I turned, but it was a close run thing. "Hello, Inspector."

In San Francisco, police detectives are known as Inspectors, which makes them sound like characters in a British crime drama. In the same mystifying way, a full-floor apartment here is called a flat, as if we were in Oxford or Liverpool. Inspector Lichlyter was the only person here besides my grandfather who knew who I was, and she knew because she was a good detective. She'd been the lead investigator the last time (but unfortunately not the first time) I'd been involved in a murder.

I think she was in her early forties although her face was deeply lined, making her look older. She was wearing the same red jacket I remembered and carrying the same heavy Coach shoulder bag. I had never thought about it before, but TV detectives don't carry handbags, and I wondered why she bothered. Her shaded glasses, which she wore even at night and even on foggy mornings, were a disguise for her mismatched eyes; one was brown, the other was blue, and without her glasses her expression projected a sort of all-purpose skepticism. I didn't dislike her; I even liked her a little. I just didn't expect to see her again so soon after all the turmoil of a few months ago.

She always called me "Ms. . . . Bogart," with that little hesitation. It was a hint of humor, or maybe just sarcasm, in a woman who otherwise appeared to have no sense of humor.

It had been more than an hour since I'd found Katrina's body, and I was shivering in the blanket someone had wrapped around my shoulders. Inspector Lichlyter headed in my direction, leaving behind a small group of uniformed officers who dispersed in several directions, looking motivated.

"Tell me what happened here, Ms. . . . Bogart," she said. She rooted about in her bag and came up with a shabby notebook. Maybe that's why she carried the bag. Like the others I'd seen her use, its wire binding was bent and coiling into nowhere at one end. Various cameras and tablets were being used by others to record the scene, but she liked and used the notebook as a prop. Sometimes, as I knew from personal experience, she abandoned it casually and strategically, to see if the contents prompted any ill-advised reaction. She rummaged again and came up with a cheap ballpoint pen, clicking it against the notebook's cover and scribbling impatiently until ink emerged. She looked up at me.

"I've already told him." I nodded at one of the uniformed officers. She just waited and I took a deep breath. "Right. I was walking along the street here—"

"Why?"

"Sorry?"

"It's cold, it's still dark, and none of the stores are open. Why were you out here on the street?"

"Not that it's any of—"

She frowned

"Right. In a murder investigation, everything is your business." I bit the inside of my cheek, irritated at the need to lay myself bare for her, and finally said, "I couldn't sleep. I walked down to the Embarcadero, then up to Russian Hill, back down California, and turned onto Polk."

"That's a lot of walking. You were out for how long?"

"I'm not sure. I wasn't in a hurry. Two hours, a little more."

"And you did or didn't see Ms. Dermody's car when you started out?"

"I went the other way, down Polk to the Embarcadero, so no, I didn't notice it then."

"Go on."

I swallowed. "I got close to Katrina's car and saw the blood on the window."

"You recognized the car?"

"It's a new Tesla. We all heard about it when she finally got off the waiting list." Oops. A little too caustic. I smiled to make it a joke and then mentally slapped my forehead; a joke was probably worse than sarcasm. She didn't smile back.

"What did you do then?"

"I got into the car and tried to see if she was still alive, but . . . well, she wasn't. I called 911 and waited here for your minions to arrive." I'd been sitting on the curb with my head on my knees when Nat arrived, ready to open up The Coffee. He found me, and he sat with me until the first police patrol car and emergency vehicles arrived.

Her lips twitched. "Minions. Yes. Did you see anyone on the street; hear any footsteps, anything like that?"

I remembered faintly hearing the buses up on Van Ness, which in daylight would be drowned out by Polk Street's own traffic noises. The near silence had been peaceful, I'd thought.

"I did hear something," I said after a minute, during which she merely looked at me. "I thought it might be Matthew. He sleeps here in the doorway on some nights," I added in response to her raised eyebrow. "There's a dumpster in the alley and he picks through it sometimes. I think that's where he got the duvet." I pointed at the shopping trolley, abandoned in the doorway.

"Did you see him?"

I shook my head.

"But he left his comforter and his shopping cart here?"

Right, the duvet was a "comforter," and the trolley was a "shopping cart." "He often does."

"And you stayed after you found Ms. Dermody and called a friend." She gave Nat, across the street behind the yellow tape perimeter, a flickering glance.

She didn't sound concerned on my behalf, just analytical. I abandoned the duvet and flapped a hand at Nat. He gave me a sympathetic pout.

"I was supposed to meet Nat. He arrived just before your first-responders and he stayed because we didn't like to leave her here alone," I said. Nat had agreed it felt wrong to leave her with strangers.

They'd separated us, questioned him, and then made him keep his distance, which was just as well since I'd seen him faint more than once at the sight of blood. He'd spent the few minutes he was with me rubbing my back and carefully not looking toward Katrina's car.

At street level the lights from all the official vehicles

were bouncing off the patchy fog, which revealed and then closed around the storefronts farther down the block. It was strange and disorienting. I was also getting flashes of Katrina's ravaged face superimposed over the scene of uniformed men and women exhibiting detached competence all around us. I had a new image to add to my nightmares. Lucky me.

Lichlyter cleared her throat. I tried to remember what we'd been talking about.

"So not just out walking, then, but meeting your friend."

"He's started a new business, reopening the coffee shop, and I've been helping him get things ready for an hour or two every morning."

"Starting when?"

"For the past couple of weeks."

She frowned.

"What time, do you mean? I've been coming at around five thirty."

She consulted the battered notebook. "So you were early today. You told the uniformed officer you tried to open the driver's side door."

You'd think it would be impossible to forget, but I found details were already hazy.

"Right. It was locked, so I went around the car and opened the passenger door."

"Which wasn't locked."

I shrugged and didn't say anything.

"The car was running when you arrived?"

"I didn't know how to turn it off."

She consulted her notebook. "The Tesla—does she usually park it on the street?"

"The renovations to her garage weren't finished in time."

She'd blistered the workmen's ears with her displeasure. At volume. "She had a charging station installed in her garage, but there was some sort of problem, with a hole or a broken pipe, I'm not sure. They had to lay a new surface on the floor, and it needs a few days to cure before it can take the heat of the tires or something." Lichlyter frowned at her notebook, and I realized I was babbling. "Anyway, the point is, she couldn't drive on it. She was charging the car at her office building." San Francisco being San Francisco, parking garages were required to have charging stations for electric cars.

"Is there anything else you feel I should know?" The mild sarcasm, with which I was all too familiar, seemed to be bringing our conversation to an end. I couldn't think of anything to add and probably looked as clueless as I felt. She glanced over at someone approaching with a cell phone in his extended hand. She took the phone with a nod of thanks and turned back to me.

"You can leave, Ms. . . . Bogart. I may need to speak with you again later, and if you think of anything . . . well, you know the drill." She didn't wait for me to respond, just flipped her notebook closed and walked away with the phone to her ear. I felt oddly snubbed. I'd remembered her being— not warm exactly, but less brisk. We'd even had a friendly moment or two in the past. Perhaps she didn't remember.

I went over to stand with Nat. He put an arm around my shoulders, which was sweet, but I almost ached to have Ben's arm around me instead. But Ben wasn't with me, and wasn't likely to be anytime soon. He'd been recalled to duty for the first time when we'd been together just a month. He wasn't allowed to tell me anything and he was gone for six weeks. He'd come home with a broken wrist and offered no explanation beyond a dry, "Bumpy flight." He was still spending two weeks a month at his civilian job in Washington, DC, and two weeks with me so, what with one thing and another, we'd only been in the same town at the same time for a handful of weeks.

Nat and I couldn't make ourselves leave. We stood together outside the crime-scene tape and watched procedures roll on like an industrial grinding machine. Men and women in uniform, as alert as border collies in spite of the early morning hour, made note of license plates up and down the block, placing small cards under windshield wipers. Two officers crisscrossed Polk Street, checking doorways, trying handles, shielding their eyes to peer into street-level shop windows, and ringing the doorbells of the apartments above. This brought out an assortment of sleepy or pissed-off locals with bed head who wandered over to the barrier or climbed back to their upstairs windows to stare down at the unfolding drama, hugging their coffee mugs.

Photographs. Video. Laser measurements. Medical examiner. Ambulance. Flickering red and blue lights. Yellow crime-scene tape. Pale, intent faces. And Inspector Lichlyter's familiar suspicion that everything I told her was, at least, filtered through my own lack of candor.

I didn't really blame her. Most people would feel that a proven liar will always lie. The reasons wouldn't matter, and I might have felt that way myself not too long ago.

CHAPTER FOUR

It was only because no one suspected anything that I was able to live here unrecognized. If anyone had connected my grandfather to his brother, the Earl, or me to my famous father, my identity wouldn't remain secret for another hour. But generally, people had no reason to think you might not be who you said you were. How often have you met someone new, heard their story from their own lips, and been suspicious that they were lying? I can tell you how often it's happened to me: Never, that's how often. Even with my own reasons, and given my own secrets, if my friend Nat was suddenly revealed as the son of a famous actor, or my ex-lover Kurt Talbot turned out to be a novelist instead of a surgeon, I'd be as startled as anyone. Added to that was the generosity of San Franciscans generally—people have come here to reinvent themselves since Oscar Wilde famously said: "It's an odd thing, but anyone who disappears is said to be seen in San Francisco." People were taken at their own valuation. If anything about my life seemed slightly odd, it would be shrugged off as mild eccentricity or simply none of their business. At least I assume that's what was happening. Grandfather wasn't well known, but a simple Google search would probably place him in his family tree, which would make my own relationship to him easier to uncover.

And once that happened, his relationship to my father, and our family disaster, wouldn't be hard to find.

My English parents had been famous and rich, and now they were dead, and the high-profile way they'd died had left me shocked, grieved, and nearly consumed by a media firestorm. After the events that had eventually driven me out of London the year before, I wanted to disappear, and I was almost too successful.

Because I was a member of the London paparazzi tribe—if taking photos of drunken friends weaving their way around Sloane Square and falling out of West End dance clubs qualified—they felt I owed them easy access to my story and resented me when I wouldn't play. I'd felt like chum for the rabid sharks of the British tabloid press. Harried and chivvied for weeks, I'd finally thrown some random clothes and shoes into a suitcase and bought a ticket on the first plane leaving Heathrow. I'd dyed my hair red to disguise my natural blonde, and exchanged Stella McCartney and Christian Louboutin for Levis and long-sleeved T-shirts. I introduced myself as Theo and took the name Bogart from an actor in one of the movies I was still watching to improve my American slang. I was even grateful that my nose had recently been broken, which subtly changed my appearance. I hoped it was enough, because there was a limit to what I could accomplish in the way of a new identity. It wasn't easy to disappear in an era of terrorist watch lists and twenty-four-hour international news cycles. It was, however, fairly easy to keep in touch with a few people via Skype without exactly explaining where I was, knowing that if anyone asked them about me, they'd be typically vague and self-involved. No one was surprised that I'd needed a break after the horrific events of that year, and I was deliberately noncommittal about when I'd be back.

Fortunately or not, I was as impulsive as ever, or perhaps simply numb. Within weeks I bought a derelict building, agreed to go into business with someone I met over coffee, adopted a dog I found mooching around my back door, and somehow signed on to serve on the board of our neighborhood association. Grieving, and without friends or family or familiar surroundings, I needed something to hold me in place. Aromas was my anchor.

My shop is called Aromas because pretty smells are what the merchandise has in common. Added to the essential oils, soaps, lotions, and perfumes, we feature bath-related items like kimonos and natural sponges. We also sell shampoo and lotions in bulk (sourced from a former meth-cooking chemist whose professional name is Smart Alex), refilling bottles our customers bring in. It's a small space, and I'd just installed a rolling library ladder so we could use the top shelves, just below the ceiling. Bunches of wildflowers and herbs, some of them given to us by customers, are jammed together to create a sort of upside down meadow on the ceiling, hiding an assortment of ugly pipes and conduits.

So I had my anchor, but I was also a prisoner of my own lies. I'd originally intended to just live quietly and anonymously for a few weeks or months, in a city where I knew no one and no one knew me. But being involved in a murder investigation in those first few months, and getting to know and like the people in my neighborhood, meant that in no time at all I had friends here; I had Ben; and trying to explain why my relationships with them were built on lies wasn't just difficult—it felt impossible.

And so the lying went on.

CHAPTER FIVE

By the time Nat and I left the scene, it was still only midmorning, but it felt like the end of a very long day. I didn't open Aromas, and Nat left the coffee chop closed—the street was still barricaded, and only residents were being permitted on the block anyway. I spent what was left of the morning and most of the afternoon trying not to remember how Katrina had looked when I found her, and taking phone calls from friends and neighbors, all of whom were agog, and couldn't wait to share their Katrina stories with me.

I heard about arguments over rubbish bins; complaints about loud music, some of which ended in police visits; fights over untrimmed shrubs blocking the sunlight to her downstairs rooms; the bitterness over her new window awning, which blocked the sunlight to someone *else's* rooms; I heard about babies being awakened by jackhammers, whatever they were, and, flying high and above everything else, impotent fury over the condo development she was championing. As a resident, she was entitled to attend association meetings, which she often did, and devising a coherent strategy to oppose the condo was impossible with her in the room. So I also heard about her threats of legal action over proposals to exclude her from the meetings for a conflict of interest. Katrina wasn't gracious in victory, and she didn't come off well in any of the stories. I was exhausted just hearing them.

Nat and I were together in my flat, and he'd spent a lot of time on the phone, too. In midafternoon he put together a meal for us. He insisted a salad of greens with a lemon and olive oil dressing would go down—and stay down—since it wasn't likely to bring up any unpleasant associations. We'd eaten the salad, and drunk a little too much wine, and then more or less collapsed on a couple of chairs in the living room. I still didn't have much in the way of furniture, but Ben had found the George Nelson armchairs somewhere; Grandfather had given me a large and valuable oriental rug; Nat had chosen the peacock blue velvet couch for me, and the coffee table with its splotches of gold leaf had been made by a friend. I was lucky because if it was up to me, the place would still be empty and I'd be sitting on the floor.

Light from the window left one side of Nat's face in shadow. I picked up my new camera and raised an eyebrow, asking him for permission. He shrugged, and I took a couple of quick shots. "Turn slightly this way. That's it. Beautiful."

"I feel so objectified." He wandered over to take the camera from my hand. "Nice piece of hardware."

"Retail therapy," I said.

Nat knew why I might need some retail therapy, and he looked sympathetic. "No word from Ben?"

"He can't while he's deployed." I swallowed a sudden lump in my throat, and grasped for a change of topic before Nat started to rehash Katrina's murder—again. He wouldn't leave it alone, and I'd had enough. "Hey, here's something I haven't told you. Haruto saw me taking a few photos downstairs, and now I have to take the photos for this year's calendar." I grabbed a couple of the old calendars from the firewood bin.

He chuckled and put down the camera. "Better you than me."

"Here's the one with the doorways leading into the Gardens."

He leafed through the pages and showed me a door painted with a six-foot Harley insignia. "That one brought in some real strange visitors to the Open Garden two years ago."

"And here's the Pets of Fabian Gardens year."

"I've never thought Mrs. Oyarzun's Chinese Crested looks like 'a skinned rabbit with a pompadour,' but that's just me." He tossed the calendar back to me. "There was nearly bloodshed that year. Too many pets; not enough pages in the calendar. Made the meetin's fun though." Nat loved the neighborhood association meetings; he e-mailed unofficial "minutes" full of snarky sidebars to his cronies, including me.

I flipped through the crumpled pages. It was an odd little anachronism, in a way, but it had its devotees, and no one on the board wanted to be responsible for eliminating it from the budget. Every Fabian Gardens household received a copy, and it hung in utility rooms and kitchens, usually a month or two behind the current date.

"I'll probably stick to flowers. Everyone likes flowers, right?"

"Yeah," he drawled. "You might want to stay away from Georgia O'Keeffe close-ups of the naughty bits."

"Oh, God."

He smirked and flopped back into his chair, leaning

down to stroke Lucy's belly, which she had presented for rubbing. I'd adopted Lucy as a stray, only later realizing that Shakespeare had her in mind when he wrote, "*though she be but little, she is fierce*." Not that I know much about Shakespeare beyond a few quotes, but he's hard to avoid at school in England, even when you try. Lucy was a small, bad-tempered terrier of some kind; she tolerated me and adored Nat. The jury was still out on Ben, although he was making inroads when he was here, largely due to his habit of giving her scraps of bacon at breakfast.

Nat kept up the rhythmic stroking, and Lucy closed her eyes. Nat resumed picking at the details of Katrina's murder. "Why didn't they just snatch Katrina's briefcase instead of riflin' it? Wasn't that kinda weird? Took time, and you'd think they'd be in a big hurry to get the hell away."

I gave him a sharp look, interested in spite of my genuine desire to forget the details. "You're right—if it was just some random robbery gone wrong, they'd grab the briefcase and run. Maybe it was someone from the neighborhood who didn't want to risk having anyone see them with it." It had a band of Russian-looking geometric designs incised into the leather, definitely one of a kind, and difficult to pass off as something from Target or the local luggage store.

"So something personal? It had to be big. I know she was a pain in the ass, but if that was enough to get someone killed, half the neighborhood would be killin' the other half."

I thought of all the fights I'd heard about and came up with what seemed like the most pressing, or at least the one with the most money at stake. The real estate market in San Francisco was the hottest in the country; ramshackle cottages in the outer neighborhoods were selling for more than a million dollars. A one-car garage in the Mission District had recently sold for $300,000. "What if it was someone who thought it would prevent the condo development somehow?"

Nat made a "maybe" grimace. Two of our residents had recently sold their adjoining buildings for princely amounts to Amos Noble, a notorious developer of third-rate condominium buildings. He'd used a straw buyer to hide his interest until it was too late for the sellers to change their minds, which was generally agreed to be underhanded. He and Katrina had made no bones about his plan to demolish the two buildings. So far, neighborhood opposition had kept the wrecking crews at bay, but no one was sure for how long. While we waited, the owners of buildings on either side of the proposed condo had also been approached to sell. They were holding out so far but, threatened with months, perhaps years of major construction next door, I could understand why they might take the money and run. If they did, the owners of two more neighboring buildings might do the same thing, and the dominoes falling would change Fabian Gardens beyond recognition. The conflict made the association meetings more contentious than usual, which was saying something. Meanwhile, the buildings had been empty for months, providing a place for rallies and demonstrations against the project and its developer, as irritating and obvious as a broken tooth.

The neighborhood had been a refuge to me; I hated to see it destroyed, and I wasn't thrilled at the prospect of a massive construction site taking up half the street, blocking off parking and filling the air with construction dust. Nat was clearly picturing the same scenario. "Doubtful. It'll go ahead—it'll be a two-year nightmare of dirt and noise and backhoes parked in the street, and sidewalks blocked off, and I'm already wishin' I lived somewhere else." He tipped his glass and finished his wine. I poured us both another glass, emptying the second bottle. "It leaves the D'Allessios as suspects number one and two, since their place is next door, but they're in their seventies, and I'm pretty sure Katrina could take them," Nat said.

"A gun trumps just about anything, though, doesn't it? If one of them was sitting in the passenger seat, they could shoot her without a struggle or anything."

"Just because they're Italian doesn't mean they're gangsters, English. They sponsor the local Grandmothers Against Gun Violence group; I'd lay money they're not packin'."

I snorted.

He went on. "On the other side it's all renters. I guess they wouldn't want to move and lose their rent controlled apartments, but Angie Lacerda's gettin' married and movin' out anyway, and Jesus and his partner, whatsisname, have been gone all month on that hike through Machu Picchu or wherever the hell they went. So they didn't do it."

"Darkest Peru somewhere. They might have paid someone, you know, a hit man," I said doubtfully.

"You sayin' 'hitman' in that accent of yours is the damdest thing I've heard all week."

I ignored that. "A couple of people switched sides recently," I said, thinking of my friend Sabina and her surgeon husband, Kurt. "Maybe money or blackmail or some other kind of pressure?"

"I don't think Katrina'd be above blackmail. Seems like just her style. She sure tried"—he stopped short—"Anyway, I wouldn't put anythin' past her."

I concentrated on not looking self-conscious, since I was fairly sure Katrina's heavy-handed hints the day before were a prelude to exactly that. It was typical Katrina, giving me a taste of her poison without actually making me swallow.

I needed the wall between my real life and my fake life to hold. For that to happen, I needed to know what Katrina had found out about me, and I suddenly realized there might be a way for me to find out.

"Where'd you go, Theo?" Nat asked suddenly.

I started and looked at him. "Sorry. Do you know what happens to a lawyer's cases and files if they die suddenly?"

"Okaay," he said, drawing it out, "quick change of topic. But you're not the only one thinkin' ahead. I already asked my lawyer friend Ricky. He says it's not unusual, 'pparently, to have a plan all organized to turn their stuff over to some other lawyer who's agreed to take care of things."

"Huh. When does that happen?"

"I guess it has to be done pretty quick so deadlines and court dates don't get missed. I bet Katrina's office will be closed up by the cops for a day or two, but they'll release it, so—any day now."

Nat was giving me the side-eye, and I tried to look thoughtful. "So—the condo project will probably go ahead with whoever this new lawyer is."

"Ricky's guess would be yes—he said a change like that at the legal end of things wouldn't bother or delay things much."

I rapidly reviewed what little I knew about lawyers. If Grandfather's solicitor here in San Francisco was typical, lawyers were belts-and-braces cautious, keeping paper files in their offices in addition to computer files on a distant server. Presumably the police had removed Katrina's computer as part of their investigation, but they would have no reason to remove the duplicate paper files—would they? And if not, they would be available to anyone with access to the file room. Whatever Katrina had found out about me would be there.

Assuming Nat was right about the police investigation time line, if I was going to get into her office to look around, it had to be soon.

CHAPTER SIX

I spent parts of the next two days checking things out at Katrina's office building to see if my half-formed plan was feasible, and buying a few things I thought I'd need. I'd never wanted a set of lock-picks before, but I learned they could by purchased online with twenty-four-hour shipping and a couple of locks to practice on. I picked up some simple white cards from the stationery store, then spent half an hour at the flower shop on the corner and made a quick stop at Out of the Closet to rummage through their shabbier offerings. Like almost every used clothing place in the city, they had an assortment of items for the drag queen diva about town, including outrageous wigs, size-14 stiletto heels, and super-sized feather boas, but I didn't need much, and everything fit into the small paper sack I carried back to Aromas.

Getting into Katrina's flat wasn't difficult, thanks to the practice locks and another sleepless night. The cousin was a potential problem, but I expected him to be asleep at the other end of the apartment at four a.m. What I didn't expect was the coffee maker to be burbling away on the counter of the open-plan kitchen. I had the door open several inches before I realized I should have allowed for an insomniac journalist. I risked a quick peek around the door, saw no one, and leaned in to grab what I needed. I didn't even step inside. I closed the door as quietly as I could, and ran with my ill-gotten gains.

I'd already made my apologies to Nat for skipping a morning at The Coffee and asked Haruto to open Aromas on Tuesday morning. Davie, my teenaged helper, was coming in after school, so if I needed it, I had all day. I hoped I wouldn't need it.

A twenty-minute cab ride and a short walk got me to Katrina's office, which was in a building on the blurred dividing line between Chinatown and North Beach on Columbus, a couple of (very steep) blocks from the heart of the Financial District. At seven a.m. it was raining lightly, and I was standing across the street under a shallow awning. We were in the middle of a significant drought. It rained so seldom that a heavy rainstorm could bring people out of their homes to marvel. A thunderstorm with lightning might just as well have been a Fourth of July fireworks display. Everyone dressed in layers, so we could deal with fog or a rapid dip or upswing in temperatures, but rain usually caught us by surprise. Groups of people tended to cluster under shelter and, even at this early hour, several people were under the awning with me, staring resentfully up at the sky.

As the rain stopped and my rain-averse cohorts moved on, a woman in the maroon jacket of the building's security guards came out of a side door into the alley. She handed a mug to a ragged man crouching under a tarpaulin stretched between a wooden pallet and a shopping cart. She talked with him for a moment or two, then went back inside.

The Beaux Arts building with its planters of disciplined boxwood wasn't new, but it was well maintained, providing a glossy and expensive habitat for medium-level legal and accounting firms. I'd watched the routine at the security desk the day before, mostly from outside, but also while casually sipping a smoothie in the small lobby café. The security guards were friendly and personable, attentive to the building's high-powered tenants. I'd checked on the location of fire stairs and emergency doors, which was always good information to have.

Gone were the days when a person—a photographer, say—could wander into a building, check the directory, and take the elevator to any floor she wished. Security had gradually become so stringent in the aftermath of the 101 California Street mass shooting that in some newer buildings the elevators only responded to chipped cards carried by the tenants. I once spent an embarrassingly long time in an elevator like that, inspecting the sleek, button-free interior, wondering how to close the doors.

Katrina's building was a little too old for that level of high-tech, but guards still inspected a visitor's ID, took a photo, had you sign a log, and then called upstairs to make sure you were expected. The only exception to the routine was early morning. Lawyers got to work early—very early—long before the support staff clocked in, and I was betting that a call from the security desk would go unanswered.

I had a moment's qualm because if I was successful, someone might lose their job. On the other hand, if I was successful *and* lucky, no one would know I'd been there.

CHAPTER SEVEN

Wearing threadbare jeans, a ragged baseball cap, and a shabby hoodie over my thrift store T-shirt, I made my way over to the security desk carrying an enormous basket of orchids in artfully moldy clay pots, surrounded by pounds of moss, several yards of gauzy ribbon, and a couple of helium balloons. The polished dark green marble floor was slippery with wet footprints and dripping umbrellas, and I didn't have to fake having trouble balancing everything. When I reached the security desk, I leaned into it and trapped the basket with my stomach to take some of the weight.

"Delivery for—er—" I pretended to check the envelope dangling from a miniature shepherd's crook, "Mr. Bhagatveer Singh Bhambra, front desk receptionist at Roberts and George, on the fourth floor."

The security guard, her shoulders stretching the limits of her uniform jacket, checked something on her monitor and flicked a few crumbs of moss off the glass counter. "Leave it here. No one's in the office yet. We'll get someone to take it up when they get here."

"The sender is proposing to his boyfriend and wants the orchids there when Mr. Singh Bhambra arrives this morning, and I have directions—"

"Who the hell proposes in the lobby of an accounting firm?"

"So can you take them up for me?" I consulted a list. "The pink ones go by his headset; the yellow ones on his chair, and the white ones are supposed to go in his rubbish bin." I looked up, wide-eyed. "I know, right? But this is all supposed to mean something to them both. Just tuck the moss around the pots." I glanced up at the huge clock above their desk. "He'll be here soon; he's coming in at, like, eight, with some musicians. God, that's confusing—I mean Mr. George will be here in half an hour, and Mr. Singh Bhambra will be in later. This sounds really lame, right? But I guess if you're a partner you can be lame. I'll have a few minutes to get some java before I have to get back to the shop." I started to heave the orchids up, dropping more moss and a few leaves onto the pristine glass reception desk.

"Java?" She smirked. "You're not from around here, huh? Look, kid, I don't know how this can work; I can't leave the desk, even for a proposal and I can't let you into the offices."

I smiled and waved the white plastic card I'd pilfered from Katrina's apartment. Luckily, it didn't contain a specific office or suite number, just the building's logo and the word "GUEST." "It's okay, Mr. George left us a card. He knows my boss real well."

She took the card, looked it over, and consulted her doughy-looking partner with a look. The partner tipped his head agreeably. "Okay, take off your sunglasses, I'm gonna take your picture and I need to see some ID."

I handed over a phony ID. It looked like the kind issued by the local legal aid program for the homeless, who sometimes needed to prove who they were and of course didn't usually have driver's licenses. It was a risk, but a small one—I'd seen her giving coffee and a few kind words to the rough sleeper in the alley more than once.

"Way to work your way up, kid," she said gruffly as she returned it, and then I felt guilty and hoped she wouldn't lose her job.

I frowned at the camera, fairly certain my green wig, nose rings, and ratty baseball cap would give me enough cover. I watched her finger on the camera button and, as it twitched, I moved slightly to coincide with the click of the shutter, just as a bit of added insurance. "Go on over to elevator B. It'll take you up to the fourth floor."

"Okay, but don't spoil the surprise. Mr. George won't be happy; he's a real prick. Sorry," I added, trying to look shamefaced.

"Yeah, that's pretty common around here," she said with a wink.

Getting off the elevator on the fourth floor, and ignoring the arrow pointing left toward the accounting firm of Roberts and George, I turned right and followed signs to Katrina's office suite.

I used Katrina's entry card on the outer door, and to my relief, the lock made several beeps, showed a perky little green light, and clicked open. I turned the deadbolt inside the door to the suite, leaned back against it, took a deep breath of copy toner, old coffee, and floral air freshener, and gave myself a mental high five. Succeeding in my ruse downstairs and opening the door with my purloined key card gave me much more of a thrill than breaking and entering probably should.

The early hour and the murky weather meant I needed

the narrow beam of bright white light from my finger-sized flashlight. The only danger was being seen from the windows of the hotel next door, but the drapes I could see over there were closed. With luck, everyone was still asleep or taking their morning showers, and not planning to fling aside the drapes to enjoy their misty view of North Beach in the rain.

I left my basket of orchids on the reception desk and walked quickly around the suite to check on the layout. It was arranged in a square, with three glass-walled offices and a conference room on the outside, each with a window, and all helpfully labeled with nameplates. A walkway went around the entire suite, separating the offices from the reception area and an inner row of cubicles, presumably inhabited by lesser beings like assistants and clerks. The central core was shared by the copy machine, a supply closet, a small break room, and the file room.

I was carrying my set of lockpicks in a case only a hair larger than a credit card. I'd once seen a friend open a lock with a hairpin, so I thought I should be able to do at least as well with actual lock picks. I wasn't fast, but I understood the principle, and by the time I'd broken into my own flat a couple of times I was confident I could open a file cabinet lock in two or three minutes. The second time my own front door took me less than a minute, I made a mental note to have a burglar alarm installed.

I pulled on the pair of latex gloves I'd brought with me— *CSI* was worth watching after all. Katrina's office door was unlocked, which was explained when a few minutes of careful rifling through her books and desk drawers yielded nothing of any interest. A coffee mug on a coaster and an expensive pen set were the only things on her desk, and the console under the window held an empty crystal vase, a handful of books, and a pair of framed photos of smiling groups of children. The kids, all wearing brightly colored T-shirts, were flanked by a couple of pleasant-looking, middle-aged nuns. The photos seemed out of character for Katrina, who, as far as I knew, had absolutely no interest in children or nuns or in fact anything except her car, her wine collection, and her work. Abandoning the office, I headed for the file room. It was locked, which gave me a chance to practice my new skill, and, as expected, the file cabinets were locked too. I used up valuable time to open them all. They used a system of numbers on the file folders, not just the alphabet, and it took me a few minutes to understand how to navigate it. I was neat, replacing everything in order, and made my way through the "B"s without finding anything. I hunted for Grandfather's name, with the same lack of results, and then finally, and with a deep sense of foreboding, found the initial of my real last name. And there it was.

I quickly sifted through newspaper clippings from my time in London and several photographs. There was a printout of an e-mail from my cousin Frederick; God knows how she'd come across that. Copies of the incorporation papers for Safe Haven Enterprises, which shielded the ownership of my building and Aromas, included my real signature. A sticker on the front had spaces for the name of the person borrowing the file, along with the date. Some of the other file folders had multiple stickers, all filled in and going back a couple of years. Mine had nothing, so I hoped it meant that no one but Katrina had read the contents. I didn't bother to read the rest of the file; I folded it in half and stuffed it into the back waistband of my jeans.

I checked my watch. The security guards were going to start wondering where I was. I flicked quickly through the rest of the files in all of the drawers, trying to be both fast and thorough. It looked as if Katrina had put together a dossier on a few of the people living in Fabian Gardens, the ones who had opposed the condo development. I wasn't sure if that was standard lawyerly procedure or some sort of embryonic blackmail effort. In for a penny—I grabbed that file too. I locked the cabinets and the file room door and went back to where I'd left my orchid extravaganza.

I quickly left the individual orchids on desks around the office with the "Condolences" cards I'd prepared, deflated the balloons with my handy Swiss Army knife, and crumpled them into the break room rubbish bin, then tucked the empty basket next to it. I was approaching the outer door to make what I hoped would be a clean getaway when I heard the tones of the electronic lock and the door started to open.

CHAPTER EIGHT

I dived into a cubicle and duck waddled under a desk as someone walked into the room. Whoever it was hesitated in the doorway, and I pulled my feet further into my hiding spot. The lights didn't come on, and I was grateful for the few seconds it took me to wonder why. That question was answered when I saw the reflection of a flashlight beam bounce off the glass office walls. I pressed back against the desk with my heart hammering, my face jammed against the fabric of the cubicle, and my legs tangled in a chaos of cables and wires.

The intruder—the *other* intruder—made faint bumps and rustles following in my footsteps. He—it was a man, judging from the shoes I glimpsed as he walked quickly past my cubicle—headed straight for Katrina's office. Without bothering to keep quiet, he started to throw drawers open and toss things around. I heard the tinkle of glass breaking and thought of the framed photos, and heard the thump of some of Katrina's heavy books hitting the carpeted floor of her office. I muttered to myself. I'd been stealthy, professional even, but this idiot was endangering both of us. The faint whine of the elevators had been growing more frequent as the morning arrivals picked up. I knew Katrina had recently come to a parting of the ways with her paralegal, but one attorney and a couple of administrative types still shared the offices, and all I needed was for one of them to arrive before I could make my escape. Crouching low, hoping he was making enough noise to shield me, I made my way toward the outer door. I was nearly there when I bumped into the reception desk. The orchid pot wobbled. I lunged for it, but it crashed and shattered on the marble floor with a noise loud enough to stop my heart. A mess of bark chunks, terra cotta shards and moss scattered over the floor near my feet.

"Hey! Who the hell are you?"

There was no way to answer that question without getting into serious trouble. I exploded out of my crouch and bolted. As soon as I cleared the doorway into the outer hallway, I made for the emergency stairs.

I slid down the first two flights without feeling my feet touch the ground as the door above me slammed open. I skidded and stumbled down more flights of stairs, three at a time, and burst through the ground floor fire door. A group of people waiting for the elevators produced a variety of startled and profane shouts as I charged through them, knocking them out of my way. I flung myself at the emergency exit crash bar, barged outside and, with the fire alarm screaming in my ears, ran hell-for-leather along the alley. With a heartbeat's incredulity, I heard what sounded like a gunshot. I didn't think the security guards would shoot me, but I didn't know for certain—this was America, after all. It goaded me to further effort. Without bothering to see if the way was clear, I dived across the busy street into the alley opposite. Brakes squealed and shouts echoed behind me as my pursuer followed.

I'd never understood the phrase "running for your life"

before. I've been chased once or twice, but mostly I was doing the chasing, after reluctant celebrities with my camera.
I'm not a fast runner, but fear of death is apparently a great
motivator, and I legged it down the anonymous alley as if
my heels were on fire. I dived for the opening at the end,
flinging myself forward as a small puff of brick dust flew
off the wall a foot ahead of me. I ran through the dust before it had time to settle. Someone really *was* shooting at
me! With some vague idea that I should be zigzagging to
throw off his aim, I slammed painfully into the opposite
corner with my shoulder and careened off it onto Stockton
Street. I burst onto a crowd of Chinese women clustered
around displays of daikon and bok choy, all arguing with a
beleaguered clerk who was trying to put out more produce
from a tower of battered cardboard boxes. I crashed into
the women, who went down like bowling pins, earning me a
hefty shove from somewhere as I stumbled over a tangle of
arms and legs and bok choy that sent me flying out into the
slow-moving stream of traffic. Several outraged shouts and
honking horns followed me as I dodged an open-mouthed
cyclist and kept running.

Around the next corner, I tore the green wig off with
my baseball hat and stuffed them in my hoodie's kangaroo
pocket and, without slowing down, shucked the hoodie and
hurled them at a homeless woman crouched beside an Italian delicatessen.

"Thanks!" she shouted after me. I was left wearing
unremarkable jeans and a long-sleeved T-shirt. I dodged
right at the next corner, kept running for half a block, then
pressed myself into an alcove containing a fire hydrant and
a pair of large, stinking wheelie bins. I leaned over with
my hands on my knees, trying hard to breathe through the

remains of my panic. After a few minutes, when I was capable of standing upright, I flattened myself against the brick wall and looked up and down the street. I didn't see anyone I knew, and I definitely didn't see anyone waving a gun around. I walked quickly to Geary and jumped on the first bus I saw.

Luckily, I had my Muni pass in my jeans, because I found I'd given the homeless woman the thirty-five dollars I'd shoved in my hoodie as I left home.

CHAPTER NINE

I was holding a plastic bag of mostly melted ice against my shoulder when Davie found me in the small office behind Aromas late that afternoon. I'd hit the alley wall hard. He got me some fresh ice from somewhere, wearing the small frown that appears whenever there's something he doesn't understand. Davie's sixteen and recently asked me to call him Davo. I kept forgetting and usually ended up with some variation of Davie-o. He's built like a UPS truck, he sounds like a foghorn, and his latest haircut left him with a mop of unruly black curls on top and little more than a shadow everywhere else. He wanted me to bleach the curls. I said I would, if he stopped threatening to get ear gauges. He was already a sensation behind the counter at Aromas, but apparently a nose ring and multiple earrings weren't interesting enough. I used my grandfather's guaranteed disapproval of the ear gauges as a persuader, since he and Grandfather had struck up an unlikely friendship, and I'm sure they drew second glances on their outings to the Academy of Sciences. I was already reconciled to spending Davie's eighteenth birthday in a tattoo parlor, although having seen some of the local tattoo parlors, I made him promise to find a place that was more hippie than Harley.

"What happened?" His frown got a little deeper.

"I tripped and banged into a wall." And why I couldn't come up with a better story than that, I don't know.

"Huh."

"It's not serious; I just want to make sure it doesn't bruise."

"Huh."

"See? It feels better already." I raised my shoulder a couple of times, which actually hurt quite a lot, and wondered if I'd torn something. I leaned over his bicycle and tossed the bag of ice into the sink in our tiny bathroom. I didn't have to leave the office, our space back there was so bijou.

"Huh."

I have no idea how he managed to communicate such a depth of skepticism, saying essentially nothing.

In a quiet moment later, trying to maintain some semblance of normalcy while images of my frantic race from Katrina's office replayed over and over in my mind, I unearthed a couple of small, flowered china bowls I'd found in a charity shop, and took them into the bathroom to wash. I thought they were probably powder bowls from an old dressing table set.

"What do you think?" I put them on an eye-level shelf.

Davie shrugged.

"I thought they might sell as soap dishes."

He reached over and picked out a couple of almond soaps in flowered paper wrapping, and dropped one in each bowl. We both looked at them, heads to one side, considering.

"How much?" I said.

"What did you pay?"

"Four dollars each. Plus the soap."

"Seventeen dollars?"

I wrote that amount on a couple of price labels and

handed them to him, and he stuck the labels on the bottoms of the bowls. I cut some raffia from our gift-wrapping supplies and tied it around the bowls to make it clear the price included the seven-dollar bar of soap.

"Mr. Pryce-Fitton has one of those bowls. He keeps his keys in it by the front door."

I was occupied with wondering who—besides me—had been in Katrina's office that morning, and what they had been looking for. And why they had come armed with a gun. But Davie was giving me a sidelong look, and I tried to remember what we'd been talking about.

"When are you and my grandfather meeting up next? He says you're teaching him about California flora and fauna."

He flushed, looking pleased. "Next Tuesday, after school. Don't put me on the schedule." I made a mental note and then decided I'd never remember, so I wrote it on a Post-it and stuck it on my computer screen in the office. When I got back, he picked up where he'd left off. "We have a deal. I tell him about local stuff, and he tells me Latin and Greek names for things. Like monarch butterflies are *Danaus plexippus*. Stuff like that." He glanced over at the small aquarium sheltering a miniature world of greenery for the eggs he collected and released as butterflies. One of them was in the process of hatching, and we both stopped work to watch. "We meet friends of his sometimes," he said suddenly.

"Which friends?" I didn't know my grandfather had any friends over here. There were none that he'd ever mentioned, anyway.

"Don't know their names. One's an older lady. White hair and everything. She has real sharp fingernails." He scowled and I wondered why he had reason to remember her fingernails.

As we watched in companionable silence, the butterfly made its resolute way from the confining chrysalis and left the husk behind. It hung from a branch, slowly moving its glorious wings, waiting for them to dry.

I left Davie happily Snapchatting and Instagramming and texting a naturalist he'd befriended online, standing behind the counter, ready for any customers who might present themselves while I walked along to The Coffee to get my usual afternoon cup of tea from Nat and share that I'd spent the morning fleeing from a gun-wielding assassin.

Nat had postponed The Coffee's official opening. ("I wanted to give people a few days to forget we'd had a murder." "Do you think that's a problem?" "Take a look at *City Beat*'s posts. It's like Jack the Ripper is hangin' around waitin' to grab people off the street.")

He had successfully combined a Paris patisserie with a Beat-era espresso bar. The café was painted and furnished in shades of coffee and cream and a sky-blue color Nat insisted was called Gay Russian Man. He'd commissioned some interesting cake stands and trays made of pale blue, food-safe resin from an artist in the Bayview, and arranged them at different heights in the display case for their payload of muffins and scones.

I'd told him I thought the take-one-leave-one bookshelf in the hallway leading to the bathrooms was a little heavy on the Josh Lanyon erotic, man-on-man romances. ("They're well written, Theo." "I'm sure that's why you read them." "A man has needs.")

I was anxious to share my morning's adventure with him, but I had to wait for a quiet moment, so I sat on the squashy couch upholstered in a patchwork of burlap coffee sacks he'd somehow beguiled from one of his suppliers and made an effort to take an interest in the reality I'd lived in until that morning.

My wandering gaze settled on the large front windows, where two people sat quietly engaged with their laptops. He'd had three different sets of curtains in three different lengths made. We'd agreed that the floor-length, burgundy velvet was more bordello than Brazilian blend. Next came the gathered and draped coffee-tan and white stripes with bobble fringe, which looked whimsically French, and I thought they'd made the cut until I came in one morning to see them crumpled in a heap on the floor. Eventually, he'd covered the bottom three feet of the window with a translucent curtain made from recycled soda bottles of all things, on a thick brass rod.

"They're an odd length," I'd said as we both stood looking at them.

"They're called café curtains and this is a café," he'd said breezily.

"But—"

He growled. "They're supposed to be short. Don't mess with me, Theo; I'm on the edge here."

I knew he was thinking about bringing someone on to help him right away, instead of waiting, as he'd originally planned. ("I'm not helping?" "'Course you are, sweetie, but you're lookin' a bit worse for wear these early mornin's, and I'm gonna get someone full time.")

While he served his customers, and produced, apparently without effort, a stream of cheerful gossip, compliments, and remarkably complicated coffee drinks, it dawned on me that I'd have to tell him my reason for breaking into Katrina's office, and I couldn't think of anything that sounded reasonable. So I had more things to keep from everyone—my file, the dossier on our neighbors, and the story of the gunman who chased me, were going to have to stay my secrets. It was an odd feeling to sit there, having been shot at and nearly killed, and yet unable to share that remarkable fact with anyone. Was this the odd dichotomy experienced by undercover cops and spies?

Reaching for the normal as he handed me my tea, I gave him a wink and tilted my head at the curtains, and he grinned back at me.

On my way back to Aromas, an argument in the street looked a couple of seconds away from turning into a shoving match. Two men, one of them with a filthy blanket around his shoulders, and the other wearing a camo-patterned jacket, were up in each other's faces, shoulders back, chests forward, pushing into each other's personal space, both of them shouting obscenities and hurling charges of theft. I saw our beat copper—thank goodness for community policing—making his measured way in their direction, and they suddenly found somewhere else to be. It reminded me that I hadn't seen Matthew in his usual spots for a couple of days, and I stopped in at Bonbons Chocolat to ask Faye-Bella if she'd seen him.

"He's been here," she said, using long tongs to put what she called a chocolate coconut haystack in a small, pleated paper cup. I reflected that since she hadn't had to ask what I wanted, I was probably there too often. I dug in my jeans for change and put it on top of her glass showcase, then picked up the treat and nibbled it. I decided I could give them up when my life was less stressful.

"He's just lying low," she said. "He didn't like the street being closed off that day. At least, I think that's what was bothering him. He came in to pick up his comforter the other day, but he wouldn't stay. You know how he repeats things; he just kept saying, 'Thief, thief, thief.'"

I stopped nibbling. "What did he mean?"

She shrugged. "He said it the same way he says everything, repeating something he's heard, but doesn't really understand."

But there was usually some meaning behind Matthew's utterances, if you could clear away his mental confusion. I'd just heard two homeless men arguing and calling each other out over a theft; maybe Matthew had heard something similar. He was out here on the street at all hours of the night, and I suddenly wondered if Inspector Lichlyter had talked to him about the night of Katrina's murder.

I didn't envy her the task of getting him to make sense.

Back at Aromas I gave Davie the orange soda I'd picked up for him, and he dispatched it in three huge gulps.

"How's everything at home?" I asked him as he lifted a carton of shea butter jars and started to take it out to the garage, where we stored extra stock. For some reason the fad for shea butter seemed to have run its course. I needed to remember to order more coconut oil, though. One of my customers had requested coconut oil tooth soap, which sounded disgusting, but I'd added it to the coconut oil hair treatments, shampoo, body lotions, sugar scrub, enriching face moisturizer, lip balm, foot cream, and nail food we already stocked.

"S'fine."

"No, Davie-o." He sighed and shook his head as if I were the lamest thing ever, as he might put it. "Really. How are things?"

"Told you. Everything's fine." He scowled. "Nothing new."

"Okay, then."

I sighed. He's only about ten years younger than me, but I'd felt *in loco parentis* practically since the first day I met him, when he tried to rob the store. I talked him out of it and gave him an after-school job. I hoped he was telling me the truth; in any case, the bruises were difficult to hide. He hadn't come in with a black eye in a couple of months. Maybe he was getting too big for his abusive drunk of a father to bully.

He spent the rest of the afternoon filling in shelves and serving the occasional customer while I worked on the schedule in the office. Davie had discovered a talent for upselling, which I told him to soft-pedal to avoid pressuring people.

"But we need the money," he said, which was undeniably true. "I just asked her if she'd tried our lemon verbena sugar scrub and body lotion. She'd already picked out the lemon body wash, so it made sense. And she bought the scrub! So that's good, right?"

"It's very good, I just meant . . ." How to tell him that the way he looked meant he was going to have to tread lightly his whole life? ". . . you know what? You were polite and thoughtful and the customer looked happy. We'll count it as a win."

He gave me a shy smile and I sighed. Nat said I clucked over him like an anxious hen, and gave new meaning to having all my eggs in one basket.

CHAPTER TEN

I had absolutely no doubt that Katrina had been planning to expose me—or, more likely, threaten to expose me if I didn't relax my opposition to her client's condo development. With the stolen file in my own hands, at least no one in her office had access to that information about me, and I could choose to tell my story, or not, in my own time. I'd stolen her dossier on my neighbors with less of a clear motive. One or two had done a recent *volte-face* on the condo development, and I was sure I'd find the reason for their change of heart in the second file. I'd felt justified, protective even, when I saw it there, but I wasn't sure reading it gave me any high ground. Eventually, I decided I was just curious, and found I could live with that.

When I finally steeled myself to open the dossier late that evening, I found a sketch of each person's life, based on their education and job history and, sometimes, their real estate holdings. Nat, for example, owned a cabin in Wyoming, which, while interesting (he seemed like such a quintessential city person to me, even though he'd started life in Texas) hardly provided material for blackmail. The papers weren't in any particular order, and most people had just a single sheet of paper, headed with their name, and date and place of birth. A few had articles or photos attached.

Ruth D'Allessio (nee Lyons), who lived next to one of the vacant buildings with her husband, had been arrested, twice, for participating in anti-war demonstrations, once in 1968 and again in 2007, which probably says more about America's bellicose history than Ruth's temper and penchant for kicking police officers. She had a woodshop in the decommissioned Hunters Point Naval Shipyard, where she designed and produced uncomfortable chairs beloved of decorators and collectors. She trained and employed young men and women who'd somehow escaped the local gang culture that put guns in the hands of children and provided the community with untold hours of entertainment in the form of regular drive-by shootings. Her membership in Grandmothers Against Gun Violence made a lot of sense in that context.

Nothing there seemed blackmail-worthy.

Her husband, Professor D'Allessio, had been a respected professor at UC Berkeley and had written several books on Italian Renaissance drama. I was surprised there was enough to say about it to fill one book, let alone five. There was a translation of an Italian newspaper article accusing him of plagiarism, but nothing had come of it and, while faintly shadowed by occasional reminders of the accusation in Italy, once he'd moved to the US, he left it behind, and his reputation here was unsullied. He accompanied Ruth on her anti-war marches (there was a photo of them together in handcuffs). Rather than damaging his academic standing, his activism seemed to enhance it. After he was pepper sprayed, and the ACLU won a judgment on his behalf, he was given tenure by the university.

The plagiarism accusation was too old to do him any harm, even if it came to light. I poured myself another glass of wine and turned the page. Moving on.

Sabina Talbot (nee D'Allessio) was a UC Berkeley alumna, a philosophy major, and a bonded motorcycle messenger and international courier until her marriage. There was a fairly lengthy list of the countries and cities she'd traveled to, often in parts of the world where postal service was unreliable or nonexistent. She'd been to Kiev and Albania numerous times, for example. She'd had an affair with a rich, married tech billionaire for more than a year. Sabina had always refused to identify him. I read his name and then wished I didn't know. She had married Kurt Talbot and the tech billionaire's baby (Sebastian) was born three months later.

The only thing I saw in Sabina's history that might cause trouble for her was the identity of her baby's father. If he didn't know about the baby, he might fight her for custody; maybe that's what Katrina was planning to threaten her with.

Her husband, Kurt, was an eye surgeon with privileges in several San Francisco hospitals. He'd interned at a famous Florida eye institute, but earlier, he'd been caught up in an investigation of medical students selling prescription drugs. He'd been exonerated, but several of his classmates weren't so lucky, and their medical careers were cut short. Reading between the lines, Kurt's well-to-do family had put him in the hands of a PR specialist who made sure his name was kept out of the media.

Okay, I could see that coming back to bite him. A doctor's reputation was his stock-in-trade; no one wants to put themselves in the hands of a surgeon with a shady past. He and Sabina had been very vocal in their opposition to the condo, which I'd always assumed had something to do with supporting the D'Allessios, who were furiously opposed to it. Then, about a month before Katrina's murder, they had stopped attending meetings and generally muted their responses to overtures to attend protests or participate in letter campaigns. So—either Katrina or something else had changed their minds.

Katrina's journalist cousin, Gavin Melnik, had been raised in Poland by adoptive parents and attended a Swiss university called ETH, which left their graduates sounding as if they had a severe lisp. ("Where did you go to school?" "Thankth for athking; I went to ETH.") I giggled immoderately at my own humor and decided I'd probably had too much wine on an empty stomach. I stopped reading long enough to make myself a cheese sandwich before settling in again. Gavin emigrated to the US when he was in his early twenties, after his parents' death in an auto accident, and he'd lived in San Francisco for twelve years. He was a little younger than he looked—only thirty-four—and his work history was spotty, but that's almost expected for a writer. After seeing some of the top-flight magazines he'd written for, I had a new appreciation for the uncertain life of a freelance journalist, since Katrina had given the impression he lived with her as a sort of general dogsbody and gofer because he couldn't afford a place of his own.

Nothing there seemed worth threatening him in any way, and he wasn't a property owner, so his support or opposition to the condo shouldn't have had much impact.

Jesus and Luis Aguardo, who lived in a flat on the other side of the empty buildings, were married in the window that had briefly opened in 2004, when San Francisco was an outlier, before marriage equality became the law of the land. They leased their flat in the Gardens and, when they weren't travelling, spent a lot of time at their *Architectural*

Digest–worthy home in Mendocino. They owned a successful wine and beverage company with outlets throughout
California, famous for both their private label wines and
for their exclusive offerings from small, specialty winer-
ies. In 2012, they were sued by the bereaved parents of an
underaged teen who had purchased half a dozen bottles of
wine with a fake ID, managed to drink it all in a matter
of hours and died from alcohol poisoning. The court case
had been brutal, the teen exposed as a binge drinking al-
coholic, his parents vilified as uncaring and interested only
in the financial settlement of their lawsuit. The mother had
committed suicide within six months. The father's whereabouts were unknown.

Jesus and Luis weren't culpable in the teenager's death,
and the entire saga had played out in the media, so there
didn't seem to be anything they could be blackmailed
with. Katrina had headed their victorious legal team, so if
she *were* planning to blackmail them, she'd been double-
dipping.

Angela Lacerda was a different story. She was younger
than everyone else in the dossier and lived in the flat underneath the Aguardos. She had undergone an abortion
when she was in high school. She was about to marry into a
wealthy Catholic family with historic roots in the city and
a well publicized, not to say fanatical, opposition to abortion. The file speculated that her current fiancé might be
unaware of her history. She owned several small pieces of
property in the East Bay, mostly vacant lots, judging from
the description. She rented her apartment—she didn't own
property in the Gardens—but her prospective family were
influencers; Katrina might have been hoping that with
the right persuasion, like a threat to tell her prospective

in-laws about her abortion, Angela would bring them into the fight on her client's behalf.

Having finished the dossier, and feeling as if I needed another shower, I stuffed it behind my pillow and tried to get to sleep. I was awake for another couple of hours. Reading it had been spectacularly unhelpful. I knew things I wished I didn't, and I couldn't see how any of it was useful in the investigation into Katrina's death unless I went to talk to the people involved. And if I did that, how did I explain knowing any of what I'd learned?

CHAPTER ELEVEN

Mixed drinks or just red and white?" Nat said he'd been coerced into planning the memorial for Katrina, although I knew perfectly well he'd volunteered.

"Just wine, I think," I said. "People can help themselves and you won't need a bartender."

"That's what I thought. And no one wants to see all those downtown lawyers liquored up and then drivin' home smashed." He admired his reflection in the window and adjusted his yellow cashmere sweater. "D'you like the color?"

"It suits you," I said, because it did.

He smirked. "Yeah, but what doesn't?"

Burial or cremation would have to wait until the police released Katrina's body, but the neighborhood, in lieu of any apparent family besides her cousin, was planning the memorial, and a small get-together. Someone in her office provided a list of professional colleagues to invite, and the rest of us were told about it on the neighborhood Facebook page. A few of our more sentimental residents were calling it a celebration of life, which seemed macabre, and I hoped we weren't supposed to have a sing-along and champagne toasts, because I couldn't think of anyone who'd join in.

Nat borrowed the key to Katrina's apartment from her cousin so he could look for a few things that might add what he called "texture" to the memorial. ("Sometimes you're really gay, you know that?" "I suppose you think it's easy bein' this amazin'.") Her cousin was supposed to meet us there, but he had something come up at the last minute, which was a mild relief to me, since as far as I knew he was still suing me, and I wouldn't know what to say to him. I looked idly round, as if I hadn't used my lock picks to borrow, and then return, the entrance card to her office suite. She'd renovated fairly recently, and everything looked new and contemporary, except for a collection of *matryoshka* nesting dolls, one or two of which were more than a foot tall. Nat was going through some boxes on her desk, where someone had made a start on packing up her things. A couple of huge rolls of bubble wrap and some duct tape seemed to promise more packing in the near future.

"She had a collection of these," I said, handing him one of the roly-poly dolls. The paint on this particular one was faded and scratched.

"You've gotta wonder why," he said. He twisted the doll at the waist. She opened to reveal another doll inside.

"They can be quite valuable, especially the larger ones," I said, and took the doll back.

"I guess we could put a couple out for people to—admire, if that's what we think they'll be doin'."

"Some of the guests might know about them, so it would mean something to see them," I said.

While Nat went through her desk looking for photographs, I amused myself by revealing all the smaller and smaller dolls inside the *matryoshka* and lining them up on a shelf. There were thirty, all the way down to a doll the size of a peanut.

"Ah, gotcha!" Nat said, and waved a slim Tiffany

photo album in my direction. I went over to see what he'd found. "We can have a couple of these enlarged," he said, "and leave the album out for people to look through the rest. I don't know most of these people," he added, flicking through the pages, "but maybe they'll be at the memorial. Look here." The photo was of Katrina, looking about twenty years old, wearing shorts and an open-necked shirt. Her arms were around a good-looking guy, who held some of her blonde hair back with one hand as the wind blew it all over the place. They were both laughing and I had to look twice to make sure it was her. When I knew her, she was always immaculately turned out, with every hair in place, and I'd never seen her laugh. Nat was still examining the photo closely. "This guy—"

"What?"

He held the open album upright across his chest for me to see. "Does he look familiar? He reminds me of someone."

I took another look. It confirmed my first impression; he was a looker, with a large, sensual mouth. His hair was thick and blonde and wind-blown. I couldn't see the color of his eyes. He was taller than Katrina, who'd been tall for a woman, but he didn't look familiar. "Who does he remind you of?"

"I dunno. It's probably nothin'." He turned the page to find a photo of her alone, perching on a large boulder, in shorts again but with a different shirt, holding one of the wooden dolls. I recognized it; the mama doll was holding a cup of tea and it was still in Katrina's collection.

"Probably started with one, and then people gave them to her for birthdays and Christmas," Nat said, as I pointed it out. "A friend of mind bought one teddy bear because it reminded him of somethin', I forget what, and before he knew it he had a hundred. People bought them when they didn't know what else to get him. And the more he had, the more people thought he liked them. He never had the heart to tell anyone he only bought the first one as a joke." He tapped the photo of Katrina. "I'll have this one enlarged; maybe someone will come who remembers her at that age. And this one with the law books in the background. Whaddya think about this one?" Katrina was glamorous in an evening gown on the steps of the Opera House.

I nodded. "Good choices—three different ages and stages of her life. By the look if it, there were no other men in her life worth a photo since that one."

"I'm surprised there was even one." He flicked over more pages. "Who's this kid, do we know?"

I looked at the photo of a boy, aged about ten. "No idea. Are there other photos of him?"

He shook his head. "Just the one. Maybe her cousin knows." He picked up the album and tucked it into his messenger bag. "Gimme a couple of those god-awful dolls." I reassembled the one I'd been playing with, and added the one in the photo and another at random.

He tore off some bubble wrap, rolled them in it, and stuffed them in his bag. "Not sure there's anythin' else. Her cousin's her executor. He said he's arrangin' for her stuff to be auctioned and added to her estate."

"That's the fellow who's suing me."

"Yeah, I know. Apart from that, Mrs. Lincoln, he seems okay."

"I wonder if he inherits anything? I never heard Katrina was married or had children. And she seemed to have plenty of money, plus her home, not to mention the Tesla. Hey! Maybe he gets everything, which gives him a motive to murder her!" I was quite excited by this flash of brilliance, but Nat shook his head.

"Sorry, Miss Marple. He said she left everything to some charity."

"No kidding? I would have thought he'd be included."

He shrugged. "He seemed okay with it." He walked away and opened each of the doors in the hallway. He called back, "Where's her wine?"

"What? For the memorial?"

He came back. "No, not thinkin' of that. It's just—she was always talkin' about what an expert she was, and what a great investment wine is; she belonged to that wine club and adopted a vine or whatever the hell. And the small bedroom set up with all the custom redwood wine racks." He opened his arms like a TV game show host. "So where's all the wine?"

We looked at each other. "Maybe she put it in storage while she was renovating?"

"It's been done for months."

"Or maybe she drank it."

"Her liver'd be the size of Montana. Take a look."

He led the way down the hall, and we both looked into the little room. She'd had a glass door fitted, and the lights were operated by a switch in the hall so the `setup could be admired without disturbing the wine. The last time I'd seen them, several months before, the floor-to-ceiling racks had been full. Now they were almost empty.

"How long had she been a collector?"

"She said she had the wine room built when she bought the building; must be fifteen years at least."

"They probably had someone in to value the wine, and they took it to sell."

"Yeah, that's gotta be it. Otherwise we're left with a cartoon image of a guy with a little black mask hauling sacks of bottles out over his shoulder 'til he drops dead of exhaustion."

As it turned out, even with its slightly unconventional setting, the memorial on Monday night was dignified and touching. One of Nat's friends owned a neighborhood antiques store, and ´the upstairs was already arranged into seating areas. The tattered silk upholstery gave the occasion a sort of world-weary, *fin de siècle* sophistication. With the addition of some discreet folding chairs, there were plenty of places for people to sit if they wanted to. Nat had taught me to have at least a few chairs in a gathering of more than five people—there was always someone getting over a hip operation or who had sprained an ankle training for a marathon or who'd just had a tough day at work. In this case, we were expecting several people on target for their sixth or seventh decade, so it was best to be prepared. Fabian Gardens was denuded of white flowers, and Nat set up large, elegant arrangements in antique vases. I thought the addition of the giant white trumpets of the poisonous datura plant might have been an editorial comment, but he maintained he just needed the drama they provided. White pillar candles reflected softly in rococo mirrors. The Tiffany album and the *matryoshka* dolls sat next to the guest book on a faded gold bombé chest. Easels around the room held the enlarged photos in gilt frames, and, seeing the young Katrina again, I found myself wondering what could have changed that carefree, smiling girl into the woman I knew and disliked.

Several dozen of our neighbors were joined by a number of well-dressed strangers I presumed were professional colleagues. Inspector Lichlyter showd up fairly early in the evening, passed some moments speaking to Katrina's cousin, Gavin Melnik, and raised her glass to me in an ironic toast. The condo developer, Amos Noble, arrived with Mrs. Noble and a teenaged daughter. The dignity of the occasion probably prevented anything worse than a few furious glares being aimed in his direction. Nat, acting as compere, invited people to speak about Katrina. Noble said a few respectful things about her, half of his audience stone-faced and the rest clueless. A priest arrived fairly late. He was a good-looking man in his mid-fifties, I guessed. He didn't speak as if he knew Katrina, and he offered the kind of free-form prayer I'm accustomed to thinking of as Pentecostal or Evangelical rather than traditionally Catholic. Afterward, he wandered around and spoke quietly to a couple of the other guests.

While two judges and the director of the city bar association each said a few words, the priest was gently flipping the pages of the photo album. I think I was the only person who saw him take a photo from the album and slip it into his jacket pocket. Before I could do or say anything—not that I wanted to shout *"J'accuse!"* at a priest—he made an unobtrusive exit and the room quieted for Nat's introduction of Katrina's cousin, Gavin Melnik, and I forgot about the photo in the surprise that followed.

Melnik fussed with a laptop the way everyone does, clicking on keys and getting flustered by failure messages until suddenly, and obviously to his surprise, a photo appeared of a dozen or so happy-looking blonde children wearing red T-shirts and eating ice cream cones. I'd seen the same photo in Katrina's office. With a rather charming, self-deprecating smile, he handed the laptop over to a woman sitting in the front row. She efficiently took over.

He cleared his throat nervously. The murmurs in the room quieted, and he flushed, as if he hadn't expected it. He was neat and attractive, with a striking combination of brown eyes and thick blonde hair in shades from almost platinum to light caramel.

"I just want to add to all the wonderful tributes to my cousin, Katrina," he said. That was a stretch. So far, the kindest thing anyone had said about her was that she was a "respected and well-known" attorney. No one mentioned, for example, that due to her efforts, several ex-CEOs were believed to be employed as Walmart greeters in Nevada.

"Before I begin, I want to thank Janine—" He dipped his head toward the woman operating the laptop who had introduced herself as Katrina's assistant. Janine smiled damply at him, bowed her head, and sniffed into her tissue. Melnik smiled at her. "As you can tell, I'm not very tech-savvy, but Janine kindly put this small presentation together for me. It warms my heart to know that Katrina was a respected colleague," he said, "and I've been pleased to meet so many of her personal friends tonight, too, but I want to share something I think will surprise everyone." His voice cracked, and he was obviously uncomfortable, but he seemed determined. Several people leaned forward in their chairs, obviously expecting something juicy, and it was, but not in the way anyone anticipated.

"Katrina and I connected through a family tracing website ten years ago. She was an orphan and I had recently lost my parents, and we found we were both alone in the world except for each other. She felt the lack of family very keenly, and seven years ago, she founded a home for orphans in her hometown of Kiev."

That caused wide eyes and some mutters, quickly hushed when a new photograph of children with a pair of shyly smiling Catholic nuns in old-fashioned black habits appeared on the screen behind him. Janine held her tissue over her mouth, nearly overcome with weeping; clearly the woman hadn't worked for Katrina long enough to learn to loathe her. The man sitting next to Janine absently patted her shoulder.

Melnik stepped forward to bend down and click a couple of keys on the laptop, and the photo disappeared. He looked momentarily nonplussed and clicked some more keys, and when nothing happened, did that exasperated shrug thing everyone does and abandoned the laptop to pick up the thread of his remarks.

"Katrina didn't want her philanthropy to be widely known, but I feel she wouldn't mind me telling you about it now," he said quietly. "She took a great deal of pleasure in the progress of the children, and I truly think it was the joy of her life. Katrina wasn't able to leave her busy law practice to see the results of her generosity, but I've seen the wonderful work being done at St. Olga's first hand. Katrina provided for the home in her estate plan, and so the good work of the sisters will continue into the future. I know that she'll continue to watch over the children." He smiled. "And, if you feel inclined to make a gift in her honor to the orphanage, perhaps she'll watch over you, too." The audience gave him his laugh and a smattering of applause. He handed the laptop back to Janine and stepped away, leaving his frankly astonished audience abuzz.

It brought the evening to a close on a positive note, made

Katrina seem more human, and eased some of the negative attitude toward her. I even felt a little sorry that I hadn't liked her more.

Nat stepped out onto the veranda and opened a basket resting on a table. Several white doves took to the skies and flew over Fabian Gardens. He hadn't told me he'd planned it, but it was very effective. I resolved to ask him to do that for me, too.

I don't know if all funerals and memorial services are so exhausting, but I fell into bed that evening at ten, and didn't stir until it was time to get up to help Nat at The Coffee. It was the best night's sleep I'd had in months.

CHAPTER TWELVE

The next morning, with the early rush over at The Coffee, Nat and I relived some of the details of the evening. The bar association's tribute, a large wreath on a tripod, had come crashing down at a key moment, which Nat said was the floral equivalent of being struck by lightning. One of the doves, relieved at being set free, left a small parting gift on his shoulder. "It's why I didn't come back inside until everyone'd left," he said, straightening the cuffs of his pale blue cashmere sweater.

"It was a beautiful send-off. You did a good thing, Nat," I said.

"Somebody had to, and I got the feelin' it was sorta 'ding-dong the wicked witch is dead' around here," he said. "I got plenty of practice settin' up memorials. Like fallin' off a log." The sheen in his eyes surprised me until I remembered his stories of families who refused to acknowledge their gay sons, even when their gay sons were sick and dying. I hugged him and he kissed the top of my head before disengaging.

He cleared his throat. "I swear that woman from the law office was the only one to shed a tear."

"She'd only worked there for a few weeks—"

"That explains it."

"She told me again how Katrina's paralegal had just quit in a huff—"

"Yeah, I noticed he wasn't there last night."

"—but Janine took up some of the slack, and she said Katrina was grateful."

"That might be a first. But she shouldn't be doin' paralegal stuff. They get special trainin' and licenses and all."

"It just sounded like an overdue report for Katrina to sign off on. Whatever it was, Katrina gave her more projects to work on, and for some reason that earned Janine's devoted loyalty."

Nat made a cappuccino for a customer and leaned on the counter to continue our conversation. "You know, someone stole one of those damn dolls," he said.

"It didn't just get knocked behind something?"

"I checked; the thing's gone. I'd say they were welcome to it, but—"

"Wow."

"Yeah. Lousy. Gavin was pretty philosophical about it. Said if somebody wanted it that much, they could keep it. He'd been thinkin' of maybe givin' them to people as remembrances. I told him what you said about them maybe bein' valuable, so he's gonna wait on that."

"It wasn't the big one, was it?"

"Nah. I wondered if maybe it was Noble's kid. I mean who else 'cept a kid would steal a doll? So," he added in a different tone, as he busied himself building a pyramid of coffee mugs, still hot from the dishwasher, "Katrina was showin' good form the other day." I pretended not to know what he was talking about. It was as close as he'd come to mentioning my scene with Katrina the day before she died, and I was flooded with the same near panic.

He would normally tease out the meaning of Katrina's spite and laugh over it with me. Instead, he looked at my no doubt pale face and launched into a story of the Coast Guard inspectors who'd made an official visit to the coffee shop the day before.

"The Coast Guard? Aren't they like the Navy? Why would they be inspecting coffee shops?"

He snickered. "They're apparently responsible for inland waterways runnin' into the Bay and someone"—his eyebrows gave the word the ironic twist it deserved—"said I'd be pollutin' the underground creek under Polk Street with cleanin' products or somethin'—I'm not sure, but anyway, they came to take a look."

I blinked. "There's an underground creek?" I'd renovated a neglected old building in the neighborhood, up to and including preparing it for earthquakes, but a hidden creek sounded like a new and unwelcome threat.

"No. Well, yeah, but it's more like a seasonal seep in a conduit, and since California's as dry as Abilene in August, I doubt it's seen a drop of water in years."

"What did the Coast Guard say?"

"Well, first, lemme tell you they were both in uniform. And you know how I love—"

"—a man in uniform, I know," I interrupted and rolled my eyes.

"Anyway, they took a look-see and said everythin's fine. They gave me a list of eco-cleanin' products to use. The cute one gave me his phone number."

"Of course he did," I said. "Are you going to call him?"

"I might. Think he'd wear the hat to bed?"

I spluttered, Nat laughed, and the awkward moment passed.

CHAPTER THIRTEEN

Aromas had made it onto the tourist trail after the publicity of a few months ago, and Katrina's murder only made a brief dip in the number of our customers. We were busy again at the end of the week. I asked Haruto to add a couple of extra half days to his work schedule, and Davie was still on for three afternoons a week, but I needed at least two more part-timers. I'd been reluctant to hire anyone in case the increased tourist business was temporary. Then I'd need to lay them off, which I wouldn't have the heart to do, and I'd be worse off than before. My former partner had left the store in some debt. It wasn't a huge amount, and I could have paid it off from my personal funds, but it had become a point of pride to get Aromas into the black and prosperous.

While I did some sums on the back on an envelope, I also wondered who—besides me—had a reason to kill Katrina. I scribbled over the numbers to make a list of potential killers. It could have been someone we knew nothing about, like one of the ex-CEOs maybe. But, if it wasn't random— and Nat's idea about her briefcase seemed to bear that out—it had to be someone who knew where she lived, who knew she'd be parked on the street, and who knew she'd be leaving for work at five in the morning. Nat was right; it wasn't business, it was personal. So it could be her cousin, Gavin, although he'd seemed pretty broken up about losing his only relative. He didn't inherit anything, so it was hard to see a motive, especially since he'd probably lost his home, too. We'd hardly seen Matthew on the street in the days since her death, but if he had a guilty conscience, he wouldn't run away; he'd be sure to tell the first person who asked. I couldn't picture either Professor or Ruth D'Allessio killing her, even if they were going to be living next to the condo development. I wondered about the priest who'd stolen her photo; I supposed he could have been trophy hunting like a serial killer, but did priests commit murder? Wouldn't they be more likely to call down hell and damnation on someone? Then there was Angela, with her secret abortion. I didn't know her, but Nat said she'd always struck him as a fairly colorless, pleasant enough woman. Still, backed into a corner and faced with the loss of her fiancé, perhaps she'd struck back. I also put a reluctant question mark against Sabina and Kurt, who'd recently given up their opposition to the condo project.

By then I'd tumbled down the rabbit hole as far as I was willing to go, largely because I couldn't imagine any of these people chasing me down an alley at gunpoint. I abandoned the list when a man who'd been hesitating in the doorway suddenly decided to come inside. Little wisps of fog swirled into the shop as the door closed. Older men often approached the shop cautiously for some reason, as if they weren't sure of their welcome. This one was dressed head-to-toe in black, even to the scarf looped around his neck. He was probably in his sixties, and a little bit portly. He had a thick patch of scarring down one side of his face and across his eyes and forehead. I gave him a friendly smile, but he looked around at the shelves of personal grooming products with faint distaste, as if he wished they weren't quite so . . . feminine. He spent a few minutes wandering around, picking things up and then putting them back, the way people do when they don't know what they want or they're trying to waste time for some reason without earning the shopkeeper's ire.

He came to the counter with a bottle of shampoo and a shower cap. He was essentially bald, so I had to assume they were a gift of some sort, although when I offered him gift wrap he just seemed puzzled. He had an accent I didn't recognize and an odd, slightly smoky smell. His fingers were nicotine stained, which is something you don't see very often now that it's almost impossible to find a place to smoke in comfort. He smiled, exposing a gold canine tooth.

"I think perhaps you are the person I am seeking," he said. Actually, his accent was so heavy I'm not sure I got that right, but I think that's what he said. The smile fell away quickly, and his face was suddenly completely without expression, which was slightly unnerving.

He asked me something so out of the blue I assumed I'd misheard. "Excuse me?" I paused in the act of handing him his purchases. The turquoise-and-white-striped bags usually gave me a little lift, even after a year in business and a lot of high-impact water under the bridge.

"I am looking for Mr. Clement Pryce. I think you might know him."

I hesitated. That sounded as if he knew my grandfather, whose name was actually Pryce-Fitton. He could just be a nice guy, ex-friend of my grandfather's, but his eyes bothered me. I'd learned to read people by watching their eyes—remind me to tell you about the kid who stabbed me in the hand with a ballpoint pen. This man's eyes were dead. They were the kind of eyes you'd expect to see on a prisoner of war or someone who'd lost his family in a fire. On the other hand, he didn't seem nervous enough to be planning to rob me, or charming enough to be a reporter. He could be a photographer from one of the London tabloids; all he'd need was a phone with a sharp camera lens. On the other hand, he was older—and better dressed—than any of the robbers or journalists I'd come across, but it wouldn't do any harm to be cautious.

"I'm sorry, I don't think so," I said, and fiddled with the glasses I sometimes wear nowadays because I couldn't wear a Batgirl mask to protect my identity.

"Ah! Perhaps this will help. I have something—" He reached into his coat pocket and pulled out a handful of small papers and receipts. He sorted through them, crushing a couple of them in his fist and tossing them on the floor, and then reached into the breast pocket of his overcoat. He pulled out one of those old-fashioned leather wallets almost the size of a paperback book, the kind people used to take on vacations because it fit their passport and oddly sized foreign currency

"It is this." He carefully withdrew a piece of newsprint, which seemed to be an ad for lingerie, and I took a step back. Robbers, reporters—I guess fetishists needed a category of their own. You might think I was unreasonably skittish, but the last time a perv had come into the shop, the few clothes he'd been wearing had been quickly dispatched for my edification. Grappling with a naked man who'd managed to douse himself in one of our more expensive body lotions was an experience I had no desire to repeat.

But he unfolded the paper and showed me the other side by smoothing it flat on the counter with his palm and then pushing it toward me with a stiff finger. I recognized the image of my grandfather. It had appeared in *The Chronicle* a few months before, during all the excitement caused by two murders, a near-fatal assault, and the arrest of one of our own. We're a close-knit neighborhood, and, speaking for myself, we hadn't yet recovered from the series of shocks.

I took a couple of seconds to regroup.

"This gentleman," he said impatiently, pointing a finger at Grandfather. The photographer had caught him walking past the front window of Aromas, frowning at the camera. It was actually a very bad likeness, and I was surprised he was recognizable to anyone but me. "He and I were colleagues years ago. Imagine my surprise seeing him in the newspaper." He blinked at me and smiled widely, evidently to encourage my participation in his astonishment. The smile disappeared almost instantly, and his oddly flat expression returned.

I picked up the clipping. "This was from quite a while ago," I said.

He shrugged, which didn't help me much.

"I don't think I know him," I lied, because lying was practically second nature. "But I can ask around, if that will help."

He flashed the gold tooth briefly in another smile. "Excellent," he said. "Thank you very much." It came out like *"Tunk you verree masch,"* which took me a second or two to grasp.

"When you find him," he said with a slight bow, "tell him Sergei was asking for him. Sergei Viktor Wolf." He shifted his scarf out of the way to reveal a Roman collar, which explained the all-black wardrobe. It was a surprise, and one that you might think would give me reason to be more trusting. On the other hand, it reminded me that I'd seen the priest at Katrina's memorial filching a photo from her album, which wasn't exactly priestly behavior. I'd have to remember to mention it to Nat and see if he knew which photo was missing.

I stopped staring at his priest's collar and pulled my phone from the back pocket of my jeans. The collar made a friendship between them less likely because my grandfather was slightly suspicious of Catholic priests. It was an unusual prejudice in a man who was otherwise very modern in his thinking, and predated the scandals of recent years, when mistrusting priests seemed to have turned into a cottage industry. I also couldn't imagine how they could have been "colleagues" in the past. As far as I knew, my grandfather spent his career in fairly high levels of the civil service, something to do with agricultural policy. When I was young, he was always going over to the countries of the old Soviet Union to discuss tractors and food production methods with politicians. I couldn't think of a time when he would have worked with a Catholic priest. Sergei's heavy accent sounded vaguely Russian; maybe that's where they had met.

"Would you like to leave a number?"

He patted his pockets, took out his phone, and clicked through a couple of screens, then recited a number with an unfamiliar area code, which I dutifully entered into my phone under "W."

Then, making conversation the way you do, especially if you're still mentally apologizing for thinking he was a

pervert, I handed him his bag again and said, "Are you visiting the city?"

"Indeed, yes. I come to visit friend, who died."

That sounded like a funeral. "I'm very sorry for the loss
of your friend."

He shrugged. "Not close friend," he said, and I adjusted
my sympathetic expression several degrees.

Ignoring my professed ignorance of Grandfather or his
whereabouts, he added: "Tell Mr. Pryce it is Sergei Viktor
Wolf. From Houston. That is very important, eh? That you
mention Houston."

I nodded, and after waiting for a couple of seconds and
blinking rapidly, he said again, "Sergei Viktor Wolf from
Houston."

"Got it," I said. He hesitated again, very obviously lack-
ing confidence in me as a messenger, but then turned and
left, closing the door quietly behind him. Another wisp of
fog floated inside.

After he left I took advantage of the store being empty,
grabbed the broom, and did a quick sweep around, since he
wasn't the only customer who threw papers on the floor. As
usual, and no matter that I'd swept the floor less than an
hour earlier, I rounded up a few sprigs of potpourri and a
receipt or two and a crumpled, and presumably used, paper
napkin. I made sure everything got tipped into the dustpan
without getting closer to it than the length of my broom.
Sometimes it's just nonstop glamour around here.

I also swept away the small drift of lightweight rubbish
gathered in the doorway. It was usually one of my first jobs
upon opening, but I'd had other things on my mind that
morning. The prevailing breeze blew in Aromas' direction,
clearing detritus from the entrance of the women's hat shop

opposite and depositing it on mine. It happened all up and down Polk Street, to the chagrin of merchants on this side and the mild satisfaction of those opposite. I made quick work of today's collection, which was as eclectic as usual, with a discount coupon to the nail salon on the next block, a handful of dead leaves, and a crumpled paper coaster featuring a golden Venus de Milo. There was also a cup from a coffee shop across town, which I hastily stepped on and crushed rather than risk having to explain the prevailing breeze thing to Nat.

CHAPTER FOURTEEN

I started to worry about Sergei. It was an odd little interlude. Grandfather was using one of several names he was entitled to use (that's the British upper classes for you), so even as "Mr. Pryce" he shouldn't have been on anyone's radar this far from home. Also, I happened to know the area codes for Houston because Nat was from there. His grandparents telephoned sometimes, and he would mouth "713" at me and roll his eyes, because they were apparently living sometime in the 1990s and their calls usually included urgent pleas for him to move away from San Francisco because they were convinced he would catch AIDS here by breathing the air. Sergei Viktor Wolf had given me a different area code. He was lying. Or, I told myself, he lived there but still had his old cell phone number. That happened, right?

"He said his name was Sergei Viktor Wolf. From Houston," I added conscientiously when I telephoned my grandfather. There was a long silence. "Grandfather?"

"Hang up the phone, Judy," he said crisply, and the call dropped. I stared at it in my hand, a little surprised. Grandfather is as sharp as someone half his age, which is about seventy, and my name isn't Judy.

Before I had time to call him back, the shop's landline began to ring. I'd been told to keep it in case the cell towers were knocked down in an earthquake, but I hadn't used it since we opened. It was a wall phone with a curly wire on the handset, and shelves had been built around it some time after brick-sized, navy blue phones had their heyday in the 1980s. It had one of those harsh bells that kept ringing and ringing while I moved things around, eventually unearthing it behind a box of body lotion samples.

"Um, hello?" I was pretty sure it was Grandfather again, but it felt odd to be uncertain. It was like being in one of those black-and-white movies where no one knew who was calling until they picked up the phone.

"Theophania, did you use your cell phone while Sergei was with you?"

"Only to put his number into my phone."

Another silence followed. I could almost hear him thinking.

"Don't use your cell phone for the time being for any conversation you don't want overheard—"

"Overheard by wh—?"

"Why don't we meet for lunch, my dear? The Garden Court at two o'clock?" He hung up again without waiting for my reply, which was worrying. Grandfather didn't do spontaneous, and he'd been abrupt to the point of rudeness. Grandfather was often abrupt, but he was never rude.

All the same, an invitation from him carried pretty much the same compulsion as a parliamentary writ, so I called Haruto, who lived above the shop in the apartment below mine, and who obligingly came downstairs to keep Aromas open, carrying his Siamese cat, Gar Wood, and telling me about surfing that morning at Ocean Beach. Gar Wood stalked around for a minute or two in the arrogant way of Siamese cats, and then settled into a sunny spot in the window and started to wash one of her back legs. She and my dog, Lucy, had reached a cranky detente. By and large they ignored each other when Lucy deigned to join me in the shop; she usually preferred to stay upstairs, solely, I was convinced, so I'd have to trudge up two flights of stairs at lunchtime to take her down for a break in the gardens.

Haruto looked like a cross between the Mikado and a flower child, with his raven black hair pulled back and wrapped into a knot with raffia. He only needed to sleep for three hours a night, so he was always looking for things to fill in the extra hours. He kept busy designing Japanese gardens and was a sort of freelance security consultant, which meant he spent the early morning hours hacking into his clients' computer systems to test their fire walls. He worked for me a couple of half days a week, mostly for the entertainment value, I think, or when I needed some extra help, and he'd expressed some interest in buying the shop. Some days I was just about prepared to give him the place, but until it was out of debt, it didn't seem like a very generous gesture.

He waggled a hand at me as I passed the front window on my way toward California Street. I got nods and smiles from my Polk Street neighbors, who had been accepting, welcoming even, when I'd opened Aromas. I'd bought the three-story building after it had been vacant for years, which meant I had refurbished the neighborhood blight and they'd seemed oddly grateful. One of them told me the building had reached the stage where they were worried about homeless squatters breaking in and setting up camp. Now, if I did say so myself, newly painted, with its climbing rose under control, and Aromas busy and attractive, it was one of the neighborhood jewels. With its new plumbing and wiring it had two full-floor flats. I lived in the top and Haruto was currently my tenant in the middle one. For a short while, Ben had lived in the ground floor studio, but nowadays, when he was in town, he stayed upstairs with me.

My immediate neighbors were Bonbons Chocolat, where I spent too much time and money, and Peter Williams Jewelry. The block also had Donna Marie's Best Buds, selling bouquets from tin containers on the sidewalk; Mr. Lee's no-name grocery on the corner; a hardware store; two antiques shops; a couple of clothing shops; an expensive hat shop, whose clientele was largely African-American women; and Hang Chuw's, which made the best dim sum and garlic noodles in the city. One of the smaller stores at the end of the block did one-hour photo printing and sold cameras. I didn't know anyone who had their photos printed, but the store stayed in business somehow, and I'd bought my camera from them. There was also our local, Coconut Harry's; a pizza and falafel place, and a small but pricey Michelin four-star restaurant, which drew people from other parts of the city. And of course now there was The Coffee, which filled our need for coffee, pastries, and sandwiches.

It was a neighborhood where people lived, worked, and shopped, on the nicer end of Polk Street, away from the rent boys and SRO hotels farther south. It meant I could do pretty much all of my errands close to home, and I didn't often have a reason to leave. The truth was, I felt more exposed, less able to protect myself, in areas of the city where strangers might recognize me. I preferred to stay where people knew me—or at least thought they did.

Most of the rough sleepers—what Nat told me are called hoboes here—who normally hung around downtown had been chased into the outer neighborhoods by one of the city's periodic "Clean Up Market Street" campaigns. In addition to Matthew, who had apparently lived on Polk Street on and off for the past year, the neighborhood now had a couple of mostly pleasant, weathered men using the street as their combination dining room, bedroom, and bathroom. Like Matthew they seemed harmless, although they were considerably more mentally together. St. Christopher's, the Catholic church on the next block, had a small overnight shelter in the basement where some of them stayed.

I caught the California Street cable car, hopped off at Montgomery, and walked the few blocks to the Palace Hotel on Market Street. In an effort to thin out what had become a sludge-slow tangle of traffic along Market, it was closed to private cars, allowing buses and bicycles and delivery vehicles to make their own accommodations with local pedestrians. I often wondered why the city streets were so much more crowded with people in those old movies, with packs of them waiting to cross the road at every intersection. More people live here now, so where are they all? In their cars, perhaps. But not on Market Street.

The sidewalks on Market were wide and gracious, left over from the time when the street was the city's main thoroughfare and the main business district as well. I knew from my movie watching that, years ago, theaters and restaurants used to line both sides of the street, but they'd been mostly replaced by discount electronics stores and fast-food places, which gave it a down-market feel. All of which meant that the uber-posh Palace, one of the city's grandest hotels, was set like a gem in a tarnished pinchbeck setting. As I reached the marble steps, a couple of ragged men with a well-fed dog on a piece of bright yellow rope were shuffling away from the entrance under the watchful eye of a doorman. For some reason, he was wearing a bowler hat, but otherwise he looked ready to bench-press a bus.

When Grandfather arrived at 1:57, I was loitering near the display cases of historical memorabilia, and I saw him before he noticed me. He attracted interested glances as he strode across the lobby—and not just from women. His hair was silver, but he was soldier-straight, with the kind of angular good looks that aged well. The Batgirl stuff disguises some of the resemblance, but Grandfather and I both have our family's standard-issue, china blue eyes. He was wearing what I always thought of as his casual uniform: gray trousers with a knife-edge crease and an elderly but immaculate navy blue cashmere jacket. He was also wearing an Eton Ramblers tie. He had his Aquascutum raincoat over his arm as usual, but the tie gave me pause—Grandfather wasn't an Old Etonian, he went to Harrow, as did Lord Byron and Benedict Cumberbatch, although not at the same time. Men of his class and generation wore their ties like labels, to help them recognize fellow members of regiments, schools, universities, and clubs. The Eton tie was as out of place on him as a scribbled mustache on a portrait of the Queen.

He placed a hand lightly at my elbow, and we were seated at one of the Garden Court's best tables—Grandfather had that effect on *maître d's*—before we had time to exchange more than our usual, slightly formal greetings.

Even though the enormous Garden Court was arranged cleverly with see-through screens and potted palm trees to provide the illusion of privacy, it was actually possible to take in the entire room at a glance, which I noticed Grandfather doing as we sat down. Then came the discussion of dishes and ingredients with the waiter, the ordering of a Manhattan for him and their signature flowery iced tea for me, and the obligatory appreciation of what was arguably the most beautiful public room in the city.

I finally interrupted him as he seemed about to launch into details about the glass ceiling dome. "Grandfather, for heaven's sake. What's all this about?"

CHAPTER FIFTEEN

Ten minutes later I was staring at him, unsure if I was being teased. Except Grandfather didn't tease.

"You're not old enough to have been involved in postwar espionage," I whispered across my salmon salad.

"My father was."

"Pop-Pop?" My great-grandfather was a kindly old gent who gave me sips of his brandy and pulled gold sovereigns from behind my ears. He'd died when I was about eight years old, leaving Grandfather as the *de facto* head of our family, even though he had older brothers and sisters. My family was privileged and wealthy and had been that way for a very long time.

"He spent a good deal of time until forty years ago traveling back and forth from the Soviet Union. As a youngster, I used to carry letters for him occasionally."

I looked at him, aghast. "Pop-Pop used you as—as a *courier*?"

He gave me a stern look. "Traveling with a child is excellent camouflage. When I finished at Cambridge I joined the—er, firm myself. Your mother, too—"

"My *mother*? Oh my God. We're a third-generation family of"—I looked around furtively—"*spies*?"

Not sure if I should feel slighted that no one had initiated me into the family business, I sat back in my seat and stared at him.

"Close your mouth, Theophania," he said. My jaws snapped shut. "How is the salmon?"

"How is the—Grandfather! Pop-Pop was a spy? You were a spy? My *mother* was a spy? Sergei—"

"Probably best if we don't use that name, my dear."

"Oh my God. Why didn't I know any of this? Why tell me now?"

He pursed his lips. "Your courage and resourcefulness recently made me reevaluate my decision not to tell you about the family . . . history." If he was giving me undeserved credit for resolving the turmoil of a few months ago, I'd take it, but—"In addition to which," he went on, "our friend's appearance at your shop is unsettling. I want you to understand what may be at stake and to be on your guard."

I dropped my knife and fork with a clatter that startled the young waiter as he approached with a pitcher of iced tea. "What's going on? Does this have anything to do with Ser—do you know why your friend wants to see you?"

Grandfather put his elbows on the table and steepled his fingers. "If I had to guess, and I do, then perhaps I have been . . . outed, and he is concerned about—er—family repercussions."

"I'm so sorry, dear," the waiter said with a sympathetic grimace, and then blushed and busied himself filling my iced tea glass before touching Grandfather lightly on the shoulder and withdrawing.

I'm pretty sure all of this went over Grandfather's head.

"Outed? How could you be outed? And by whom? And why? And whose family are we talking about having repercussions?"

He pulled on one ear. "Remember, my dear, this is conjecture. The family in this case is our American cousins. They will be concerned that their own, er, sons and daughters will be exposed also. Our friend was a colleague twenty-five years ago. But he was injured and left the firm, entering a Catholic seminary to study for the priesthood." He pursed his lips again. "Truthfully, I wondered if he was in deep cover. He had been involved in a particularly brutal operation in Eastern Europe, and afterward he apparently had a Damascene moment. He eventually went through with his ordination. I couldn't imagine the firm taking things that far, so I assume he had experienced a genuine conversion. I haven't heard from him for—it must be twenty years. The last thing I knew, he was in South America. Colombia, I think."

I had no idea where to locate Colombia on a map. I was on slightly firmer ground with South America, but the only thing I associated with Colombia was drug smugglers and death squads, having watched an episode of *Narcos* at an impressionable age. Grandfather moved on while I was still trying to catch up.

"The Americans are extremely sensitive and don't really trust us—or anyone, really," he said thoughtfully. "His appearance here might mean that something, somewhere, has gone wrong with—well, it would have to be an historical operation. Or I suppose it could be something unrelated, and he needed my nonprofessional help."

I tried to keep my expression neutral as I chewed a mouthful of something. He gave me one of his fleeting smiles, and after a short pause, he took a small, leather agenda from the breast pocket of his jacket and slid it toward me. "Please write down the telephone number he gave you."

I pulled out my phone. "I could just—"

"Write it, please, Theophania. And then erase it from your telephone."

He glanced at the number and then tore out the part of the page where I'd written it, then kept tearing it until it was practically dust and put some of the dust on his empty plate and the rest of it in his pocket. He took my telephone, scrolled and tapped through several screens, changed a setting or two, and returned it to me. I had no idea what he'd done, and I didn't like to ask.

He raised a hand, and our waiter instantly appeared with the bill for lunch in a discreet folder. Grandfather checked it cursorily, handed it back to him with a black credit card, and then waited until he was out of earshot. "I will telephone our friend and meet him later today. I need to catch up with him this afternoon because I have a meeting to attend this evening." He seemed to think for a minute. "Hmph. If his situation isn't toxic, and doesn't cross too many national borders, I might invite him to join us."

"A meeting? National borders?"

"A few old colleagues who get together every month or so for dinner and drinks."

"Old colleagues." I took a deep breath. "You mean— spies? Other spies?"

"Well, former military intelligence officers, for the most part."

Of course. "Former intell . . ." I had a sudden qualm. "Are they all American?"

"Hardly, my dear; I'm a member, after all. My group in

London is more geographically diverse, but even here we have quite a representative sampling of international—"

"Oh my God, there's a group in London?"

"We have several chapters."

I choked on my iced tea, coughing and spluttering, and finally managed to get out a croak as another thought occurred to me and I bent low to whisper across the table. "Do you mean Russians? Are you friends with Russian . . . um . . . intelligence officers? Can't you be deported for that?" I looked quickly around to see if anyone was listening, which seemed to amuse him.

His hand absently touched the Eton Ramblers tie, and his lips twitched at my no doubt appalled expression.

"Is the tie for . . . our friend, instead of a red carnation in your buttonhole?"

"It's been some time and that photograph didn't capture me very well. In fact, I'm a little surprised—I thought the tie might help him to identify me, since he's an Eton Old Boy. It was a joke between us years ago. His eyesight has been poor for quite some time. An acid attack, I believe. You said he was wearing a Roman collar, Theophania, so unless he's *in mufti*, that will help me, even if he has changed a good deal."

My struggling brain caught up. "Oh, God, an acid attack—his face is badly scarred. But why would he come here to try and find you?"

"I can't imagine. The—er—codes he used are very out of date, of course. Viktor and Houston are, or were, in the nature of an SOS." He thought for a moment. "No, not an emergency; more like a call for assistance.

"But why did he come to me?"

"You said he had a photo of me taken outside your shop;

perhaps it was simply the only place he knew where to begin." In a different tone he asked, "Who have you told about your hiatus here, Theophania?"

I assumed the subject of MI5 or 6, or Her Majesty's Secret Service and the family business, was finished. When Grandfather moved on, he moved *on*. "I'm in touch with a few friends in London through text or video apps, but I haven't told them where I am." When it came down to it, I didn't trust any of my harebrained friends not to sell me to the UK tabloids, which were zealous and unmerciful.

"What about Frederick?"

My cousin Frederick—Freddie—was the family black sheep and chronically short of cash. With any kind of financial incentive, he'd hand me over to the tabloids without a second thought. "Especially not Frederick. He thinks I'm in the Canaries."

"Ah," he said. We considered the dessert menu in silence for a minute or two. "He is coming for a visit."

"Oh, God, really?" Frederick wasn't anyone's idea of an ideal houseguest. He tended to overstay his welcome, often by months.

"I'm afraid so. He thinks I'm antelope hunting in Wyoming. I may have to lease a hotel suite in Jackson Hole so he can visit me there." He smiled faintly, and I did a mental double take. I'd thought he was simply being courteously reticent and quintessentially English when he'd taken to my strange new life, and my new identity, without a hint of disquiet. I'd obviously been mistaken. He was thoroughly enjoying himself.

Even with most of my thoughts in turmoil, I knew how very lucky I was to have him in my life. Within weeks of telling him where I had landed—it didn't occur to me even for a moment to keep it from him—he followed me here and leased a home on Telegraph Hill. He'd never said so, but I assumed he felt I needed some adult supervision. He'd given up his very comfortable life in Kent, surrounded by horses, hunting hounds, and Capability Brown landscapes to live in a city where, honestly, he was a fish out of water. I was vaguely pleased that he had some friends—even if they were spies. Ex-spies.

"Thank you, Grandfather." He looked at me with a raised eyebrow and then at our coffee cups, as if he thought I were thanking him for lunch. I hurried through the next bit: "For moving here, for helping me, for everything."

His expression didn't alter. "Our sojourn has been interesting for me," he said, "and, if you don't mind my mentioning it, Theophania, I felt you might need some . . . support after . . . the events of last year. In any event, I was glad to do it, my dear."

I tried to swallow the lump in my throat, recognizing the partial truth hiding his refusal to say that he, too, had needed some propping up. The comforting idea that I'd been any help at all was fairly remote. "Grandfather—"

But he cleared his throat and briskly checked his wristwatch. "I should telephone our friend right away; if his personality hasn't changed, he will be pacing the floor waiting for me."

"I thought he might be a news photographer," I mumbled.

Grandfather laughed like a seal barking.

CHAPTER SIXTEEN

My father had been famous; not just a little famous, a lot famous. I couldn't imagine how my mother had been able to live a secret life next to the spotlight he worked in. I was starting to feel crushed under the weight of my own lies and prevarications after little more than a year, but she had done much more, year after year, constructing two completely separate lives for herself. How had she managed it, and had my father known?

By the time Davie came in to work after school, I wouldn't have noticed if my customers had walked away with half the store and I couldn't make change without counting everything twice. Even Katrina's murder had been shoved into the background by images of my mother and my grandfather running from spies, or possibly chasing them, across the back alleys of Europe. I counted out the same roll of quarters in the cash drawer several times and found I was staring out the window at Matthew's comforter, rolled neatly in the doorway of Bonbons Chocolat.

"I haven't seen Matthew around," I said at random, wondering if the reunion between Sergei and Grandfather had happened and what Sergei could need Grandfather's help with.

Davie silently relieved me of the quarters and closed the cash drawer. "He's okay. He's just scared," he muttered.

"Do you know where he lives when he's not on Polk?"

"He's got a squat up near the panhandle. Don't know where, exactly," he added before I asked. "The priest at St. Christopher's might know."

"Good thinking, Davie."

He snorted. "Davo. FTFY, Theo."

I didn't know what that meant and I didn't want to ask. He didn't often talk in Internet acronyms, but I think that was one. It occurred to me as he turned back to his work that the insistence on his new name, like finding the ice to take care of my shoulder, indicated a shift in our relationship, and it left me a little off-balance. He was in the habit of coming upstairs to my flat for a snack or a meal several times a week. The last time, he'd put out the placemats and cutlery on the table, as if to separate himself from the kid who up until then had been happy to eat on the couch with his feet on the coffee table. Of course, until recently I hadn't had placemats.

My dreams that night were full of running footsteps and formless terror. There was nothing specific for me to be afraid of, but I was overcome by dread. I knew I couldn't escape, that I should turn and face it, but instead I always ran, my feet tangled in ropes and wire, or bogged down in mud and quicksand.

I sat up in bed, heart pounding. Nothing too mysterious about the symbolism in that one. Lucy stirred in her sleep, and I stroked her and stared at the ceiling for a while. I turned my head to look at the empty pillow next to me, and then patted the books and papers on my nightstand until I found my phone to check the time. It was only three o'clock.

I took a hot shower and made some tea and took a cup back to bed with me, and dug out the files I'd stolen from Katrina's office.

I looked over the information Katrina had discovered about me again. If she'd planned to threaten me with exposure, she had plenty of ammunition. The incorporation document for Safe Haven Enterprises, with my real name and signature, and a copy of Haruto's lease, with my current name as owner, were particularly revealing. He and I had exchanged documents and signatures via an online document signature service, which I'd been assured was secure. Katrina might have used the same service, but surely that wouldn't give her access to everyone's documents.

The photos she'd found online included one of me and a few friends in the fountains of Trafalgar Square, celebrating my eighteenth birthday. That one actually made me smile. Grandfather had been less amused when he collected me from the local police station. The file included a copy of the police report from that night. Other photos included the one taken of me the night of my mother's death. There were copies of some of my e-mails, too. I wasn't sure what level of expertise was required to get these things. The incorporation papers might be public records, but the e-mails and the lease shouldn't be, which implied some kind of advanced computer skills. The only computer whiz I knew was Haruto, and I trusted him. Maybe I shouldn't. That was a new thought. There were no originals, just copies, so I set them aside to burn the next time I had a fire.

I didn't know what to do with the other folder. I'd stolen it in a confused impulse to protect my friends and neighbors, but now I couldn't decide if it would be creepy to keep it or better to destroy it.

I closed it and stuffed it under my pillow again.

I fell asleep still pondering and didn't wake until nearly seven thirty. I sent Nat a quick apologetic text and walked up to The Coffee, shivering a little as usual. There were no other people on the street, unless you counted Matthew, who was just waking up in the doorway of Bonbons Chocolat, wrapped in a pink flowered duvet. I was remarkably relieved to see him; I hadn't realized until that moment how concerned I'd been by his absence. He sat up as I approached him and looked blearily around.

"Hi, Matthew," I said, and he nodded, eyes to the comforter, his fingers tracing the flowers, one-by-one. He counted them quietly to himself as I tried to get his attention. "Would you like a muffin? How about a coffee?"

"Black, no sugar; black no sugar," he muttered nearly under his breath. "Muffin, muffin, muffin."

He didn't speak much and what he said didn't always seem rational, although even his oddest remarks had some sort of real world underpinnings if you thought about them enough. He'd been muttering, I thought, about mats, for several days a few months ago, and I thought he meant he wanted one to sleep on, so I bought him a yoga mat at the variety store on the next block. But he'd just rolled it carefully and added it to the assortment of mysterious packages that hung from his waist on ragged strings. Then one morning he'd handed me a grubby piece of paper with *MATTH* printed crookedly in pencil. Finally grasping what he'd been trying to tell me, I asked him if he was Matt or Matthew and he smiled at the ground.

"Matthew, Matthew, Matthew," he'd said, so Matthew it was. Sometimes he seemed relatively clean and at other times, like today, he and his clothes were filthy and he smelled terrible, as if he'd been dumpster diving or digging in the dirt somewhere. A small insect ran out of his beard and along his jawline, and without thinking, I reached down to pick it off his face and crush it between my thumbnails. He didn't take any notice, concentrating on his count of the flowers on his comforter.

Someone from St. Christopher's occasionally persuaded him to take a shower and sleep for a night in the small shelter there. One of the volunteers either washed his clothes or, if they were too far gone, wrapped them up in a bundle, which he invariably insisted upon keeping, and gave him an assortment from their donated clothes bin. He refused to relinquish the incredibly grimy and bedraggled raincoat he wore every day. During the day, bundles of greasy clothes dangled from strings around his neck and from the piece of rope tied around his waist. He used them as pillows when he slept outside. His shopping cart was usually half full of the cans and bottles he collected, and he protected it ferociously.

He might still be in the doorway when I returned with his coffee and a muffin, but sometimes he just wandered off to wherever he spent his days. If I left him now, he might not be here when I came back. He usually left his comforter in a tangle in the doorway; Faye-Bella rolled and saved the comforter for him, and often she ran it through the washer and dryer, too.

I called the rectory and explained that Matthew was in a fairly bad way, and the man I spoke to said he appreciated the call and would send someone.

"I tried to bring him in last night but he wouldn't come," he said.

"Bring him a coffee, will you?" I whispered into the phone. "I'll stay with him until you get here."

But Matthew shoo'd me away brusquely when I tried to linger. I sat on the edge of the planter outside Aromas, trying to keep an eye on him without crowding him. In ten minutes or so I was surprised to see Katrina's cousin, Gavin Melnik, approaching. I was even more surprised when he reached Matthew, crouched down, and handed over a paper coffee cup.

Matthew took it and started mumbling: "Coffee, black. Coffee, black. Coffee black."

"Right, I remember. Coffee black," Melnik said. "So how about coming over to the shelter? Maybe get you some new clothes, what do you say?" He stood up slowly.

"Coffee, black. Coffee, black. Thief. Thief. Thief."

Melnik hesitated, as if he wasn't sure how to manage, but then he rallied. "Sure, we'll have more coffee, too. Want to come with me? I won't let anyone take your stuff."

Matthew stood up and let his comforter fall to the ground. Then he just waited, with his head down. Melnik reached out his hand slowly and gently took his arm, but Matthew threw him off with surprising force. Melnik took a couple of steps back and raised both hands in a "surrender" gesture.

"No touching today; I get it," Melnik said gently. He bent his head to look up under Matthew's tangle of greasy hair. "Sometimes Matthew likes to touch, but not today, right, Matthew?"

Matthew flung his head up, and his eyes darted from left to right and back again; he seemed to be anxiously consulting people only he could see. "Not today. Not today. Not today." I couldn't tell if he was talking to us, or if his imaginary companions needed reassurance. Melnik stood up straight and said to him, "Father Martin will be at the rectory, and we'll get you some more coffee." After a brief hesitation he started to move off down the sidewalk, and Matthew followed a couple of paces behind, pushing his shopping cart. I watched them until Matthew caught up after half a block. He grabbed a handful of Melnik's sweatshirt and held on as they made their way slowly toward St. Christopher's. For the first time I realized that, although he looked much older, Matthew was probably only in his twenties. Melnik, who had several years on him, actually looked younger.

I didn't know if Inspector Lichlyter had spoken to Matthew about the night Katrina was killed, or if she'd get anything coherent from him if she had. But if he had seen something, he could be a helpful witness, given the right encouragement. Or he might be in danger. As soon as I thought of that, I left her a message to let her know where he'd be for the next hour, if she wanted to interview him.

After a busy day, I spent most of the night reading and rereading online encyclopedias and English news stories from the time just before I fled London. If my mother had been a spy, I thought—hoped, I suppose—that there was something more to my parents' story. But there was no hint, anywhere, that it was anything but a tragic murder followed by a remorseful suicide. It left me feeling depressed and anxious and reliving the worst time of my life, when my life had changed forever and I found myself alone and hiding in a strange city.

My father was more-or-less a penniless artist when he and my mother met. She had surprised her parents by taking a first in classics at Oxford, and surprised them again by turning down more eligible suitors to marry him. Within twenty years, specializing in portraits of the rich and famous, my father was so well known that he was rich and famous himself.

When I was a young girl, I learned to sit quietly if I wanted to stay in my father's studio while he worked, and it eventually became so much a part of our routine, I think he often forgot I was there. When he wasn't working, standing like a giant at his easel, he was reading. If his model was present, then he accompanied them out of his studio, but if he was working alone, there was almost no time between setting his paints down and picking up a book. It was part of the same movement—left hand releasing the giant palette onto his table; right hand onto the book of the moment, opened to the page where he'd left off reading, so there was no delay, no time for thought, before picking up the threads of his novel. He would walk away from his easel already reading and quietly sink down into an armchair where he might stay, almost unmoving, for ten minutes, or an hour, or even three hours without raising his eyes from the page except to occasionally glance over to his work in progress. Sometimes I'd be reading, too, but often I'd leave while he was still engrossed. He would stay there until my mother called upstairs that lunch—or dinner, or the car— was waiting, and was he coming down? I can still see the slight frown, the almost glassy-eyed concentration, as he transferred from one state of mind to another. It was only later that I thought it strange, that it was almost as if he were afraid to have time to think, even for a minute, without distraction.

I was slightly drunk the evening I came to their home in Holland Park to find him, comatose in his studio, covered in blood, with my mother dead at his feet. I pried the bloody knife from his hand, which he barely noticed, and telephoned my grandfather and then the family solicitor, who told me sharply to call the police emergency number. When I opened the front door to the police minutes later, I was confronted by hard-faced officers who wouldn't let me go back upstairs, one of whom broke my nose when my shocked acquiescence evaporated and I was suddenly struggling and screaming like a banshee. The house filled with people in the next few hours as I was questioned by a series of uniformed, and then plainclothes officers, my clothing replaced with a Tyvek jumpsuit and slippers, my mother's body taken away and my father cautioned and under arrest. The front page of a national tabloid the next day was a photo of me, wearing the jumpsuit and holding something against my face to stem the bleeding from my nose. The police weren't particularly sympathetic, and even seemed to take some satisfaction from how far the mighty had fallen and been slain in high places. It took me a while to realize that I was a suspect, having left my fingerprints on the murder weapon, and I was left to the tender mercies of the press. It took the police weeks to investigate my father's guilt, even after he confessed. The day he was found hanged in his cell, I ran for Heathrow and the first plane leaving the country.

Grandfather's lunchtime revelations about my mother's secret life were shedding light into the dark corners of my parents' lives, and I wasn't enjoying it much. Even without the resurrection of every emotion I'd spent the last year trying to forget, I'd had a fairly complicated week, one which included finding a dead neighbor, being chased by a gunman, and learning that my family was deeply imbedded in espionage. All of which could be why it took me a while to notice I was being followed.

CHAPTER SEVENTEEN

The fog was spreading its cool, damp presence like a living creature, clinging to everything and making the sidewalks glisten. I was an hour from home on one of my nighttime prowls around the city, and I'd more or less decided to tell Nat about my breaking and entering and the files I'd stolen. I was walking along the Embarcadero, near the bow-and-arrow sculpture no one seems to know the name of, enjoying the smell of the damp and salty fog moving off the Bay. At first I just had a prickling sort of awareness of someone else nearby. I looked around casually, because I'm a city girl and it's smart to be vigilant. I didn't see anyone, but the feeling wouldn't go away. As I walked on, although I couldn't hear them, I could almost feel footsteps behind me.

By the time I was half a block from home, I'd gradually picked up the pace until I felt like one of those race walkers—heel-toe, heel-toe, hips wiggling and elbows flying—but I still hadn't seen anyone. My nerve broke. I ran up my front steps, fumbled with my key, and slammed the door behind me. I leaned against it for a few seconds to catch my breath and took the inside stairs two at a time. I crossed the front room in the dark and sidled up against the closest window frame. Keeping to one side, I peered down onto the street, almost convinced I'd imagined the whole thing, but as I watched, someone crossed the street and stood in a doorway opposite. He was in deep shadow, his head covered by a hoodie and his hands stuffed in the pockets of a hip-length padded jacket. Next door, I could see Matthew's legs and bottom half, wrapped tightly in his duvet, emerging from the doorway of Bonbons Chocolat. As I watched, he shifted and rolled over. My shadow didn't move. I pulled back, leaned against the wall, and tried to catch my breath.

I peered down onto the street again, but the doorway opposite was empty. He was either standing in Aromas' doorway underneath my perch, or he'd left. It was deeply unsettling to think of him loitering below me, but if he meant harm, I couldn't leave Matthew out there alone.

Out of habit, when I walked alone at night I carried my keys poking through my fingers like a knuckle-duster, which Nat assured me was called brass knuckles, but sterner methods seemed to be called for. I raced through the apartment and dug out my gun—unfortunately, I still hadn't taken the marksmanship course that went with it—from its box in my bedroom closet. I stuck it in the back waistband of my jeans, where I hoped it wouldn't go off accidentally and shoot me in the backside. I took it out and checked the safety again, then replaced it. When on earth had I become a person who took a gun to a—a brass knuckle fight? When had I become a person who took a gun anywhere? I opened my outside door as stealthily as I could and looked in both directions, but I saw no one except for Matthew.

I approached his comforter warily. "Hey, Matthew," I whispered.

He didn't move and I heard nothing, just the residue of silence, of something that had been there, and now wasn't.

"Matthew?"

He shot upright, his eyes wide, and thrashed around in the comforter cocoon until he freed his arms. "Thief! Thief! Thief!" He was shouting

"No, not a thief. It's just me. It's Theo, from the soap store."

I tried to shush him with some "calm down" motions of my arms, which he misread as an invitation to continue fortissimo, because, dear God, he was still shouting. "Theo! Theo! Theo!" He started to pant and I had just enough time to realize I should have left him to sleep peacefully when I heard the pad of running footsteps fading in the distance.

Matthew wouldn't come indoors, even into the garage, but I was finally able to persuade him to make a nest of his comforter in the tiny paved yard behind Aromas. He insisted on bringing his shopping cart, too. The space was clearly deficient in some way because he wasn't happy about it, inclined to grumble about thieves, the rattle of the cans in the bottom of his shopping cart, sounding like stage thunder rolling across the dark and empty gardens. I took him a mug of hot milk and a cheese sandwich, and he eventually settled down. He drank the milk and stuck the sandwich in one of the grimy plastic bags hanging from the rope round his waist, and all I could do was hope he didn't plan to eat it.

I went upstairs. Lucy's nails clicked on the hardwood as she made her way down the hallway. She waddled in my direction only to discover that, for the umpteenth time in our life together, I had come home without dog treats. She sniffed my hands and huffed her disappointment at me before turning and heading back to bed. I lay on the bed next to her and stared at the ceiling.

My first thought, as always, was for the relentless British tabloid press. A single photo of me on a San Francisco street would blow my carefully crafted new life to smithereens.

Paparazzi would be dropping out of trees and camping out on my doorstep to capture the first photos of me since my "mysterious" disappearance from London more than a year before. I resented being afraid, but I was even more puzzled. A nighttime pursuit made no sense. Next, I thought of Sergei Viktor Wolf, because Grandfather had implied that his appearance could mean some sort of danger for me. I didn't think he'd be able to produce the light, running footsteps I'd heard, carrying his overweight. Besides, if Grandfather had been in touch with him, he'd have no more reason to follow me.

None of my thoughts were conducive to getting any sleep.

Over the next couple of days, with my nerves set on hypervigilant, I thought I identified two men, one slightly taller than the other, and a woman. They wore a variety of hats and scarves, but they were at a disadvantage, since my daytime routine was basically spent in the Gardens, where they couldn't follow, and on the half block between Aromas and The Coffee, which didn't leave them much scope for staying incognito. All the same, they didn't come close enough for me to get a good look at their faces, and they had a talent for melting away if I walked in their direction. Being followed wasn't a new experience for me, so I thought I knew the difference between seeing someone from the neighborhood a little more often than usual, and pursuit by a stranger. It used to happen a lot but now, when I was living anonymously so far from home, it shouldn't be happening at all.

I was forced to rethink my assumptions. Tabloid photographers were basically hit-and-run artists and wouldn't be bothered to follow me for longer than it took to capture a few frames of me looking furtive and anxious, which, frankly, they could achieve anytime they watched me for more than five minutes. So who were they? And, equally important, what did they want? My next guess, that it had something to do with the lawsuit against Aromas, seemed all too possible, and I should probably have thought of that first. Just because Katrina was dead didn't mean the lawsuit had died with her, and I'd heard nothing, one way or the other. Did private investigators get hired over slip-and-fall lawsuits? And was this how Katrina had discovered what she'd discovered about my life? But if Katrina had hired him, wouldn't the contract have ended with her death? I'd believed the lawsuit was a personal vendetta, but was the property developer, Amos Noble, somehow involved?

And what could I do about it? My shadow, or shadows, hadn't threatened me, or even come close to me. And in broad daylight on a busy city street, it seemed somehow embarrassing to make elaborate, or indeed any, preparations for self-defense.

I was wary of telling Grandfather. I was almost sure he wouldn't think I was imagining ways to include myself in the family business, but it was enough to make me hesitate. He'd just begun to think I was resourceful and brave; it hurt me to think of disappointing him. I couldn't confide in anyone else. Any sensible person—even Nat—would insist I report it to the police, who were certain to ask me why I thought I was being followed. Explaining without telling them I was living here under an alias would be complicated. I thought of consulting Inspector Lichlyter, who at least knew who I was, but the same lack of concrete evidence applied—no one had approached me, or tried to run me over, or left threatening notes.

But I gave up my late night walks.

CHAPTER EIGHTEEN

I was alone when Gavin Melnik walked into Aromas late one afternoon, about a week after my lunch with Grandfather. He somehow kicked over the basket of natural sponges just inside the door, giving me a quick horrified glance before stooping to right the basket, grabbing an armful of the scattered sponges and tossing them in before making his way over to the counter with a huge one clutched in each hand. He and Katrina both had blonde hair but little else in common as far as I could see. He was nicely put together but without Katrina's height. Since awkwardness seemed to be his hallmark characteristic, bulletproof self-confidence clearly wasn't a family trait, either.

I was at a bit of a loss. It seemed a little weird to call my lawyer to ask what I should do with Melnik already in front of me. Did I acknowledge him? Ignore that I knew who he was? He hadn't spoken to me at Katrina's memorial or when he'd come to deal with Matthew. Was there some sort of protocol for the interactions between plaintiff and defendant? Was there an established etiquette? We stared at each other like startled meerkats.

Then he cleared his throat. "I'm Gavin Melnik. I wanted to speak to you at Katrina's memorial, but I was afraid you wouldn't want me to approach you." He glanced at the sponges in his hands with what looked like genuine confusion.

When I didn't immediately reply, he looked away, first to the shelves of gallon jugs of shampoo and body lotion behind me and then up to the ceiling of wildflowers and herbs. Maybe he didn't remember being in the store before, since he'd been carried into an ambulance on a gurney feetfirst with his eyes closed.

"I remember you," I said finally. "And I saw you with Matthew the other day."

He looked puzzled for a second and then his face cleared. "Yeah, I volunteer up at St. Christopher's. Look, I'm really sorry," he blurted. He blinked nervously. "The lawsuit wasn't my idea; Katrina said she would get me twenty-five thousand dollars."

Judging from his rather shabby varsity jacket, the money would have been welcome. He stood up a little straighter, chin out, his eyes fixed on the wall behind my head. I once read of a soldier executed by firing squad who refused the blindfold he was offered and bravely faced down a firing squad. The irony of course was that he was being executed for cowardice. He must have looked much the same as Melnik, with the same mix of defiance and *hauteur* in the face of certain death.

"I wanted to, you know, tell you I won't be continuing the lawsuit," he said to the wall. "I don't drink much," he added confidingly to the counter standing between us, "but it was my birthday and I was out of control that day. The whole thing was my fault." He transferred both sponges to one hand and pressed them to his chest, then changed his mind and dropped them on the counter. He held out his hand in a tentative sort of way, obviously expecting me to brush him off.

The lawsuit could have been a serious financial drag on the business, which I'm certain Katrina intended. But his apology seemed sincere, and I had enough to do without holding onto a grudge. I extended my hand. His face lit up, and he moved toward me so quickly he knocked the sponges and a box of seashell soaps off the counter. He bent down to pick them up and banged his head on the counter so hard it must have rung like a bell.

"Ow!" He rubbed his head and then darted an anxious look at me. "Don't worry; I won't sue." It was an awkward joke and, given the topic of our conversation, exasperating.

He lurched forward again, this time knocking over a display of candles in small floral tins, but, with some quick sleight of hand, somehow managing to prevent them falling to the floor. He shoved them back into order, then grabbed my extended hand and pumped it vigorously.

"Thank you! Thank you! I've been so worried about this. Katrina was . . ." His voice dropped. ". . . well, she was very forceful. And I owed her a lot. I don't know why she didn't like you." He paused, perhaps hoping I would enlighten him, and then soldiered on. "I really admire you for standing up to Katrina like you did. But anyway, I was sort of hoping we could be, you know, friendly, if you stop being mad at me."

I couldn't decide if that was brazen or courageous, but it surprised me into an amused snort. He puffed out a big breath and he gave me a shy smile. "I thought you might throw me out or call the cops. I'm sorry about spilling everything. I get clumsy when I'm nervous." He grabbed a couple of stray tins and pushed them back into line with the others. I stuffed the sponges under the counter, next to the box of dusty, gun-shaped soaps I keep out of a sort of nostalgia for my ex-partner, who'd originally bought them.

He hesitated. "Would you like to join me for a cup of coffee? I noticed a coffee shop down the block and it would mean a lot to me to talk to someone who knew Katrina. I miss her, you know?"

I wasn't up to watching his wistful expression change when I explained that he might be the only person within fifty miles to be sorry she was gone. "I'm afraid I'm alone here at the moment."

His shoulders drooped, and he extended his hand for a farewell handshake. "Right. Some other time. I'll just . . ." He jerked his thumb over his shoulder and turned to go, then hesitated before looking back. "I'm—I'm looking for a job. I'm a writer," he added with gentle pride, "but you know how it is; I need a day job, too. I don't know much about computers, but I have some bookkeeping experience if you use QuickBooks, and I'll do just about anything." He looked at me hopefully, and honestly, he reminded me of a fledgling swan, all fluffy and helpless.

"I already have an accountant," I said, and his face fell.

"Sure, I understand. It's been tough finding work that I can leave behind at the end of the day, so I have the time and energy to do my writing. I volunteer at St. Christopher's shelter a few hours a week, but I really need to find a paying job."

I thought of Nat, who wanted to hire someone for The Coffee, and then had almost instant second thoughts. He was shy and almost comically clumsy, and given all the steaming milk and hot coffee, an accident-prone barista could have a short, painful career. Although if his entry into Aromas was any indicator, Nat would be able to see him in action and make that judgment call.

"My friend Nat owns the coffee shop," I said. "He might be looking for someone."

"That's great. If he's there now—" I nodded. "I'll go along and talk to him." He held out his hand and I shook it again, reflecting that most Americans would find all the handshaking funny—or be pulling out the hand sanitizer. I wondered if he'd picked up the habit in Europe, or if it was just another sign of nerves. He left, looking as if he'd shed ten years. I felt lighter myself, knowing that the lawsuit wasn't going ahead. I telephoned my insurance company lawyer and gave her the news, although, lawyer-like, she said she'd wait for official notification before assuming anything.

Twenty minutes later, Melnik poked his head in the door as I was dealing with a store full of customers and gave me a dazzling smile and a thumbs-up. He looked happy, and I realized he'd looked woeful or nervous every time I'd seen him until that moment. I waved, and he went on his way. He was cute, if a man in his thirties can be cute. And with him on board at Nat's, maybe I wouldn't have to get up every morning at the crack of dawn.

I got a text from Nat: *He'll do but not my type. Next time send . . .* I snorted. He'd added a photo of a shirtless Channing Tatum.

The next day, Melnik ("Call me Gavin") stopped by to tell me he was apartment hunting, since he wouldn't be staying on at Katrina's apartment once it was folded into her estate. "I thought I'd start looking; it could take a while to find somewhere. This is a great neighborhood, but I need somewhere cheap, if that's even possible."

And I had an empty, ground floor studio. He arranged to move in the following month, when he would need to move out of Katrina's apartment. He said he didn't own much—a few small pieces of furniture, some cardboard boxes, and a couple of garment bags would be easy to move over from the other side of the Gardens. I was relieved that the studio's Murphy bed meant he'd have somewhere comfortable to sleep, at least. I waived the security deposit, but he said he could come up with the first and last month's rent. I did an Internet search—I'm not a complete idiot—but he wasn't a convicted serial killer or a sex offender, and he wasn't on the city's unofficial landlord blacklist. He was volunteering at St. Christopher's, his credit rating was surprisingly good, and I knew where he worked. Fair enough. San Francisco is a rent-control city, and in any event Fabian Gardens landlords were restricted in the amount of rent we could charge by a provision in the community covenants. As part of her campaign to be a thorn in everyone's side, Katrina had fought us on that. She'd lost, and hadn't been happy. The rules meant that the community was more economically diverse than some other places in the city. We did have a few millionaires, including a dot-com baby millionaire who, rumor had it, had furnished her place with nothing but vintage pinball machines. But we also had a number of blue-collar retirees who had lived here for decades, and some solidly middle-class families and couples, along with twentysomethings who shared some of the smaller apartments or lived solo in a studio while they took classes at USF, Hastings, or San Francisco State.

I went with Gavin to the coffee shop for his first morning shift and my last day as a barista. Nat had already given me my pink slip and told me to get some more rest. I stayed long enough to realize that I wasn't needed. Gavin seemed less clumsy, or maybe just more cautious. He and Nat got along well together, and he willingly did everything asked of him, up to and including using a glass jar to capture a spider and release it into the alley. Nat was afraid of spiders, and I didn't like them much either, so we were usually reduced to playing rock-paper-scissors. The spider escaped twice, and its eventual liberation involved a spatula, a box of coffee stirrers, and two of Nat's customers, one of whom was apparently a member of PETA and who took it upon himself to assure the spider's comfort during its ordeal.

I left Nat and Gavin reading PETA brochures and walked back to Aromas feeling more cheerful than I had in weeks. The spider was free. The lawsuit was off my plate. Business at Aromas was good. The recent neighborhood association meeting had been remarkably harmonious without Katrina's spiky presence. I hadn't noticed anyone following me for a couple of days. I'd even managed to take a few photos for the calendar. True, Katrina's killer was still at large, and Ben was still potentially in danger somewhere overseas, but the other side of the ledger was looking pretty good.

Two hours later, I was straightening a rack of kimonos when Nat clattered through the door, so winded he almost couldn't talk, as if he'd run from The Coffee on a single breath. He bent over at the waist and tried to gulp in some air. I went over and patted his back, and he gasped out the problem. Nat has this smooth-as-honey Texas accent which, if you have a clipped English accent like mine, rests in the ear like music. He was saying something that sounded like "Hand. Bleedin'." I smothered a snort. Nat fainted at the sight of a paper cut, so I thought he'd cut himself trying to make a sandwich or something. Then I realized he was actually shaking, and thought maybe it wasn't so simple.

He stood up straight and tried again, his face ashen and his eyes frantic. "Theo! You've gotta come."

He hustled me out of the store without giving me a chance to lock up, down the block, into the coffee shop, where a microwave oven sat on his counter in a nest of bubble wrap. Gavin was sitting at a table with his head in his hands. He looked up when we arrived and passed a hand over his face with trembling fingers. Nat waved a hand at the microwave. I approached it warily and opened the door.

A bloody hand was sitting on an equally bloody and crumpled cloth. It looked like some sort of nightmarish flower, sitting upright with the fingers twisted and pointing in different directions. I frowned, trying to figure out why it looked so misshapen, because obviously that was the important thing, when I heard a sort of retching noise and half-turned to see Nat give up the struggle and collapse in a graceless faint against the wall.

I took some of his weight and lowered his head gently to the floor, knowing from experience that he'd come around by himself in a couple of minutes. I waved Gavin over. Frankly, he looked green, but I thought taking care of Nat might focus his mind. He flicked a cloth off his shoulder and held it under the cold water tap, then folded the cloth into a pad. He crouched down and pressed it onto Nat's forehead and the back of his neck with surprising competence. With none of his usual dithering, he looked up at me and said, "You should call the police."

"Yes. Right. I'll do that." Then I hesitated. I understood Nat's impulse to find a friend to help him with—I looked quickly at the hand again and then wished I hadn't. Inspector Lichlyter wasn't exactly a friend, but at least I knew her and she knew me. She'd know she didn't need to go digging any further into my past as part of a new investigation.

She must have had caller ID because I was still trying to frame my first sentence when she said, "Miss . . . Bogart. What's happened now?"

CHAPTER NINETEEN

The police took my microwave," Nat said mournfully over a glass of wine that evening. "It was a good microwave. Good and big, and it was cheap, too."

"They'll bring it back."

He looked revolted.

"Or you can get another one," I added hastily. "Did the police tell you anything?"

"I can't get another one for the price I paid for that one. I bought it at the sale of Katrina's stuff. I only picked it up yesterday. And no, I don't know anythin' more than I knew this morning, which is basically nothin'."

"Was it—empty when you bought it?"

He gave me a look. "No, English, it came with a bonus gift."

"I just thought—"

He leaned over and patted my knee. "I don't know. It was all done up in bubble wrap. I didn't open it up until this mornin' and found . . . all wrapped up in that kitchen towel thing, and when I unwrapped it . . ." He was looking a little sketchy, so I didn't press him, but the microwave being Katrina's—that was significant, wasn't it?

"How did you come to get the microwave?"

"It was handled by an estate liquidators south of Market.

I was needin' a microwave, and I remembered Katrina's kitchen had this almost-new one from when she did the reno a few months ago, so I put in a bid." He shuddered.

"And it came from the liquidators already in the bubble wrap?"

"Yeah." He took another gulp of wine.

"Was it an auction? Was there a preview day or anything?"

"Yeah. The girl had taste, I'll say that for her. I saw a couple of decorators there eyein' her stuff. What are you thinkin'?"

I swirled the wine in my glass and then shrugged. "It feels, I don't know, significant. But if anyone had access to the microwave, I guess not. So the hand—"

"It wasn't a hand, 'pparently."

"It was a hand; I saw it. Sort of deformed, I thought."

"That's 'cause it was parts of two hands sorta wrapped together. God, how awful is that?"

"Pretty awful," I agreed, feeling a little sick. "So someone is—"

"—wanderin' around with a finger and thumb missin' on both hands. It's gonna make it hard to—forget it; I can't think of anythin' that isn't disgustin'." He looked miserable.

"Will you keep The Coffee open?"

"I'm closed while the cops go over the place with a flea comb, but it doesn't look like it was the scene of the crime, I guess. I may leave it an extra day to air the place out."

By the time I saw him the next day, he'd cheered up a little and it was clear from his airy disregard for the happenings of the previous day that, for the moment at least, it was a closed topic. Nat said he'd decided to do without a microwave; it would be seen as a positive by people who wanted to avoid things like GMOs, high tension power lines, and cell phone radiation. I helped him put back a couple of tables the crime scene people had moved out of place while Gavin cleaned fingerprint powder off the bathroom fixtures.

"I don't think microwaves have anything to do with GMOs." Science wasn't one of my best subjects in school, but I was almost sure I was right about that.

"No, but I can put a sign in the window that says *No GMOs. No Microwaves;* appeals to the same demographic."

"Listen to you, all business-speak."

He grinned. "What else? What about peanuts, maybe? Everyone's allergic to those. Remember when you could eat peanuts on planes? Okay, *No GMOs, No Microwaves, No Peanuts.* Anythin' else?"

"You're serving free trade coffee."

"'Course I am; d'you think I could get away with anythin' else?"

"And organic, non-antibiotic milk," Gavin said as he passed by on his way into the kitchen with a cleaning tote. He and Nat high-fived.

"And one hundred percent post-consumer recycled paper napkins," I added. "I suppose you'll need another list of the things you *do* have, and add the free Wi-Fi."

Gavin came back and held out a plastic spray bottle. "Did you know this glass cleaner is organic?" He looked befuddled and sniffed the nozzle gingerly. "How can glass cleaner be organic? It smells like vinegar."

"Huh. I'm gonna need a bigger sign." We both giggled.

"What's funny?" Gavin was still inspecting the glass cleaner bottle.

I left Nat to explain as I headed back home.

Haruto and Davo were handling things in Aromas, and instead of going inside when I reached it, I waved and kept walking. Matthew was missing again, and it worried me. I was also thinking about the other homeless men who'd been living on Polk Street recently. I didn't want to jump to any conclusions, just because they were basically strangers. They might not be guilty of anything, but maybe they'd seen something. And then I wondered if any of them were missing fingers.

Once the idea occurred to me, I couldn't get to St. Christopher's fast enough. The shelter was open every evening and, unlike most shelters that opened only at night, there was a day room with a few tables and chairs. Volunteers ran the place, and I gathered they served a hot evening meal, and let people take a shower. Once a month, someone gave haircuts and a volunteer was there to answer questions or help them fill in applications for ID cards or get Social Security benefits. Too many of them were former military veterans, fallen on hard times, and they couldn't get things they were entitled to, like disability benefits, unless they had an address to receive mail, or a bank account to transfer funds.

The church had a residence attached to it at the back, facing onto an alley. It was fairly civilized, no dumpsters or nasty smells, although it could have used some tubs of flowers to replace the torn black plastic and chunks of pine bark in the spaces on either side of the entrance. The rectory mimicked the Mission Revival architecture of the church, with decorative wrought-iron bars across the lower windows which, given everything, was probably a good idea. A grand curved staircase of shallow steps had a bronze handrail full of cavorting, fleshy nymphs leading up to the front door. Nat told me once that the congregation insisted they were angels. He said the railing had been rescued from the 1906 fire, and the owner's wife considered it too racy to install on their rebuilt mansion. Why she and her philanthropist husband thought it would be appropriate for a church, I have no idea. Maybe that's why it was hidden away in the alley. I rang the doorbell, which produced several bars of the "Ode to Joy," and turned to look in the window at the side. It was open, but all I could see through the gauzy curtains was a ketchup bottle on a table pulled up to the window.

"What is it?"

I was so startled by the barked demand and the sudden appearance of the good-looking priest from Katrina's memorial that I took a half step backward and nearly fell down the stairs, arms windmilling until I was able to get my balance. By which time the door had been slammed shut. Nice.

I gathered myself together and rang the doorbell again. This time I was prepared when the door flew open. He was wearing jeans and a short-sleeved black shirt with a stiff Roman collar. I could see him preparing to slam the door again.

"Er . . . Father?"

He narrowed his eyes, as if he knew the form of address didn't come naturally to me. He'd be right—I even called my own father by his first name. "What is it?"

"My name is Theo Bogart," I said. "The owner of the soap store? I'm a friend of Gavin Melnik's," I added finally, since nothing else brought about any appreciable hint of recognition.

He turned and strode down the hallway, leaving me to follow, or not. I closed the door behind me and followed him into a small room crowded with dark furniture. He threw himself into a cracked leather armchair I was pretty sure I'd seen on the sidewalk a few months before. He didn't ask me to sit down.

None of this seemed like very priestlike behavior, somehow. The elderly prelate who occasionally played chess with my grandfather in England was almost my only in-depth experience with members of the clergy. He was courtly and gracious, with a tendency to tell jokes with Latin and Greek punch lines. Seriously, could this fellow really be a priest or was he just another one of the local homeless guys with more enterprise than most, squatting in the rectory? I perched on the edge of a hard-backed chair opposite him.

He frowned at me, and I nearly stood up again. "I'm sorry, who are you again?"

"My name is Theo Bogart. I own Aromas, on the next block. You might have seen me at Katrina Dermody's memorial service."

"Right. Sorry about . . ." The apology seemed to cover his greeting at the door. He extended a hand. I half rose from my uncomfortable roost to shake it, but he just leaned over to slam shut a drawer in the small table at the side of his chair. I sat back, feeling awkward.

Since he said nothing else, and in fact was inclined to stare out of the window, I said, "I was wondering if the police had asked you about the men you shelter here, if any of them had gone missing, or—well, suffered an injury lately."

He dragged his eyes from the window and made an obvious effort to pay attention. "What?"

"You haven't heard?"

"I've been away on a retreat. I came back to the city for Ms. Dermody's funeral and then went back to the gold country."

"Oh, right," I said, unsure what a retreat was except in a military sense, and this priest didn't look as if he'd back down for anyone. "Well, my friend Nat found a hand in his coffee shop, you know the new one down the block on Polk?" He nodded. "Well, there."

"Eeuuw," he said unexpectedly. "No, I haven't heard anything. And one of the volunteers would have told me if any of our guys has gone missing. If they don't show up for a few days, we go looking for them. They usually drift into the same underpass or park or wherever."

I nodded glumly. "Well, it was just a thought. I suppose you'd notice if anyone was missing some fingers."

"I thought you said it was a hand."

"I thought it was at first, but it turned out to be parts of two hands."

He went still and his face lost color.

"Does that mean something?" I asked. "Is it something done by some local tong or a street gang or whatever?"

He said, as if reluctantly, "Was it the part of the hands with the thumbs and index fingers?"

"I thought you didn't know anything about this." He frowned and I hurried on. "Yes, it was."

He put one hand up to his face and then dragged it through his thick blonde hair. "It could be a priest," he said heavily. "I saw it in . . . South America. A drug cartel in Colombia wanted to get rid of local priests without killing them because the locals wouldn't stand for it. So they kidnapped them and tortured them and then cut off the index finger and thumb of both hands. Then they dropped them back into their villages."

"Gross and cruel. But why? Was it a—a signature, so everyone would know who had done it?"

"More than that." He leaned forward with his elbows on his knees. His face was very pale. "When a priest is ordained, there's a special blessing given to the index finger and thumb. It's how he holds the Host—the wafer—as it's consecrated during the Mass. Without that part of his hand, he can no longer say Mass. It's an intensely cruel mutilation."

"But who would do that here? I mean, what the hell? *Heck*, I mean."

He shrugged. "I don't know why, but I can almost guarantee your fingers came from a priest who did something to piss someone off, probably connected to South American gangs."

If this was a coincidence, it was a weird one. Grandfather's friend Sergei was a priest with South American connections. Grandfather and I hadn't spoken since our lunch at The Palace. We'd both left a couple of messages for each other, but somehow hadn't connected, and I wasn't sure if he'd met with Sergei as he'd planned, or if it was all a forbidden subject between us. I'd been prepared to wait for our fortnightly visit to open the conversation again. I was still trying to absorb the information he'd shared about his murky past and our family business, not sure how I felt about him keeping something so important from me for my entire life.

"You should call the police inspector in charge of the case," I said. "I don't think they know anything about who

the fingers belong to, and that might help. Her name is Lichlyter."

"Yes. I'll do that."

He stood and ushered me down the hallway toward the
front door. As he reached above my head to open it, I hesitated and then grasped the nettle. "Why did you take the
photo from Katrina's photo album?"

"I don't know what the hell—or *heck* if you prefer—
you're talking about," he growled. The door slammed in my
face.

CHAPTER TWENTY

So Katrina was dead. My grandfather was a spy. Someone was mutilating priests. Or one priest, anyway. People were following me. And yet, the mundane continued to be important, too, which became all too clear when I took Lucy down to the garden to do her business and followed her around with a plastic bag at the ready as she chose and then discarded a number of potential spots. It always took her a while because the property behind all the buildings on this block had been combined into a private pocket park about a hundred years ago. The result was surprisingly large—bigger than two American football fields—with the buildings taking up about a third of that around the perimeter. It formed a green and leafy refuge, with pine bark pathways, a couple of neatly shaved lawns with untidy groups of Adirondack chairs, a lush, raised-bed vegetable garden, lots of trees, a few of which were over a hundred years old, a koi pond, and even a ruthlessly trimmed knot garden. There was a playground with swings, a firepit for cool evenings—which was just about every evening—and a ramshackle little wooden shed where the volunteer gardeners kept their tools. On sunny days I sometimes brought a sandwich out here and sat in an Adirondack chair while Lucy lay down at my feet, panting and vigilant, ready to harass the nearest rosebush if it turned into a threat. She'd once been witness to a fairly frightening scene out here, and she'd never quite let down her guard since. I liked to think she was protective of me, but it's more likely she just enjoyed intimidating the shrubbery.

The garden was used by everyone who lived here. The swings were empty, but the younger kids would come out after school. The vegetable garden was leafy, which meant there would be potatoes soon, or maybe something more exotic. The volunteer gardeners got first dibs, but most of the produce was distributed first-come-first-served on Saturday mornings. There were rules and a computer spreadsheet, so no one got more than their fair share. I usually steered clear and got my veggies at Whole Foods.

I looked over at the two empty buildings, five million dollars on the hoof, as Nat would say, and yet about to be demolished to cause a wound on the neighborhood gestalt. A young woman—I thought it was Angela Lacerda—wearing a tasseled, black-and-white *kufiya* around her shoulders was slowly walking the narrow paths of the knot garden, her hands occupied with a simple metal bowl. She was caressing the edge of the bowl the way someone might stroke a dampened finger around the rim of a wineglass to make it sing. The tone the bowl made was slightly eerie but not unpleasant, and it somehow overrode other random noises. In addition to the *kufiya*, her outfit included jeans tucked into the tops of lemon-colored socks. Lucy growled at her as she approached. Angela took it as an invitation to join me on my bench. Lucy growled again.

"The calm before the storm," she said. "I like to come out here before the kids show up in the afternoon." She was thin, and not unattractive, but she was colorless, and most girls would have compensated for that lack of sparkle with makeup. She was wearing a sweater in a pale, muddy color, which needed something to brighten it up. I decided the lemon-colored socks must have been a gift. I quickly glanced at her left hand. No engagement ring. Interesting.

She bent down to place her metal bowl, which was half full of water, on the floor near her feet, and picked up a twig. She waved it enticingly at Lucy, who ignored it. "I'm Angela Lacerda. I think you own the perfume store, don't you?"

"Theo Bogart," I said. "And I know what you mean about the kids."

"If I had any of my own, I guess I'd be happy they had a safe place to play." Her eyes suddenly filled with tears. "Sorry," she sniffed. "Recent breakup."

"Been there," I said sympathetically. I thought of Katrina's dossier and the high school abortion. "Men can be dicks."

She scowled at me. "My fiancé—ex-fiancé"—she sniffed again—"isn't a dick. He's kind and generous and—It was all my fault," she wailed suddenly. "His family is wealthy, and I wanted to prove my value, I guess. So Jason wouldn't think he was being burdened with a delicate flower who couldn't pull her weight, you know?"

"Did—er Jason think you were—"

She faltered. "I could tell his parents were singing that song, and he'd started to say a few things—I'm not a mogul or anything, but I'd bought a few pieces of property for things like back taxes and made a little profit on them. I thought if I showed them, I could play with the big boys—I got involved in a business deal that didn't turn out well, thanks to our late friend Katrina Dermody." The twig snapped in her fingers.

"Anyway, that's all over," she said, before I could follow her down that intriguing trail. She sniffed once more and straightened her shoulders, and her face assumed what was probably a more typical, capable expression than the tears. She adjusted the *kufiya* around her narrow shoulders and bent over to secure the hems of her jeans into her lemon-colored socks. "Ticks," she said.

"Ticks? Here in the Gardens?"

She narrowed her eyes. "Can't be too careful. You're on the association board. I recognize your name. And who's this?" She leaned down to hold out a tentative fist to Lucy, who growled again.

"That's Lucy. She doesn't bite. She's just prickly."

"I understand. She's cute."

I eyed Lucy's lopsided little face doubtfully. "Not many people think so, but thanks."

I started to ask her for the story of Katrina's involvement in the business deal and the broken engagement, but Gavin was strolling across the garden toward us. He raised a hand in greeting.

"Hi, Miss Bogart," he said as he reached us.

"Call me Theo."

He looked shyly pleased. "Theo. Hi," he added to Angela, sticking out his hand, "I'm Gavin."

She blushed and shook the proffered hand. "Angela. Good to meet you."

Now they were both flushing, both apparently suffering the agony of being shy and awkward. "This is Lucy," she said. Gavin stepped back, onto the edge of the metal bowl, and it spun away, splashing water.

"Oh my gosh, I'm sorry. Is that a standing bell? Is it yours? Are you a Buddhist?"

He shook a few drops of water from the bowl and handed it to her. "I'm so clumsy; was the water charged? I'm really sorry."

"I just use it to meditate," she said, reassuring him even as she took the bowl and held it tenderly in the crook of her arm. "I'm not religious or anything. Are you Buddhist?"

"Gosh, no. I'm just interested in alternative spirituality, you know?"

"Me too. I love how many different ways people have developed to, well, to hold back the night, I guess."

I stood up and patted my thigh to get Lucy's attention, then tucked her under my arm and strolled away. I don't think they noticed.

With the calendar in mind, I took a few minutes to assess the gnarled and ancient purple clematis growing on the garden shed. The weathered shed had some old and rusty garden tools nailed to one of the outside walls as a sort of declaration of ownership by the volunteer gardeners, in case anyone got it into their head to think they could store their model boats there or something. The Garden Gnomes were both vocal and territorial. (That was Nat's name for them, not mine, but it was hard to think of them any other way once the idea took hold.) A varied assortment gathered every Saturday morning carrying water bottles or mugs of coffee, rubbing their eyes like sleepy kindergarteners on a field trip, some of them wearing red knitted hats in an ironic *homage* to their nickname. In my experience, this makes them nearly unique, since Americans often don't recognize irony unless it sits up and begs. The English, of course, use it all the time, whether it's appropriate or not.

Professor D'Allessio, the current *über*-gardener, handed out grumpy orders to anyone who wandered by, so I was always careful to avoid catching his eye. He'd been retired from UC Berkeley for a decade or more, and the garden was his passion. We all knew him as Professor, and no one ever called him anything else, even his wife, Ruth.

If Lucy ever finished her perambulations, I thought I might stop in to see them and find out how they were taking Katrina's death. And I supposed I could have a word with Angela Lacerda if I could pry her away from Gavin. I looked at them, heads close together, as they strolled down the garden.

In the meantime, I had the photos to take for the calendar. I was planning to pair O'Keeffe-style close-ups of the flowers with a wider view of their location, while taking Nat's advice to avoid the sexual subtext in O'Keeffe's art. If I took everything from unexpected angles maybe they'd focus on that. I'd include the shed's rusty tools in tight close-up, with a flower from the clematis vine growing up over its roof; I could crawl under the bench down the way and shoot upward from ground level, with one of the nasturtiums growing through the slats; the datura, with its protective ring of picket fencing, would look interesting from the viewpoint of one of its large trumpet-shaped flowers, and the kids' swings, with that vine growing on the crossbar. Or maybe that was a weed.

The rosemary in the knot garden/labyrinth was in flower. I could pair a close-up with an overhead shot to show off the rigid geometric precision of the hedges. I looked up and worked out the angle. My friend Sabina's top-floor flat looked like a good vantage point.

While I was thinking about it, Professor D'Allessio

sneaked in under my radar. He marched in my direction, with his hoe at parade rest as usual. "Ah," he shouted, raising his hoe to get my attention. "Soap girl! You!" He had nicknames for all of us, and mine was actually a slight improvement over the original. Nat was "the furry one"—no clear idea why. For some reason the professor liked Ben, and so he was "Ben, the lawyer." He referred to Sabina, his granddaughter, as "my little Sabina," although she towered over him by several inches and was about to become a mother for the second time. Her husband, Kurt, was "*il biondo,*" which I think means "the blonde," which, fair enough, as Kurt was about the palest blonde I'd ever seen. I'd never heard if the professor had a nickname for Katrina, but I was about to find out.

"So," he said, reaching me and holding his hoe upright like a staff of office. He kept the thing honed to a razor's edge, and I worried he'd lop off an ear one day. His face, topped with a cap of wiry white hair, looked carved from redwood. I waited, resigned, to hear his latest complaint. His English wasn't perfect, but he never had any trouble making his opinions known.

"Calendar for this year," he said unexpectedly. "You do photographs, yes?"

I nodded.

He waved a hand, encompassing the entire garden with a grand, Italian gesture. "Do photographs of garden." He frowned at me ferociously. "No animals. Pah!"

"That's a good idea, Professor," I said, because it was always best to agree with him whenever possible.

"Yes. Not so many fights." He nodded firmly, once, and started to move away.

"Speaking of fights—" I said hastily, and he turned back. "About Katrina—"

"Ah. You mean did I, Guillermo D'Allessio, kill the bitch?" He spat on the ground near his feet.

I must have looked as shocked as I felt; I'd never heard him utter even the mildest of crude language.

He narrowed his eyes, thumped his hoe on the ground, and doubled down. "She was a bitch. She try to destroy the Gardens." Then he shrugged. "But I don't kill her. Plenty of others, maybe," he cackled and waved his hoe at Gavin and Angela, now halfway down the garden, engrossed in conversation. He grimaced. "My little Sabina knows I am *distrowt—distrowt*! And she says don't worry. Maybe someone will kill her. She try to make me feel better." He shrugged. "That is all I know."

He stomped off, swishing his hoe rhythmically and decapitating weeds daring to show their heads in his path.

I picked up Lucy, who'd finally achieved her objective, and dropped the resulting plastic bag into one of a pair of dedicated waste bins we'd recently installed over the objections of our pet-haters and to the satisfaction of our pet-owners. The bins had an airlock entrance to cut down on escaping smells, and we'd had them painted in a sort of botanical camouflage, all of which made them difficult to find unless you were practically on top of them. Like even the simplest changes to the gardens, the bins represented dozens of hours of my life and the lives of the other neighborhood association officers.

Lucy grumbled at me, although her heart didn't seem to be in it, as I hitched her under one arm. I had to carry her or she'd stay to argue with our resident raccoon, and anyway, pets weren't permitted in the garden unaccompanied. She was usually impressively obedient, and she walked to heel around the neighborhood, but apparently being out here made her brains dissolve. She'd arrived already trained, by the way, so it was surprising when no one claimed her. After I turned her in, I kept checking in with the kindly people at the city animal shelter, hoping she'd be reunited with the poor soul who owned her. She'd been surly, argumentative, and miserable there, and after a month she was due for the chop. They waived the adoption fee, with fixed smiles on their faces, and by the time I remembered "The Ransom of Red Chief," she and I were already on our way home.

We headed over to Sabina's flat; maybe she'd tell me why she told the professor someone might kill Katrina. It was Kurt Talbot's flat, too, but I preferred not to think too much about former lovers, especially ones I no longer liked very much. Kurt played golf on Wednesday afternoons and then came home to change before going back to the office for evening appointments. I thought I might be able to catch him for a few minutes and ask them both . . . whatever I could think of to ask them about Katrina.

Sabina had exchanged her skin-tight motorcycle leathers (and the motorcycle that went with them) for figure-hugging stretch dresses, which made her small baby bump obvious. Today's was dark green with a subtle glitter in the fabric and, as always, she was stunning. She was also carrying a vicious-looking knife with a set of wings and the number 666 on the handle. It probably says something about both of us that I didn't even blink.

"Hey, Theo! Hi, Lucy."

Even though I'm tall, she had to bend slightly from her

six-foot altitude to kiss my cheek, and her long, fiery red corkscrew curls tickled my face. She exchanged the knife for a chopstick she grabbed from the kitchen counter, bunched up a handful of her hair, pulled it into a casual knot, and impaled it with the chopstick. When I've tried that trick, the chopstick usually ended up on the floor. Then she filled a mixing bowl with water and put it on the floor for Lucy, who ignored it in favor of sitting upright by the back door, ready to leave.

"I'm putting my knives up in the hallway; come look." She guided me along to their central hallway where, sure enough, she had her collection of knives in shadow boxes arranged with subtle lighting from somewhere. "Decided before Sebastian gets old enough to walk I needed to put them somewhere he can't get his hands on them, but I didn't want to lock them away. What d'you think?"

"It looks great," I said, because it did, although I will never understand Americans' love affair with their weapons. She grinned at me. Sabina understood me. Or at any rate, she understood the person she thought I was.

I told her about my calendar project, and she cheerfully led me into their bedroom, which overlooked the gardens. One of the bed pillows was on the floor, and the mattress was askew. She blushed when I looked at it and said, "Nice," in an admiring tone, and then she giggled and we bumped fists. I looked out of the window down at the potting shed and the knot garden below. "This is the perfect angle," I said. "I'll come back with a camera if that's okay."

She turned around from rummaging in her closet. "Sure. Hey! Would you like to buy my leather jacket?" She held it out in my direction and looked it over. "I'm never going to wear it now, and it's about your size."

It was black, a little scraped and dinged, with heavy zippers in unlikely places. It was left over from her former career as a motorcycle messenger, and I loved it. I'd been a clotheshorse, once. Now I had fashion apathy. I didn't even have any jewelry here, except a pair of earrings and a bracelet I was wearing on the day I left London. My Louboutin heels ended up at the Salvation Army store in the Mission, and I now owned half a dozen pairs of ballet-style flats to go with my wardrobe of jeans and long-sleeved T-shirts. But I could use a warm jacket.

CHAPTER TWENTY-ONE

She tossed me the jacket. "Try it on. I'll pour you some wine and get some snacks; come out when you're ready and we can catch up while Mariana gives the kiddo his bath. Are you hungry?"

"Not really. But wine sounds great."

On my way past the hall bathroom, I glanced in. "*Hola*, Mariana."

She looked up "*Hola*, Miss Teo." She had her arms full of Sebastian, so I said, "*Hola*, Sebastian," and wiggled my fingers at him. He gummed his fist and kicked his legs happily like a frog.

Kurt looked a little startled when I smiled at him as he came up the stairs. I didn't usually.

"Hi," I said. "Sabina's offered me a glass of wine."

"Sounds good," he said cautiously. He leaned into the archway leading to their sitting room. "Pour me a glass, would you, Sabina? I'll be right there."

I settled myself into a comfortable chair, leaving the sofa for them because they were sort of tactile, with a tendency to gaze into each other's eyes a little too much. Sabina came out of the dining room with a third glass, and a plate of Brie, grapes, and crackers. She poured wine into a second glass and poured herself a glass of sparkling water. I heard

Kurt cooing at Sebastian in the next room, which, frankly, I would never have believed if I hadn't heard it myself. I turned to Sabina and opened my mouth to say as much, but she preempted me. "Sebastian will be asleep when he comes home this evening; he wants to get his baby fix."

"Everything is good?" I asked.

A smile lit up her face. "Better than good."

"So. How is parenthood?" I asked when Kurt joined us. I thought that was a safe topic, since they were both good for twenty minutes on the subject of Sebastian's latest acts of brilliance, which, since he wasn't yet three months old, you'd think would be fairly limited.

When I'd known him better, Kurt had the emotional depth of a flounder and a chilly mien to go along with his pale good looks. I thought he'd behaved out of character by marrying Sabina while she was pregnant with another man's child. I was still suspicious and always watched him carefully for signs of disenchantment, but to all outward appearances he'd entered his marriage and fatherhood with enthusiasm. Sabina had told me he was participating in parental duties wholeheartedly, although what that meant for either of them with a full-time nanny on hand, I wasn't sure. Sabina was pregnant again at the recommendation of their family therapist (this is California, after all), who felt a baby who was wholly theirs would cement the family bonds. I was raised on the unfortunate dynamics of the stepfamilies in the Brothers Grimm tales, so it sounded a risky strategy to me, but so far seemed to be so good.

After the stories of Sebastian's weight benchmarks reached and cleverness displayed, we all sat in silence for a couple of minutes, Kurt and I drinking our wine. They seemed very happy, and six months ago I would have bet money that Kurt wasn't capable of the depth of warmth I saw in his cool, gray eyes every time he looked at Sabina. He looked like a man who couldn't believe his good fortune. Sabina's attitude was a little more . . . wry. But judging from the condition of their bed, she was happy enough, too.

I introduced Katrina into the conversation gingerly, and they both made regretful faces.

Sabina said, "We knew about the orphanage."

"Katrina asked us for a donation, and I was happy to help," Kurt said. "Seemed like a really worthwhile cause." And yet they hadn't gone to the memorial service.

"The Professor said Katrina being murdered wasn't much of a surprise to him," I said gingerly.

Sabina's expression darkened. "He was worrying himself into a nervous breakdown. I'd have said anything to ease their minds a little, and I could have killed her myself for putting them through that. But Kurt came up with a better solution."

Kurt had a golf tee in his left hand and he rolled it between his fingers like a magician preparing a sleight-of-hand trick. He tossed it upward, caught it, and took a deep breath. "When the condo plans fell through, and the buildings were still sitting there empty, Katrina and I put in an offer."

My jaw may have dropped. "The condo plan fell through? When? Why? How long have you known, for god's sake? No one told the neighborhood." He shrugged. He had a great line in shrugs if you weren't on the receiving end. "You don't think life here would have gone a bit more smoothly if we'd known? Jesus, Kurt, the association meetings alone— and Katrina might still be alive."

He frowned. "What are you talking about?"

"Suppose someone thought killing Katrina would stop the condo project?"

He snorted and put down his wine. "Are people really that dumb? She was only the lawyer, not the principal."

"Some people thought of the project as life or death for the Gardens. That didn't make them dumb," I said stiffly. Although, yeah, it probably did.

"Katrina thought if everyone was still furious with Noble, we'd slip in under the radar without too much opposition." As usual, Kurt had thought of himself first and to heck with how things affected other people. I bet he only gave a donation to the orphanage because he could deduct it off his taxes.

He went on. "I thought it would preserve the nature of the Gardens for the people who already lived here and owned property." He darted a look at Sabina, who smiled and patted his hand. Okay, maybe he didn't always think of himself first. Just mostly. He cleared his throat. "So we made an offer on the buildings, but—Theo, this is complicated; do you really want to hear about it?"

"Are you kidding? Of course I want to hear about it. Why was it complicated?"

"Noble was tired of all the protests and the city on his case for months. Two months ago he was looking for a way out, and Katrina found it for him. The title on one of the buildings wasn't secure. He backed out of financing the purchase. Unfortunately, Angela was stuck with properties she didn't want. I think it put her in financial hot water, too."

"Angela?"

"Angela Lacerda. She'd purchased the buildings on his behalf originally. It isn't that unusual," he went on, at my surprised exclamation. "If people know there's someone with deep pockets interested in their property, the price goes up. A developer has a front person do the purchasing so his name doesn't come into it."

I thought of Angela's left hand, which used to be weighed down with a three-carat diamond engagement ring. No wonder she blamed Katrina for her troubles. "So, simplifying here, Angela bought the buildings for him, but Noble refused to reimburse her, and she was stuck with them. And it was Katrina's fault."

He ran a hand through his hair. "Basically. After the title thing was cleared up, Katrina and I wrote her an offer, but Angela rejected it. She ripped Katrina a new one apparently, insisted there wasn't anything wrong with the title, that the sale to Noble was being held up for no reason."

"Was she right?"

He put his wineglass on the coffee table and avoided meeting my eyes. "The title issue was cleared up, that's all I know."

"So what happens now? Do the buildings stay empty?"

"With Katrina out of the picture, I couldn't handle the purchase alone. I mended fences with Angela, told her if she decided to hold on to the buildings, and did a build-out to suit me, I'd be her first tenant. I offered her a year's rent up front, and we're guaranteeing her a ten-year lease. She'll recoup her money and then some. It's property in San Francisco. Money in the bank. Look, I'll show you."

He took up the bottle of wine, and Sabina and I followed him into the dining room, where he unrolled an architectural rendering and some technical drawings onto the table. He leaned across to anchor the top corners with the bottle and a potted orchid.

"The view from the Gardens side will look pretty much the same as now; she'll put retail space with large windows on the street level, but most of the work will be interior. Upstairs, we'll have plenty of consultation spaces, good space for the admin staff, natural light. Space like that downtown would cost us twenty-five dollars more a square foot. The permitting process was fast-tracked, demo has started, and it should be ready in six to eight months. And after that, my commute will be five minutes instead of twenty-five." He and Sabina exchanged a smile. His surgeon's hands were delicate and sure as he rolled up the drawings. "If I'm honest, I'm relieved it turned out this way. Katrina was—she hadn't been completely—" He didn't finish the thought. "If you're interested, I'd offer to show you the space, but I'm doing a video consult with a surgeon in Australia, and if that somehow runs long it could be a while."

"Would you like to see it, Theo?" Sabina asked. "We could walk over. It's mostly just a construction site, but it's kind of interesting to imagine the 'after.' Almost as good as HGTV. I was there a couple of days ago checking out the closets." She snorted. "The plans call for eliminating some of the storage spaces, but I'm thinking we need to put them back into the design." She shrugged. "Anyway, come on over with me and you can tell me what you think."

Kurt checked his watch. "I have to change and get back to the office." He hesitated. "I didn't mean to cause trouble by keeping this all under wraps, Theo. Katrina wanted it kept on the down-low. We don't need neighborhood association approval for the build-out, because nothing much will be different on the outside, but if you want to share it all with them, I'm fine with it. Maybe they'll think I'm one of the good guys, for a change."

If it weren't for the fact that he's an arrogant bastard I would have said he looked unsure of himself. I knew he wasn't popular in the community, mostly because of that arrogance, and I certainly wasn't a fan, but maybe he had some good points hidden under the façade after all.

Sabina pulled on a sweater. "Come on, Theo—I'll show you what the new space will look like. There's already been some problem with the plumbing, and I imagine there's a lot more of that kind of stuff to come." She rolled her eyes.

I put down my wine glass. "What's the plumbing problem? Is it anything to do with the stream under Polk Street?"

"There's a stream?"

"Apparently."

"The builders called yesterday and said some storm drain must have backed up, and it's causing a stink. Luckily, not our problem. If we'd bought the buildings, on the other hand . . ."

Most of Sabina's height was in her legs; her jacket fit me perfectly. I put it on as we left.

CHAPTER TWENTY-TWO

think the power is on," Sabina said, clicking a switch.
A sconce in the wall flickered on and then died. "Maybe
we don't need the light," she said hastily and clicked the
switch off again. She stepped over a small drift of fast-
food bags, candy wrappers, paper napkins, and several coffee cups swept into a neat pile. I thought I caught a glint of
gold and bent down to look.

Sabina looked back. "Have you found something?"

I sifted through the pile with my toe. "I thought maybe
someone had dropped a gold charm, but it's just a shiny
logo printed on a napkin." I pointed it out. "Have you ever
been to the Venus de Milo Club?"

"God, Theo, why would I want to go there? It's all naked
women and bachelor parties."

"Really? Huh. Never mind, then."

"Come on up. I'll show you where the buildings will be
thrown together upstairs." She wrinkled her nose. "I see
what they mean about that smell. Sorry, Theo, I didn't realize it was this bad. It should be better upstairs."

Within minutes we were opening doors onto closets and
bathrooms, trying to find the source of the stench and calling back and forth, stifling giggles and trying to come up

with the most ridiculous ideas of what could be causing it, when Sabina suddenly went silent.

"Sabina? Have you found the pile of dead fish?" I turned a corner, and she was staring into a closet with one hand holding the door and the other hand over her mouth. She looked up at me, and tears spilled onto her cheeks.

I took a cautious look inside the closet, at the body partly wrapped in a padded blanket and duct tape. He'd been dead a while. His scarred face was gray-green and horribly distorted, his eyes distended behind his glasses. His swollen tongue was erupting from his mouth, forcing his lips away from his teeth. One of the teeth was gold, otherwise I might not have recognized him. Built-up gases had bloated his body so that his clothes were stretched and looked much too small for him. His scarf was digging into the flesh of his neck, covering his Roman collar, if he was still wearing it.

Feeling as if I knew far too much about what to do next, I took hold of Sabrina's arm and guided her downstairs as I pulled out my phone. In the few minutes before the police arrived, I telephoned Grandfather and left an unsatisfactory message along the lines of *our mutual friend has turned up dead*—I couldn't think of any creative, spy-like obfuscating language to disguise the news of Sergei's death and the fact that I was freaking out.

"Tell me again, Ms. . . . Bogart, how you came to be in the empty building." Inspector Lichlyter had looked resigned when she'd arrived to find me with Sabina, who was still weeping quietly under the care of an EMT.

"My friends Sabina and Kurt Talbot have been renovating the buildings, and Sabina brought me over to look at the work they'd done. We could smell something bad, and we were looking around to see if we could find the source of the smell, and we found . . . him."

I looked over to where people in bunny suits and masks were photographing the corpse in situ. I envied them their masks. With the closet door open, the smell was indescribable.

"Do you recognize this, Ms. . . . Bogart?" Lichlyter held up a see-through plastic evidence bag, the inside smeared with blood.

I didn't realize until that moment that hair actually did stand up on end. In fact, my hair seemed to be trying to crawl off my head. Recognize it? I've been familiar with that hoof pick since I was eleven years old and gave it to Grandfather for his birthday. He used it to hold his keys, which were still attached. It was a ring of heavy brass, a bit more than two inches across, with a sharp hook attached to one side with a hinge. The hook folded into the center and turned it into something that could be safely carried in the pocket of, say, a pair of jodhpurs, but easily extended to clean a horse's hoof of hard-packed sand, or to remove a stone. The hook was extended and bloody.

"I don't think so," I lied. "What is it?" That struck the right note of polite curiosity, although she gave me a sharp look, and I reminded myself to be careful, that she was far from stupid.

"We think it's the murder weapon." As if the blood hadn't given me my first clue. "The victim had it in stuck in his jugular."

Which was sickening for more than one reason.

"His wallet has a driver's license and some credit cards in the name of Sergei Wolf. Is the name familiar at all?"

"No," I said, lying again automatically, and then, prompted

by God knows what, blurted, "Did Father Martin from up at St. Christopher's get in touch with you?"

"You think this is related to the hands in the coffee shop?" she said sharply.

"I don't know," I said hurriedly. "I just wondered." I nodded toward the crime scene. "Are his hands . . . intact?"

Her face closed down. "We'll know more after the autopsy. What else can you tell me?"

"Nothing. No, really, nothing," I said, and carefully didn't look at the hoof pick in the plastic bag.

"Your friends Dr. and Mrs. Talbot, they own the building?

I shook my head. "The owner is another local; her name is Angela Lacerda."

She wrote that down in her notebook, but within minutes Angela had arrived, flustered and appalled and disinclined to be helpful. "I'm not answering any questions," she said brusquely when Lichlyter approached. "You can talk to my lawyers. What is going on here?" When she got her first whiff of the body, she gagged and covered her mouth and nose with her hand. "God! Let me out of here." She turned and stumbled back outside. When I followed her out, she turned on me, her face red and tear-streaked. "What on earth is happening—are you involved in this?"

"No, of course not. I just found him."

"It's the second body you've *found*"—incredibly, she made air quotes with both hands—"I guess he who hides can find, right?"

"No, that's not what—"

But she spun and strode away from me down the street, sobbing angrily. What she hadn't done, I realized as she marched away, was ask anything about the murdered man.

CHAPTER TWENTY-THREE

When Lichlyter let us go, I saw Sabina home and mobilized Sebastian's nanny. Mariana didn't speak much English but understood that there was a crisis and went into nurturing mode with warm blankets and cups of hot tea. Sabina had stopped weeping, but the EMT said she was in shock, and I could believe it. I tried to rub some warmth into her freezing cold hands, and we talked quietly until Kurt got home, taking the stairs two at a time, his Australian colleague abandoned after my call.

As soon as I felt I could leave, I made a beeline to Grandfather's home on Telegraph Hill and rappelled down the stairs to his front door. The homes there are built on a series of small plateaus, accessible by steep flights of stairs, and the light is soft and filtered through a thick green canopy. It's not the ideal place for a seventy-year-old man to live, in part because some of the homes could kindly be described as quirky, but Grandfather said he liked the trees. One of the first things he'd arranged, while he was still staying at the Ritz-Carlton on Cathedral Hill, was a lease on a Bechstein grand piano. ("It's huge, Grandfather. Where will you put it?" "I don't need a dining room, Theophania, but I do need room for a piano.") The thing is nine feet long.

Hauling it up the four hundred steps from Filbert Street must have been worth a hefty tip.

Neither he nor his housekeeper came when I rang the bell, so I pulled out my key and let myself in, jittery with nerves and wondering vaguely where he could be and why he hadn't returned my call

His home was small but lovely, glowing with silver and fine, polished furniture, and comfortable, linen-covered chairs. Things looked normal, but it was unusually quiet. He often had music playing, or he was making his own at the piano, or his housekeeper, Mrs. Munn, was making small noises at the back of the house. Not today.

"Grandfather?" I took a cautious step inside. "Grandfather, are you home?"

Birds chattered and fluttered in the trees outside, but the house was silent. I went cautiously into each room and found his phone on a charger in the kitchen. I unplugged it, taking it with me and checking his voice mail. I have texts and voice mail messages on my phone going back to the day I bought it, but he always deleted his messages as soon as he'd listened to them. My message was still here, so he hadn't heard it. I also checked under the beds and inside the closets. I'm not sure why, except Sergei had been found in a closet, and you never know.

Each room except one was completely orderly. An oil painting in the living room was on the floor, leaning against the wall. My father specialized in portraits, but this was one of his fairly rare landscapes, and Grandfather had included it among the items he'd shipped from England. As a reminder of our family tragedy, I would have thought he'd never want to see that particular painting ever again.

Instead, it had pride of place. I tugged on the door of the small wall safe it usually disguised, to make sure it was still closed, then quickly replaced the painting and went on through the house. As I rifled in a drawer, trying to find some paper and a pen to leave a note, I heard a noise at the front door and spun around to see him, looking hale and hearty, if a little surprised to see me.

"Theophania? Is everything all right my dear?"

"I was about to ask you the same. I have something to tell—"

He gave a lightning quick glance at the wall safe painting. I wouldn't have noticed, except I was staring at his face, which had a large graze and purple bruise on one cheekbone. "What happened? Did you fall? Do you have any peroxide?" The injury didn't look fresh, but my mother had used peroxide for everything and it was almost the only first aid I knew.

His hand touched the bruise, and he winced slightly. "It's nothing, my dear. My meeting with Sergei was a little more confrontational than I anticipated."

I tried to capture his attention as he glanced through the window and frowned slightly. "Your friend Inspector Lichlyter is approaching," he said.

I pushed his phone into his hand. "Oh God, before she gets here—Sergei's dead, and he had your hoof pick in his neck!"

He gave a demonstration of the reason British aplomb is admired throughout the world by raising an eyebrow instead of bursting into horrified questions. "Ah? Then perhaps I'm about to be asked to assist the police with their enquiries." He calmly put the phone in his pocket.

"I told her I didn't recognize it," I said quickly.

"Just so, my dear. Ah, good afternoon Inspector," he said as he opened the front door. "Won't you come in? How can I help you?"

She looked a little nonplussed, possibly by my presence, and refused his offer of tea or a glass of sherry after she took a seat on the sofa in the window. I thought that was a good sign; on *Law & Order* the police never sit down to do their interviews unless the perp is in handcuffs. She dropped her shoulder bag on the floor and bent over to rummage in it until she came up with her phone, and a notebook and pen. Grandfather fussed a little, adjusting the drapes, moving a small table where she could reach it. I thought he was laying it on a bit thick, myself.

She lifted her telephone, perhaps to show him a photograph of Sergei's face, and then had second thoughts and dropped the phone back into her bag. "I'm sure Ms. . . . Bogart has told you about the unfortunate death of Mr. Wolf. I understand he was a friend of yours?"

Grandfather settled into an armchair, fussing at the pillow behind his back. "May I ask how you know that?"

"He had your name and telephone number on your card in his pocket."

"Ah, yes, I see," he said thoughtfully while I understood more clearly his habit of shredding even small slips of paper. "He was scarcely a friend," Grandfather said. "In fact, I think it's fair to say we barely recognized each other when we met again a few days ago." He smiled. "I suppose the years make a difference to one's appearance, even if we tell ourselves that we haven't changed. I knew him twenty-five or thirty years ago, when we worked together briefly. Are you aware that he is—was—a member of the clergy?"

"No. I didn't know," she said shortly. I watched her absorbing the information.

"Well, we knew each other before he studied for the priesthood."

"He was a Catholic priest?" I could almost see her adjusting Sergei's status. "In the diocese here?" Now she was mentally running through all the protocols for calling the Bishop. I was unsettled by how familiar she'd become. So Sergei hadn't been wearing his Roman collar. I tried to decide what that meant, if anything.

"He was on vacation. I believe he had recently lived in South America, but I'm afraid I don't know specifically where he was—er—posted. Are you certain I can't get you a glass of sherry?"

"No, thank you. How did you come to meet again?"

"He was here for a few days on business and contacted me to renew our acquaintance. I met him last Wednesday, I believe, we talked about old times, and after an hour or so, we parted."

"What time did you meet?"

"We arranged to meet at four o'clock; he was a few minutes late."

"How did he contact you?"

"I beg your pardon?"

"You gave him your telephone number during your meeting. How did the two of you connect before that?"

"Through a mutual friend," Grandfather said, without hesitation. "We had been fellow members of a small social club. One of the other members in England gave me his telephone number, allowing me to choose, or not, to contact him."

She wrote something in her notebook and looked up at

him. "I'd like to contact him or her. Would you tell me their name and how to reach them?"

"Yes, of course." He took the proffered notebook and wrote something down. "I believe she is traveling in India at the moment, but I'm sure a message left at that number will reach her eventually." He smiled blandly and returned the notebook.

Lichlyter bit the inside of one cheek. "Where did you and Father Wolf meet?" I noted the automatic respectful address. Sergei was no longer simply a dead body; he was a dead priest. I could see that it made a difference.

"He said he hadn't yet had an opportunity to see the murals at Coit Tower, so we met there and spent our time together strolling through the tower."

"So just at the top of the stairs here, in fact?"

"Indeed. When we parted I gave him my telephone number." He shrugged. "I didn't anticipate hearing from him again, but I thought it was a friendly gesture."

"He didn't come to your home?"

"He had another appointment, and we parted at about five thirty," which I thought was an admirable example of telling the truth without answering the question. I think Lichlyter noticed, too, but she didn't follow up. "I believe— yes, I took a photograph." He reached into his jacket pocket, pulled out his phone, and flicked through a few screens before finding what he was looking for.

Lichlyter glanced at a three-quarter photograph taken from the side, as Sergei—I couldn't think of him as Father Wolf—bent to examine one of the murals in extreme close-up. A section of the WPA-era mural stretched into the middle distance.

"Any of the two of you together?"

"No. I thought I would send him this one as a souvenir of his visit."

"Do you know who he was meeting after he left you?"

"I'm afraid not." Grandfather frowned slightly, as if in thought. "He said he had originally planned to meet with another person he knew, but that it wasn't possible. He hoped this other person could tell him something he needed to know. He told me he had been traveling recently as part of his work. Something to do with one of the churches here, I assume."

"Did he give you any details?"

"He did say he was trying to solve a puzzle for a fellow priest, off the clock, as it were. I think he felt under an obligation to his friend, who had recently died."

I raised my head sharply, and Lichlyter gave me an inquiring look. I gave her a casual shrug, and she turned her attention back to Grandfather, whose expression hadn't changed.

"Do you know anything else about this obligation, or about his friend?"

"Only that he was killed in a hit-and-run accident."

Lichlyter's attention sharpened. "Where?"

"In Ukraine."

That surprised her. "His friend died in Ukraine, but he was solving a puzzle on his behalf here in San Francisco?"

"So he said. He also said it was quite like old times," Grandfather said.

Her eyes narrowed. "Why would it be like old times? What kind of work did he do?"

"He was what I believe today would be called a forensic accountant, but that was a very long time ago. I don't know what kind of work he did in recent years beyond what I assume were regular parish duties."

"And you don't know any specifics of this task he had undertaken?"

"I'm sorry to say not. I can't imagine it would stray too far from his work for the Church. Perhaps something to do with one of the local parishes? He told me one or two stories of uncovering malfeasance, without mentioning any names, of course," he added, raising a hand as if to forestall the question. "I'm sorry to hear of his death, and I don't know of any reason that he would be killed."

"Given his extreme lack of visual acuity, did it surprise you that he chose to spend time viewing artworks?"

Grandfather smiled. "That didn't occur to me."

"Can you tell me where you were yesterday between approximately ten p.m. and two a.m.?" That surprised me; I was fairly sure Sergei had been dead longer than that.

"I was with a friend and, if it's satisfactory, I would like to let her know you might wish to speak to her, and why, of course. I'm certain she will corroborate my, er, alibi."

I tried not to look as shocked as I felt. "Her" who? Did Grandfather have a-a lady friend I knew nothing about? Being together from late evening until early morning didn't sound as if they were playing cribbage.

Lichlyter shared a shrewd look between the two of us and chewed the inside of her cheek. "How did you injure your face, sir?"

Grandfather touched it lightly and then winced. "I can only blame my advancing years. I tripped and fell."

"It looks painful."

"A little."

"When did this happen, sir?"

"A couple of days ago."

"I would have thought longer from the color of that bruise."

She dropped her notebook into her shoulder bag and rose smoothly to her feet. "I think that's all for now. Please call me later today with the name of your friend."

Grandfather walked her to the front door, giving a masterful performance of an elderly man a little unsteady on his feet.

She stopped on the doorstep, thoughtfully inspecting the highly polished brass lock and handle on the dark green door. She turned back and spoke to me. "Would you mind coming into my office tomorrow afternoon? At about three, if that works for you."

"Okay, I mean, of course. Three o'clock at your office. Um, where is your office?"

"The Hall of Justice at 850 Bryant."

I nodded and she finally left.

"My fingerprints will be on my hoof pick, of course. The next thing she'll want is a blood sample or a DNA swab," Grandfather said thoughtfully as he watched Lichlyter leave. "Theophania, I gave Sergei my key on the hoof pick. He said he felt unsafe at his hotel. I thought he was being dramatic. He asked if he could stay here, and I had no real reason to refuse." He raised a hand absently to the bruise on his cheek. "I explained that I didn't spend every night at home, but that he was welcome to stay and to leave the keys as he left. He took me up on the offer for a night; that would be Wednesday night. Do you know how long he had been deceased?"

"Several days, by the look of him," I said, and thought

how odd my life had become when I could say that with some confidence. "Perhaps as long ago as Wednesday or Thursday. One thing, though." I chewed the inside of my cheek. "Sabina told me that the closet where he was found was empty two days ago, and the smell was only noticed today."

He nodded thoughtfully. "So he was killed somewhere else, and possibly stored there, before being moved yesterday night. It explains why the Inspector was so specific about the time frame."

He disappeared into the back of the house and came back carrying a small, folded cloth. He opened the front door and rubbed it over the handle, knocker, and mail slot.

I watched in stunned silence as he came back inside and made his way through the sitting room, carefully wiping the hard surfaces.

He took down the painting again and wiped the safe, then placed his fingers on each key on the touch screen before replacing the painting and wiping the frame.

"Grandfather, what on earth—"

"Did you notice if the good Father was wearing a ring when he came to your shop?"

"He had a heavy gold signet ring on his right ring finger. Is that how—?" I nodded at the graze on his cheek.

"He took exception to a remark I made about Catholic charities."

I goggled at him. "You made a—what did you say, for heaven's sake?"

"He goaded me." He looked a little shamefaced. "I said their bookkeeping left something to be desired."

"That doesn't sound very inflammatory."

"Well, no." He sighed. "A Roman collar is so often a

prima facie case for integrity, which of course is why some people find them so useful. He had changed a good deal—he was slender, with a full head of hair the last time I'd seen him—but I knew the remark would bite if he was, er—the real McCoy, because it was the last thing I said to him when he left us to join the priesthood. He hit me then, too," he said reflectively. "But then he'd been under a great strain for some time."

"So you didn't really part on good terms, then, all those years ago."

"I'm afraid not. Which made his attempt to reach out to me all the more surprising."

"Did he say anything about the problem he needed you to help him with?"

"He did, Theophania. He said he thought he knew why and by whom Katrina Dermody was murdered."

CHAPTER TWENTY-FOUR

I took a second to recalibrate at the unexpected introduction of Katrina. "How could he have known that? And who did he say it was?"

"I should be more precise. He didn't say he knew who it was, just that he'd deduced their existence from the effect their activities produced. He also asked me to discover whether anything was amiss with an orphanage in Kiev."

"Anything amiss? An orphanage in Kiev!" Apparently I had decided to repeat everything he said to me. I tried to stop doing that and grabbed onto the only question that came to mind. "Was he from there? Where is Kiev? Russia?" My education had some unexpected black spots, and geography was one of them.

He gave me one of his pitying looks. "It's in the Ukraine. I know that he was *persona non grata* in Kiev, in fact in the whole of the country, and couldn't go there himself to investigate. He felt that his friend, this other priest, had been killed deliberately, not in a simple traffic accident."

I abandoned the orphanage. "But the Internet—"

"Of limited value in this case, Theophania. The orphanage certainly has a website with some photos of the staff and a discussion of their—er—mission I think they call it."

"Did Sergei want you to go to Kiev?" I said blankly. "That seems like a lot to ask."

"He hoped to persuade me. However, I am also *persona non grata* in Ukraine. He did not know that."

I sat back in my chair and stared at him. Honestly, I was having trouble with all of this. I had always thought he'd had a fairly significant but boring job as a senior civil servant, and occasionally, and in an amateur sort of way, did small jobs for the Foreign Office.

"Since the Russian invasion of Ukraine, and the annexation of Crimea, modern day Kiev is like Mos Eisley." He paused and then quoted unexpectedly, "You will never find a more wretched hive of scum and villainy."

I did a mental stutter; I thought the only movies he watched had subtitles. I recognized the reference because Ben had an unexpected inner geek and he insisted that the Star Wars movies were as important to western culture as the Greek myths.

Grandfather pulled on his earlobe and looked into the middle distance. "That is Kiev. Agents of the Russian government, anti-Russian forces, assassins—"

"Assassins!"

"Car bombs, weapons trafficking, poison—"

"Poison!" I was reeling, and apparently back to repeating him.

"The city is like the old Wild West in America. Being a journalist, opposing Russian influence, criticizing the government, being any kind of activist—they are all extremely risky. People die simply for offending the wrong people. In any event, I cannot go there, and I told Sergei as much when we had finished our disagreement and begun to talk. He was very disappointed."

"What was supposed to be wrong with the orphanage in Kiev? Were they dealing in black-market adoptions or something?"

"He was concerned that someone might be relaying funds to anti-Russian forces using the orphanage as a cover. Or that possibly it was some kind of money laundering operation—" He sighed. "It's difficult to know. And now that he's gone, we may never know. When he realized I really couldn't help him, he was less forthcoming. He implied that something that was supposed to be happening at the orphanage was not happening." He frowned and made an impatient gesture.

"I know a little something about an orphanage there. It's called St. Olga's," I said, happy to have something to contribute to an increasingly bewildering conversation.

"Indeed, Theophania?"

I nodded. "Gavin Melnik visited there fairly recently. He said Katrina was its benefactor, and she was concerned that the orphanage was spending more money than it should. Gavin reported back that, as far as he could tell, everything checked out, but he isn't a-a forensic accountant or anything. If Sergei thought St. Olga's was the orphanage connected to Katrina's death, shouldn't we do something? Try to find out—"

"Under no circumstances, Theophania. This is far above our, er, pay grade. If his priest friend did not die accidentally, Sergei's is the third murder associated with whatever is happening there. It is certain to be extremely dangerous and, as I said, very difficult if not impossible to investigate. An investigation of that scope requires resources and manpower. Now," he said in a very different tone of voice, "I heard Mrs. Munn arriving at the back door. No doubt she has been to the shops. Shall I have her make us some tea?"

"There must be something we can do," I insisted. "We don't have to go to Kiev; we could probably find out at least some of what we need to know here, where Katrina and Sergei were killed."

He didn't respond but went off to speak to Mrs. Munn, who, sure enough, produced a steaming teapot and some slices of cake in short order.

I dutifully poured cups of tea and doled out cake slices for a couple of minutes before I raised the issue again. "What about the members of your ex-spies group? Can they find out anything—surely they must have contacts in Kiev?"

He made a thoughtful grimace. "It's possible." He sipped his tea and carefully examined his slice of cake without adding anything.

"Please, Grandfather! You know Lichlyter is going to find out you own that hoof pick, and don't you want to find out who killed Sergei?"

He smiled at me.

"What?"

"You are apparently not considering that I might have killed Sergei myself."

I recalibrated again. "Oh. Right," I said blankly. "It did occur to me when I saw your hoof pick." He gave me an approving look. "Did you? Kill him, I mean."

"No, my dear, I didn't." He pursed his lips and gave me a searching look. "I'll have a word, Theophania, with one or two of our members and see if they feel comfortable talking to us."

The "us" gave me a little bit of a glow, and I had to be content with that. I flopped down onto his sofa. "This has been a very weird day," I said, and then remembered something I should tell him. "When I got here, *The White Cliffs of Dover* was on the floor."

He lifted the painting, looking it over front and back, then opened the safe, glanced inside, and shifted a couple of things aside. He shut it again, replacing the painting much as I had.

"Is everything where it should be?"

He nodded. "Everything." He bit his lip. "Do you remember the combination, Theophania?"

"I wrote it down and put it in my safe deposit box, but I don't know it offhand."

"It's your Great Uncle Teddy's investiture date. Can you remember that?"

"Um, not really."

He gave me what I could only describe as a pitying look. "Let's find something simpler for the time being. We'll reset it to"—he hesitated—"the name of the magazine where you sold your first photograph."

"How do you remember that?"

I got another look. "I don't, Theophania, but I assume that you do?"

"Yes of course." He stepped aside and I reset the electronic lock. "It's—"

He stopped me with shake of his head and handed me the small agenda and gold pen he'd withdrawn from his pocket. I wrote down the name, he glanced at it, then ripped off the part of the page where I'd scribbled the name and tore it into small pieces before placing half the pieces in his pocket and burying the others in the soil of a large potted aspidistra. Obviously, I'd been cavalier all my life, just tossing things into the recycling.

He opened the front door and stared at it for a moment, in much the same way as Lichlyter had, and then down at the spotless front step. "How long had you been here before I arrived, Theophania?"

"Just a few minutes. Why?"

He smiled at me. "No special reason."

After we finished our tea, I headed back to Aromas, handing over another small fortune in cab fare. It occurred to me that, while I couldn't fly to Kiev, I had my own computer hacker; maybe Haruto could find out if anything was odd or wrong about St. Olga's. If he found anything questionable, I could follow up with Gavin.

I telephoned him an hour later as I followed Lucy around the Gardens. I could hear Gar Wood yowling in the background.

"Haruto—seriously, doesn't that cat ever shut up?"

"Says the owner of the worst-tempered dog in San Francisco."

"Okay, fair point. Would you do a bit of research for me?"

"Sure, what d'you need?"

"It may involve getting into the financials of a nonprofit in Eastern Europe."

"I can do that. If I find anything I'll tell them I can break their firewall and they need better security."

"I need you to find what you can about an orphanage in Kiev. That's in Ukraine," I added self-consciously. "It's called St. Olga's. Maybe start with their website, and see if that gives you any leads to information about their finances—maybe nonprofits over there have to report their donations to the government like here—the number of kids they have, news items from when they opened. And contact information—telephone numbers, e-mails; anything you can find."

"Okay, that all?"

I thought for a minute. "No, one more thing. See if you can find anything about a priest dying in Kiev in the past couple of months."

He nodded. "Interesting," he drawled. "Okay, done and done. I'll see what I can find tonight."

I was at home when Haruto texted at five the next morning, saying to find him when I woke up. I left Lucy asleep on the bed, walked down the back staircase of the building—a second way out in case of earthquakes—and knocked on his back door.

"Jesus, Theo—what are you doing awake at this hour?" He was wearing a blue and white kimono jacket over jeans and tatami sandals. Gar Wood was pushing her head between his ankles, vocalizing as usual. Do all Siamese sound like crying babies? I don't know how Haruto puts up with it.

"Hi, Gar," I said, and gave her chin a token obeisance, after which she shut up and stalked away. "Can't sleep. What's up? Got any more of that?" I inhaled the coffee smell from the mug in his hand.

"Sure. Don't tell Nat." He poured coffee into another mug and handed it to me on his way to getting a carton of half-and-half from the fridge.

"So what's up?" I said, blowing on my coffee.

"Come inside. I have something to show you."

I'd slipped off my shoes and left them by the door. He'd never said anything about this little shoe-shedding ritual, but there was a small shoe rack by the door with his shoes on it, and a couple of pairs of sandals for guests, so it seemed only polite to follow his example. I liked his place; he shared my aesthetic, which is to say, there wasn't much in it. We had never discussed religion, but I think he was a Buddhist. He had turned his smaller bedroom into a meditation space, with tatami mats and a *noren* curtain painted with mountains replacing the door. Almost the only furniture in the rest of his apartment were a large antique *tansu* chest against the wall opposite the fireplace, and a handful of legless chairs on the beautifully finished hardwood floors. He had done the refinishing here, and in my flat, in exchange for a break on the rent. I knew his second bedroom was full of blinking, high-tech equipment, but he kept the door closed, so nothing disturbed the serenity of the apartment.

He draped himself onto one of the chairs, put his coffee on the floor, and picked up his laptop. It looked almost miniature in his big hands. "I started by looking for a priest who'd died or disappeared, and I found two."

That was a jolt. Truthfully, I hadn't really expected him to find anything.

"Who were they?"

"I'm not sure how to pronounce it, but the first one, six months ago, was Yaroslaw Hryhorenko. He was in his eighties, and he died of pneumonia. He'd been parish priest at the same church for, like, fifty years; his death and funeral made the local papers."

"Who was the other one?"

"His name was Artem Ponomarenko. Killed in a hit-and-run a couple of months ago. No witnesses; no one was ever charged."

"Was he a parish priest, too?"

"Nope. He was secretary to the local bishop, which is a bigger deal than it sounds, apparently."

"Wow. Poor Sergei."

"No, his name was Artem."

"I meant, I'm pretty sure he was the friend of a friend, and the friend's name was Sergei."

"Was?"

"He's dead, too."

"Okaaay. Anyway, they were the only two in the last year."

"Right. What's next?"

He grinned. "The first thing to know is that I'm good, really good, at breaking through firewalls."

"I don't doubt it," I said.

"The second thing to know is that I would never expect an orphanage, even one in Eastern Europe, to bury their data and bounce it all over the world with fake IP addresses."

"Wow. Truly?"

"I got there in the end, but whoever did this has something to hide."

"So what did you find out?"

"On the surface everything looks legit. Without mad skills"—he grinned at me again—"no one looking at it would have any idea things aren't what they look like. They bank online. Money comes in; money goes out, and it's spent on what you'd expect: food, the light bill, books, stuff like that."

"But?"

"The accounts are phony. There's no there, there."

"But that doesn't make sense. The orphanage exists; it must have bills to pay. Where's the money going?"

"Still don't know. And that's not all. I'm not sure where the money's coming from, either. That's where things start bouncing around." He shook his head. "It looks like simple bank transfers, but—it's not." He shrugged. "That's all I can tell you. I'll keep looking if you want. The only trouble is, if I haven't already, it might set off a red flag somewhere. After a while, when I realized things weren't kosher, I used a sniffer program to help me avoid notice, but before that . . ." He shrugged again. "Not sure."

"Who would know how to set up something like this? I mean, is it the Pentagon, or some kid in his mum's basement?"

"It took some serious skill, but I could do most of what I've seen so far. It could be one person."

"Or a small government program? Like, I don't know, a bunch of spies?"

"I suppose . . ."

And I knew how to find a bunch of spies.

CHAPTER TWENTY-FIVE

The Hall of Justice on Bryant Street had a blocky, ominous look, or maybe that was just my guilty conscience. The immediate surroundings weren't seedy, exactly, but a lot of uniformed police officers were coming and going, police patrol cars were parked on the street in significant numbers, and an assortment of rather shattered-looking people were wandering around outside. All of the nearby storefronts housed bail bond agents. The most prominent was Honest Eddie's Bail Bonds. Good grief.

The other people waiting in line to go through the metal detectors seemed to be mostly family or lawyers visiting inmates at the jail on one of the upper floors. I had to empty my pockets to go through the metal detectors, but I was allowed to take my three-inch Swiss Army knife through the barricades and into the elevator. I kept my fingers around the knife in the pocket of my jeans, in case someone escaped from the jail and tried to take it from me. I didn't want to be responsible for anyone getting taken hostage. I was still defending myself against imaginary accusers when the elevator doors opened again, and Inspector Lichlyter was standing there waiting for me. It took me a second to recognize her without her red jacket.

She led me past what American crime dramas called the

squad room. I looked around curiously, hoping for something less mundane than tidy desks, battered office chairs, and out-of-date computer monitors. Most of the desks were empty—I guessed their owners were all out solving crimes. She stopped briefly to pick up a tray holding a manila envelope and a file folder from one of her colleagues, scribbled something on the file folder, and ushered me down a hallway into a room just big enough for two chairs, facing each other across a narrow table.

The floor was carpeted, and the walls sprouted large, asymmetrical bulges and ridges covered in dark fabric. It had a weird dampening effect on sounds, which I suppose was the point. Our conversation was easy enough to hear, since we were only two feet apart, but everything else was muffled. Small noises, like closing the door, fell instantly into the abyss. It was also too warm in there and, unlike the larger room, felt oddly threatening.

"I won't be recording our conversation, Ms. . . . Bogart," she said, indicating a video camera on the wall in one corner of the room. "For now, the equipment is turned off, and you are just assisting me as a helpful member of the public."

"Right. Okay," I said. Perhaps she meant it to be calming.

She picked the file folder out of the tray and opened it in front of her, leaving the lumpy manila envelope in the tray.

"I understand Ms. Dermody was suing you on behalf of Mr. Gavin Melnik," she said. I was surprised our conversation was apparently to be about Katrina and not Sergei, and tried not to look it.

"Right. Yes," I said. I abandoned my knife to clasp both hands on the table in front of me. "It was a trip and fall lawsuit. The details were being handled by my insurance company."

"I understand also that Mr. Melnik has dropped the lawsuit since Ms. Dermody's death."

"He told me. He said she had pressured him into suing me."

"That seems strange. Why would she do that?"

"Katrina didn't like me."

"Is there any particular reason for that?"

I told her about Matthew and my adversarial role on the neighborhood association board, and my conviction that she'd sent Gavin Melnik to Aromas to make trouble for me.

"So there was some animosity between you and Ms. Dermody?"

"Not really." I hesitated. "Perhaps on her side."

She shifted some papers in the file folder. "Your grandfather moved to San Francisco with you?"

"A couple of months afterward."

"He must be very protective of you," she said pleasantly. She reached for the manila envelope and shook it gently.

To my absolute horror, the plastic bag containing Grandfather's hoof pick landed on the table.

"We've identified this item, Ms. . . . . Bogart."

I felt the color drop from my face.

"Apparently, it's a hoof pick," she said. "People who ride horses often carry them, and as you can see, this one is also being used as a key ring. Do you ride, Ms. . . . . Bogart?"

"I have in the past; I don't anymore."

"I imagine your childhood in England being full of ponies and horses, is that right?"

I nodded.

"And other members of your family probably ride horses, too."

"My parents didn't ride. My mother didn't have the time, and my father never learned. They—"

She held up a hand. "But other family members. Your grandfather?"

I swallowed. "Yes; he's a life-long rider. But he had, you know, grooms and people to take care of his horses. He wouldn't need a hoof pick." Another lie. All riders carry one.

"Odd that you didn't recognize what it was when I asked you before."

"It doesn't look like a hoof pick," I lied. "They're usually more like small screwdrivers or large pocket knives, not that circle thing."

"It's neat, isn't it?" She picked up the plastic bag and pressed it around the contours of the hoof pick. "Easy to slip into a pocket I would have thought, and, as you see, there are keys attached." She raised an enquiring eyebrow.

"Is there—did you find fingerprints? I mean," I added more firmly, "that would help you identify whoever handled it. Maybe it belongs to someone who isn't the killer." I wiped my hands on my jeans. "I mean, fingerprints would tell you who handled it, but not necessarily who the killer was." Oh God, shut up.

"Yes, we've gotten that far, thank you," she said dryly. To my surprise, she went on, "There are some partial prints of interest. We're waiting on the identification now. It doesn't take long if the prints are in our system."

She put the hoof pick back into its envelope. "Thank you for coming in today, Ms. . . . Bogart."

"That's it?"

She raised an eyebrow. "Unless there's something you'd like to add?"

I started to shake my head. "No. Yes—before I go—the

fingers in Nat's microwave. Did they belong to the body I found?"

"It looks that way," she said. "At least, Father Wolf's body is missing those parts of his hands. We'll know for sure when the medical examiner has finished with him. The ends of the bones will be compared, the DNA matched, but for now I'm satisfied that they belong together."

I wasn't sure if that was good news or not.

"Some South American gangs mutilate priests in that way," I said, as if I knew anything about South American gangs.

"So we've heard. We're taking that into consideration, of course." She returned the hoof pick into the envelope and showed me politely to the elevator.

What did she mean to accomplish by showing me the hoof pick again? If she meant to rattle me, mission accomplished. Was I a suspect? Was Grandfather?

I got on the wrong bus by mistake because I wasn't paying attention to anything outside of my own head. By the time I got home, everything had changed, and not for the better.

When I walked into Aromas, Haruto stuffed his phone into his jeans. "Theo! Thank God! I was just calling you."

"What's happened?"

He gulped. "Davo's been picked up by the police for questioning. Something about his fingerprints on a murder weapon. What the hell? He'd never do anything like that."

"God, no, of course not." I pulled out my own phone.

Haruto dragged a hand through his hair. "It was his stupid friends who got him into trouble for tagging."

"What? What does that mean?"

"You know—spray painting graffiti on billboards and bridges, harmless shit, but his prints were in the system."

My phone rang, and I picked up the call on autopilot. Nothing had ever sounded so good as Davie's foghorn voice, and the relief threatened to knock my legs from under me. I grabbed hold of the counter.

"Davie! Where are you?" I looked at Haruto, who mouthed something I couldn't decipher. "What's happening? We have a very good lawyer, and I'll call him right away."

"Don't worry, okay?" he said anxiously in my ear. "I dunno what this is all about, but Juvie isn't so bad." I could almost see him shrug. "One of my friends is there," he added, as if I'd find that comforting. "They won't let me leave with just anyone; if they can't reach my dad, I'm stuck here 'til Monday."

I bowed to his superior knowledge of the criminal justice system. It was already four o'clock. After making what I hoped were comforting promises, I hurriedly told Haruto what was happening and then telephoned my grandfather's attorney, Adolphus Pratt, who promised to see Davie immediately. "He's a minor and I can't reach his father," I told him. "Do we need a—a barrister? I mean I know they don't call them that here, but a lawyer who specializes in criminal cases?"

He made soothing sounds, explaining that he was capable of navigating the preliminaries and would bring a criminal attorney aboard if and when it became necessary.

"Hurry," I said. "God knows what's happening to him. And he's just a kid."

I left Lichlyter a vaguely threatening message about the proper treatment of juveniles in custody. I wasn't all that surprised when she didn't call me back.

I got to the apartment Davie shared with his father in

the Tenderloin as fast as I could—in an Uber this time. Maybe I needed to rethink my decision not to have a car in the city. I'd been there once before, in an unsuccessful attempt to have Mr. Rillera arrested for neglect and child abuse. At the time, fifteen-year-old Davie outweighed his father by about fifty pounds, which, added to the denials of both, weighted the scales of justice on his father's behalf.

The elevator still didn't work, and I climbed three flights of rubbish-strewn, sharply aromatic stairs with flickering light fixtures behind metal cages giving a sinister liveliness to the graffiti on the walls. I rang the Rilleras' doorbell, which I decided wasn't working, since I couldn't hear it even with my ear pressed to the cracked wood of the door. I knocked, but with no better result, even when I abandoned polite taps for a side-of-the-fist hammering. I began knocking on doors up and down the hallway. The woman in the apartment at the end of the hall reluctantly appeared after I'd answered her litany of questions to uncover if I was from the police or "the immigration."

"Please, it's really important. It's about his son."

The door opened a few more inches, pressing hard against three security chains, and I saw an eye and part of her nose. "Davie in an accident?" she said sharply. "His father's a waste of skin, but Davie's one of the best."

"I agree. No, not an accident, but he really needs his father right now."

Her eye flicked to the card I'd slipped through the gap and then brightened. "You're the soap store girl. Yeah, Davie talks about you. I'll tell his father if I see him. Knowing him, it'll be late," she added with a sniff.

The only other person I roused came to the door in his boxers and an undershirt and didn't know—or refused to say—when Mr. Rillera would return. "I got a shift tonight," he grumbled. "Stop all th' damn banging and hollering."

I gulped. "I'm really sorry but it's an emergency. His son needs him."

"If his long shot came in at Golden Gate Fields, he'll be on his first beer at the Venus in North Beach. He's got a thing for one of the dancers. Just keep it down," he said sourly, and shut his door

I checked the time. It was ten minutes to five. There wasn't anything else I could do. Unless Adolphus Pratt was able to work a miracle, Davie would spend the weekend with his friend at Juvenile Hall.

While I was still on the bus heading home, my grandfather telephoned in answer to my frantic messages, and I told him about Davie being taken in for questioning.

"They won't question him without a parent or guardian *ad litem* present," he said. "The boy needs an attorney—"

"I've asked Adolphus to go down to see what he can do."

"Ah. Good, well done, Theophania. I'm sure he will telephone you after he's spoken to the boy."

"He'd probably rather speak to you. He thinks I'm an airhead."

"I'm sure that isn't true, Theophania," he said, although he didn't actually sound very certain. "Now I must speak to your Inspector Lichlyter. I will keep you informed. And Theophania?"

"Yes?"

"Instead of worrying, try thinking of something pleasant, like the white cliffs of Dover."

He hung up abruptly.

Knowing my grandfather as I did, he was heading downtown to confess to owning the hoof pick and explaining how

Davie's fingerprint came to be on it. I was puzzled about that for a minute, until I remembered Davie saying something about the china bowl where my grandfather kept his keys. He'd obviously picked them up at some point.

I took another Uber to Grandfather's house and, multitasking like nobody's business, I spoke to Adolphus while I took down *The White Cliffs of Dover* and found a telephone number written on the back in pencil.

Adolphus said Davie would have to stay in custody until his father could be found. He'd already received a telephone call from my grandfather, who had walked into Inspector Lichlyter's office to admit to ownership of the hoof pick and was, he said, assisting the police with their inquiries. It didn't help his cause when he was asked his blood type, and it was the same as the blood found on Sergei's ring.

"I told him not to answer any further questions," Adolphus said. He sounded irritable. "Anyone who watches television knows not to answer questions without a lawyer present."

"It was because of Davie," I blurted. "He would want to make himself the object of the investigation; not Davie."

"It apparently didn't occur to him that the police might think he had an accomplice," he said, crossly.

I drew in a breath. "Oh God—"

"Please don't worry. I've done everything I can. Until young Mr. Rillera's father is found, and Clement is arraigned, and bail is set, our hands are tied. And visitors," he added repressively, "are not permitted."

So I paced in my living room, with Lucy pacing beside me, and tried to tame my anxieties by listing them. This was a trick I'd tried before, and it never worked, but I didn't know what else to do. Grandfather had been detained, on the strength of his ownership of the hoof pick and his blood type on Sergei's ring. Davie might or might not be detained due to his fingerprint on the hoof pick but, as a minor, he could only be released into the custody of a parent or guardian. Davie's father was MIA, and Grandfather's bail hearing wasn't until Monday. In the meantime, I wasn't permitted to visit them. Nope. Still didn't help.

Lichlyter's hints about Grandfather being protective of me aside, I was sure he hadn't killed Katrina. He was much more likely to use Adolphus Pratt against an adversary than a handgun. He had given me my small revolver for Christmas a year ago since, as a woman living alone, I was apparently in need of one, but it hadn't occurred to me until now to wonder if he owned one, too. He hadn't killed Sergei. He told me so, and I tried to have faith that Lichlyter wouldn't be able to prove that he had. I told myself he was a grown-up, capable of taking care of himself; he probably had handcuff keys and a metal file hidden in the heel of his shoe. Did they let you keep your shoes in jail? Oh God, would they make Grandfather wear an orange jumpsuit? Was he really arrested, or just being held for questioning, and what was the difference? And I was frantic about Davie. He'd sounded okay when we spoke, but I recognized bravado when I heard it.

After telephoning Adolphus Pratt so often with questions that even he ran out of patience, I telephoned Honest Eddie's Bail Bonds. I was expecting whoever answered the phone to sound like a character from *Guys and Dolls*, but he sounded more like an insurance agent.

"If bail is granted—" he said smoothly.

"If!"

"It sounds as if your grandfather is being arraigned on

a capital offense. The judge may decide he's a flight risk—didn't you say he was a foreigner?"

"No. He's English."

"Right. Foreign. So if he's feeling generous, the judge will take his passport and set a high bail."

"How high?"

"Could be a million; could be several."

"Dollars? Yes, of course dollars. So I would have to raise the money and turn it over to the court before he can be released?" Grandfather was wealthy, but I'm not sure he, or I, could raise multiple millions overnight.

"That's where I come in. You raise ten percent of the bail, and I lend you the rest. It means I'm on the hook to guarantee your grandfather's appearances in court. When he shows up, if the charges are dropped or he's tried and found innocent, you pay me back what I loaned you, and I keep the ten percent as my fee. If he's found guilty"—I made a noise I wasn't proud of—"the same applies. I hope that's clear?"

I swallowed. "Yes. How quickly can this be arranged?"

"As soon as bail is set, come to my office. If I think it's a reasonable risk, I'll pay the bond. It might take a day or two, but we'll get your granddad out of jail, okay?"

CHAPTER TWENTY-SIX

Grandfather's last comment about the White Cliffs of Dover had been cryptic, but I can take a hint. The woman who answered when I called the telephone number had a harsh, husky voice, but wouldn't give me her name or speak on the phone. I didn't want to assume anything, but I did wonder if she was the friend Grandfather had been spending his nights with.

She wouldn't meet me until the next morning, which meant another nearly sleepless night. At a few minutes past eleven, I was standing on a mat decorated with a line drawing of a "tipsy" martini glass and a stylized letter "B" at the doorway of a 1940s apartment block near Lake Merced. It was a pleasant neighborhood of trees and lawns close to the city's southern edge, near San Francisco State and the golf course.

I realized, as the light glinted on its lens, that the doorbell was also a camera. I'd heard of them but never seen one. Haruto told me they send a live feed to a smartphone or computer. She opened the door, slipping her phone into the pocket of her slacks.

"Come in," she said. She had high, wide cheekbones, hazel eyes, and thick, creamy hair, which she was wearing in a complicated chignon. She was in her late fifties or early sixties, I thought. She wore black suede shoes with a gold buckle across the front and the kind of heel often called "sensible;" fine, black wool slacks; and a white cable knit sweater with a red scarf tied jauntily around her neck.

Her appearance was a surprise in more ways than one. I'd seen her in The Coffee, and she had jogged past me on one of my walks a few nights ago. I'd also seen her walking briskly along the Embarcadero more than once. So either she and I shared a penchant for early morning walks in the same parts of the city, or she was following me for some reason. I felt as if I were holding a kaleidoscope utterly still, before all the bits of colored glass moved and changed everything.

She closed the door, after glancing outside in both directions, drawing a two-part metal crossbar lock across the width of the door. I'd only ever seen one like it in movies set in high crime areas of New York City. Her fingernails were bright red and sharply pointed.

She led me into a light-filled room in the middle of the small apartment. Oddly, it had no windows, just a large skylight. Instead of a couch, she had a quartet of armchairs arranged around a low table. She went over to a metal-and-glass bar cart. "Please have a seat. Would you like a drink? I have sherry, or scotch, or I can make you a gin and tonic." She smiled at me briefly. "No limes or lemons, I'm afraid."

It wasn't even noon. What the hell. "Scotch, please," I said.

She poured a couple of inches into two heavy crystal glasses from a bottle I didn't recognize, and downed hers in a single swallow as soon as she'd handed one to me. She didn't cough or splutter, which was a feat I couldn't have copied if my life depended on it. I took a wary sip. It tasted smoky and expensive. She refilled her glass and sat across from me, taking occasional sips of her refreshed drink.

"Well, what can I do for you, Theophania, is it?" I nodded. "I'm Valentina. Valentina Kompanichenko."

"I was wondering," I said awkwardly, "if you had heard from my grandfather."

"Ah?" She sat forward and put her glass on the table, then casually slipped her hand down between the arm of the chair and the cushion. "Is he missing?"

Her expression had changed. The angles of her face were harder, her eyes more focused. I felt, suddenly and ridiculously, as if my life might depend on what I was about to say. "Nothing like that," I said, and she relaxed slightly. "I wasn't sure if you knew, and perhaps I'm overstepping here, but he's not able to be in touch, and I thought he would want you to know that he's been arrested for murder," I said, and put down my own glass, making sure both my hands were in full view.

"Pah! Ridiculous. I told the Lichlyter woman that he and I were together every night for the past three weeks."

"You were?" She shrugged gracefully, leaving me to guess whether she was telling the truth or not. "There's a new situation, another murder, and he's implicated. In a way. I mean, I know he didn't do it, but there are—well, it's a situation," I said miserably, and not very coherently.

"This second death is related in some way to the lawyer?"

"I don't know. His body was found in the same area, and it's possible there's a connection between them. I wanted you to know that Grandfather's arraignment or bail hearing, I'm not sure of the difference, is on Monday, and we're hoping he'll be home that afternoon."

She relaxed back into her chair. "I see. Thank you for telling me."

I nodded, then hesitated.

"Ah, but there is more," she said shrewdly. "Are my intentions honorable, is that it?" Her hand was still tucked beside her seat cushion.

"Not really." I took a gulp of my scotch and tried to look harmless.

She didn't hazard another guess, just took a sip of her drink and looked at me calmly over the top of her glass.

"I've noticed you in my neighborhood, and I was wondering if you'd, well, seen anything, or done anything, that could have a bearing on these murders. My grandfather is in real trouble, and I'm not sure how to get him out of it."

She frowned. "Are you saying you believe I had something to do with this man's death? Hah! I can think of many reasons to kill a priest, but it was not I."

"Yes, he was a priest," I said slowly. "So you knew about his death. He was a former colleague, I understood."

"He was no colleague of mine." Her mouth drew into an uncompromising, hard line. "He was a devil who killed many harmless people in a village in Ukraine two and a half decades ago." She was quietly biting off her words, as if they tasted bitter.

"It was a mistake, apparently," she added after a pause. Her eyes flashed and she showed her teeth in a grim smile. "It was a mistake which cost me my husband and my child, and other families their loved ones." She refilled her glass.

"I'm so sorry. I had no idea." The kaleidoscope shifted.

She went on, as if she couldn't help herself. "And then he undergoes a miraculous conversion, enters the priesthood, and is absolved of his many sins." She took a gulp of her scotch. "This is not a sin that can be wiped away like that—" She snapped her fingers. "Reasonable people know there is no afterlife of reward or punishment, only this life. I would wish him to live a long life to consider how terrible were his sins and to suffer. So no, I did not kill him. Others, perhaps, might have a wish to kill him." She emptied her glass, got up to pour another, and sat down again. She didn't seem to be in any hurry to see me gone, but it took me a while to think of any follow-up to the story I'd just heard.

"Who do you know who might have had a wish to kill him?"

"I know of four people," she said. "His mistress, his son, a priest in Kiev . . ." She hesitated. "I lie, there are more than four people because I must add the family members of everyone who died because of his mistake."

"Can I assume that the mistress was from the time before he became a priest?"

She shrugged.

"And his son—where is he?"

"He lives in Northern California, in a small town called Willits."

That was uncomfortably close to San Francisco.

"How old is he? What is his name?"

"His name is Pavel. I am not certain of his age."

"You know his name, but not his age?"

She shrugged again. "The dead lawyer who was murdered?" I nodded. "She was his mistress."

"She was—Katrina was Sergei's mistress? But she was so much younger—"

She shrugged. "War heightens the emotions, no? Age matters little at such times."

"War?"

"How is it that young people know so little? Yes, war. It was a time of great upheaval and many people died."

"The priest in Kiev—"

"A priest who risked his life to provide information which was—misused."

"He—if it's the same priest—was killed in a hit-and-run accident earlier this year."

She narrowed her eyes. "The priest was Artem Ponomarenko. He was a very brave man, and the information he provided should have saved many lives."

"That's the one; he died a few weeks ago."

She absorbed the news calmly. "I . . . see. And you know this how?"

"Sergei told my grandfather he was here to do Father Ponomarenko a favor, or get justice for him or something. He wasn't clear." She frowned and said nothing. I labored on. "So Katrina and Sergei were . . . together. And Sergei's son, Pavel—who was his mother?"

She narrowed her eyes. "That is all I know. Now I am finished talking about it."

The doorbell rang, and she checked her phone. "Sit here. Do not move," she said sternly. Nothing would have persuaded me to disobey her. She left the room and I heard her operating the lock on her door ,and then a mumble of voices. She returned, leading what looked like a pack of spies coming in from the cold. Overcoats and scarves and hats were discarded and tossed onto a side chair. The pack resolved into three well-dressed, middle-aged people.

"Anthony, Ruby, Joseph—this is Theophania, Clement's granddaughter." They nodded like mandarins and took seats around the coffee table. I nodded in return and didn't dare to say or do anything.

Valentina stood in the doorway, a foot or two behind one of her guests, who shifted slightly to keep her in view even as he leaned back in the chair next to mine and crossed one leg over his knee. It was a casual pose, but he didn't look relaxed. "Anthony," he said to me, holding out his hand.

I took it in my own. It was cold and dry. "How do you do?" I said formally. I looked at the other two people in the circle, but they said nothing, so I kept quiet, too.

"How did you get in touch with us?" he asked pleasantly enough, although his eyes were as cold as his hand.

"My grandfather left me Valentina's telephone number. I didn't know her name and I don't know anything else." I was anxious to establish that fact before our conversation went much further.

"But whatever you told Valentina caused her to reach out to us, I see." He pursed his lips. "And what was that?"

"That my grandfather was taken up by the police yesterday under suspicion of murdering a priest by the name of Sergei Wolf. Or possibly Sergei Viktor Wolf."

His eyebrows rose. "Ah?" He looked back at Valentina, who nodded.

If this was Grandfather's social club, it was terrifyingly unlike any I'd ever come across before. They were all practically rigid with displeasure; my head actually started to ache from the atmosphere.

Ruby and Joseph exchanged a glance. She had long bangs and a cap of glossy chestnut hair crowned with a purple beret. She was wearing a thin sweater with a tightly cinched belt over a wool skirt. His shoulders were round inside his green sports jacket, and he had salt-and-pepper hair with a side part. Neither of them was smiling.

"She will need to speak with Jacob," Valentina said.

Anthony pursed his lips and then nodded. The other two, after a slight pause, also nodded.

"Can any of you tell me anything about an orphanage in Kiev?" I blurted out.

He looked back at Valentina, who nodded again. "Why is this orphanage your business?"

"It's possible Father Wolf was investigating them and was killed for it. I'm worried that a friend, Gavin Melnik, may be in danger, too."

If anything, the tension in the room ratcheted up a couple of notches.

"Melnik," Anthony said flatly.

Ruby stood and began to put on her outerwear, pulling on leather gloves and finishing with a large scarf worn like a shawl, knotted around her shoulders over her coat. Unexpectedly, she took her phone from her coat pocket, aimed it at me at arm's length, and took a photo before I realized what she intended. Then she casually picked up her purse and left without saying goodbye to anyone. I heard the door close quietly behind her. Valentina followed her out, and I heard the locks being engaged.

"I'd like to be sure," Joseph said quite suddenly, revealing a broad Southern accent of some kind, and the other two nodded. He held out his own phone to me. "Please take this and press your thumb and index finger to the screen."

I opened my mouth, but no sound came out. I suppose I intended to ask him if he were serious, but his expression answered that question for me. I did as he asked.

"The child knows nothing," Valentina said, in her harsh voice. "We will need to find out what we can, and do what we can, without her assistance."

"I can help!" I said. "Just tell me what to do, and I can do it." I was met with blank stares. I rubbed my hands on my jeans. "Okay, maybe not. What do you know about Gavin?"

"We know the name," Anthony said. "The boy is the son of a former colleague from Kiev."

"A former colleague—of yours?" Were there only a dozen people living in Kiev at any given time?

No one said anything. Anthony and Joseph stood and started to pull on coats and gloves. They took turns exchanging very Russian-looking cheek kisses with Valentina, then she followed them to the front door and locked it behind them. Neither of them said goodbye to me.

"Come with me," she said when she returned. "Have you eaten? I was about to make myself a sandwich." She walked out of the room, taking her drink with her. For a couple of stunned minutes, I stayed where I was, trying to make sense of what she'd told me and what the spies hadn't told me. I was turning the kaleidoscope to see the new pattern, but it still just looked like chips of colored glass.

I picked up my scotch and followed her, glancing at the side of her seat cushion on my way past. I could see the handle of a knife.

The kitchen was small, with a pale green and cream tile counter, cream painted cabinets, and appliances that could have been original to the 1940s-era building. There were no decor items—no chicken-shaped egg baskets on the counter or little framed pictures on the walls, no flowered tea towels hanging in front of the sink, no souvenir magnets on the fridge. Everything was immaculately, almost clinically clean. She snapped on an honest-to-goodness radio tuned to NPR, raised the volume, tossed a couple of heavy pot holders over it, and turned it to face the wall, which muted the sound on our side, but must have given the people next door ringside seats to Terry Gross.

She opened the refrigerator and rustled inside it before looking over at me. "Do sit down." She nodded at the built-in table and benches on one side of the room. "I'm having Havarti cheese with sliced tomatoes, but I also have bologna." She pulled out a plastic bag of bread, jars of mayonnaise and mustard, a tomato, a small lettuce, and something—the cheese presumably—wrapped in plastic, and assembled all of it on the counter. She opened a drawer and withdrew a small knife, which had been sharpened so much its blade was almost worn away, and efficiently used it to shred a pile of lettuce leaves. "I always have an early lunch," she said. "Usually a sandwich or sometimes soup." She looked at me.

Even though thirty seconds before I'd been about to say I didn't want anything to eat, I found myself saying, "A cheese and tomato sandwich would be lovely. Thank you."

"Good. It will take me only a jiffy to put this together. A jiffy. A jiffy is a real thing, you know, in chemistry, in physics." She waved her knife. "But it is a very, very small thing. It will actually take me many jiffies to make our sandwiches. English is a very imprecise language," she said seriously.

I felt like apologizing for my mother tongue. And then wondered if it was also her mother tongue. On balance, and thinking of her name and her painstakingly correct grammar, I thought probably not, although she had no accent that I could discern.

I watched her preparations very carefully, unwilling to blink in case I missed the addition of something untoward in my sandwich. I wasn't certain, but I thought it likely that I was about to eat lunch with an ex–Soviet spy. Or, I suppose, she could be a current one, but surely she'd be unlikely to join a club for ex-spies if she were still a working agent. Unless that was a sophisticated double bluff, double cross.

She sliced the tomato into slices so thin I could almost see through them and arranged them on a small plate she took from a stack at the side of the sink. She put bread on two more plates, and added two slices of cheese on each slice of bread. "Mayonnaise or mustard?"

"Mustard, please."

"Pepper?"

"Just a little salt on the tomato."

She efficiently built two sandwiches, piling the shredded lettuce on top and, maybe it was just me, but slicing the tomatoes so neatly seemed redundant, since she divided all of the thin slices between the two sandwiches. She cut them in half diagonally and put each one onto its own plate, put everything else back in the fridge, and brought the plates over to the table. She went back for two sheets pulled from a roll of paper towels, and went back again and filled two glasses with ice and then with water from a jug in the fridge. I would have preferred individual, unopened bottles, but at least we were drinking from the same container.

"I have ice cream for dessert." She sat down and raised her scotch in a mock salute. "Alla vostra," she said, "and death to our enemies."

"Oh, um, right. Same here." I took a mouthful of water and picked up half of my sandwich. "Um—have you known my grandfather very long?"

"For more than forty years, my dear. Cambridge." She swallowed most of her drink.

It was having no obvious effect on her.

"Oh, er—"

"No. Not like that." She made an unladylike snort. "Your grandmother would have skinned me alive."

"You knew my grandmother."

"I did. And now your grandfather and I are friends with benefits, isn't that what you young people say?"

I blushed and she laughed. It was an uninhibited, joyful sound, which was oddly alarming coming on the heels of her coldness minutes before. I remembered Sergei having a similar on-off switch, Maybe it was a professional asset in certain lines of work.

"Are you Russian?"

"I was born in Ukraine, as a matter of fact, but yes, I lived in Russia for most of my childhood."

"Did you . . . are you . . . I mean, who did you—"

"Which service did I work for?" I nodded. "I think that's need-to-know, and you don't need to know." She wasn't kidding.

I munched my sandwich. I wanted to know why she'd been following me. And what else she knew about Katrina and Sergei. And I was practically alight with curiosity about her relationship with my grandfather.

I took another bite of my sandwich and chewed thoughtfully. "So you and my grandfather met up again when he moved here?"

"At a meeting of our former colleagues, yes."

"Where does the group—?"

"That's need-to-know, as well."

"Right." I looked uneasily at the radio, then around the kitchen, through the archway leading to the living room. "Um—"

"Sometimes here, and sometimes at his home on Telegraph Hill," she said.

"And, er—"

"About twice a week." Now she wasn't trying to hide her amusement, and I suddenly didn't want to know any more. Twice a week bettered my own record, in any case. I finished my sandwich in silence, and when she served up small bowls of vanilla ice cream, without asking me if I wanted any, I ate that, too.

She looked at me thoughtfully. "Your grandfather didn't kill our friend," she said suddenly. "We were not, in fact, together every night for the past three weeks, but that is for you alone to know."

I swallowed. "Do you think this terrible history of Sergei's past might explain his death?"

"I do not know," she said flatly. "I knew her, you know," she added in a different tone.

"Who?"

"Katrina Demchyshyn, the woman who was killed. I knew her cousin, the young Gavin, too. Or, at least, his father."

"Her name was Dermody."

Another shrug. "Perhaps she married; perhaps she just changed her name."

"Anthony said Gavin's father was a colleague. He meant of yours?"

"Yes, of mine. Dead now, of course, or I wouldn't have mentioned it. His son was a shy little thing."

"I think he still is."

She hesitated. "Yes. Is there any thought of him having killed Katrina? Family is often involved in sordid cases like this. They lived together in close quarters; often emotions are heightened."

"Close quarters" being relative, considering the size of Katrina's apartment, I thought. "They seemed friendly and he was . . . proud of her, I think. At the moment, all the attention is on my grandfather, who I know didn't kill her, and a young friend of mine. It's ridiculous to think they conspired to kill Katrina. I mean, why? And how, for that matter?"

"I agree that it is unlikely."

I wish she'd said it was impossible.

"It's odd that Sergei, and his wife, and Katrina, and this priest who hated him are all dead."

"Odd. Yes." Suddenly, as if she'd just made up her mind about something, she said, "You should consider the priest at St. Christopher's. He was in love with Katrina. If she spurned him . . ."

"Surely—"

She snorted. "You might consider the young St. Augustine's wayward prayer: 'God make me chaste—but not yet'!"

CHAPTER TWENTY-SEVEN

The man who answered when I rang the number I received in the form of a text later that afternoon also refused to speak on the phone. We met in Sutro Park in the Outer Richmond. Even though I was early, he arrived before me and was sitting on a bench, stroking the head of a big yellow dog, as he'd said he would be. The dog was an improvement on a red carnation or an Eton Ramblers tie, anyway. He stood and offered his hand when I approached—I was holding an empty Starbucks cup, as instructed—and the dog wandered off.

With a mild shock, I realized he was another one of the people who'd been following me. I recognized his coat, of all things. "Call me Jacob," he said, and I wondered if that was really his name. He was tall, dark haired and rosy-cheeked, wearing an overcoat and gloves, with a scarf neatly tucked around his neck. His faded blue/green eyes were almost hidden in pouches and folds, his face mapped with deep wrinkles. I sat next to him on the bench and wondered what on earth to say. After a couple of silent minutes, I decided the only way forward was to take the first step.

"Your colleagues seemed to think I should talk to you, but they didn't explain why."

He shrugged. "I am the president of our small club;

there's probably no other reason." We were on a small stone-and-grass viewing platform, facing a long, sloping lawn in one direction and some steep, rocky stairs leading to a lower pathway in the other. A harsh, wet, and salty wind was blowing rags of fog past us and gradually filling the park.

"Great little park, this," he said, peering over the low balustrade into the murk. He assured me that if the day were sunny, we could see a panoramic view of the wide sands of Ocean Beach. He pointed into the completely opaque curtain of fog. "You can see the windmill at the edge of Golden Gate Park, too. I don't know why more people don't come here."

"It's a puzzle." I hugged myself with both arms and wished I'd worn my new leather jacket. Pretending my hoodie was a fur-lined anorak wasn't helping.

He snapped his fingers to call his goofy dog, who'd wandered away and was already invisible. The dog galumphed back, with a squeaking animal about the size of a young rabbit between his jaws. Jacob pried it from between his teeth, to the dog's obvious annoyance, then efficiently twisted its neck and dropped the little corpse over the balustrade. "Gophers," he said with a shrug. "They're a scourge." The dog, tongue lolling, sat down and leaned up against his leg.

It took me a minute or two to refocus. "My specialty back in the day was teenagers," he was saying. "Of course it's been a while since I could make that believable." He chuckled and I tried to smile. "For years, most of the work has been electronic surveillance and the analysis of the data. Now the post-Soviet Russians are poisoning their own agents in their new homes in the West. It is so—so

1973," he said, with a small, wrinkly frown, from which I inferred that he wasn't joking.

"Was Sergei Wolf a member of your organization?"

"He occasionally attended meetings in"—he hesitated—"somewhere in South America. Our chapters have reciprocity. Your grandfather is a member of the London group, of course." He chuckled. "Some of our members find rubbing shoulders with an earl a new experience. But it's true what they say: everybody loves a lord."

"He's not actually—"

"But I owe your grandfather a great debt. We will put out feelers and see what we can find out. Is there anyone who you feel might be the guilty party?"

"I just know Grandfather didn't do it. They've also got a young friend of mine in custody—his name is Davie Rillera."

"And he didn't do it, either?"

"Definitely not," I said firmly. "I've met several of your members now, and they're all—mature. Do you have any younger members—I mean, people who would be capable of chasing someone through the city streets and shooting them?"

"The retirement age in our profession varies." He smirked, as if at a familiar, oft-told joke.

"So yes, then?"

He waggled his hand in a "maybe yes, maybe no" gesture.

"Very helpful," I said crossly. "How many members does this group have?"

"Eleven now. We have some rather exclusive membership criteria." He rearranged his rubbery face into another clown-like grin.

"How does someone join?"

"By personal invitation from another member, who provides us with the details of his or her career. Then we all meet with the candidate individually, and then we vote."

Thinking of Valentina, I asked, "How many women members do you have?"

"Two lady members, at the moment."

I had a feeling their "lady" members were, as one of my noir movie characters might put it, no ladies.

He went on. "We lost one of our ladies a few months ago. Of course she was in her nineties, so not entirely unexpected. She was our chapter's last World War II agent. Brave girl. Parachuted behind enemy lines and slit the throats of some highly placed SS officers." He stroked his dog's head, and I thought of the casual dispatching of the dead gopher and wondered if Jacob had slit some throats, too. Or perhaps cut off some fingers.

"Do you know anything about Sergei's personal life?"

"He has a son who lives in Northern California, I believe. Mendocino, perhaps."

"And there was a mistress?"

He shrugged and didn't answer me.

"Tell me about this village where he's supposed to have killed everyone."

"Ah, you've been speaking to V." He stroked his dog's head again. "Her losses prevent her from seeing that the deaths she still mourns were caused by nothing more or less than a tragic accident. The nineties were a terrible time in that part of the world. The entire decade was filled with war, revolution, and vicious ethnic cleansing." He shook his head. "Such a bloodless phrase to describe the bloodiest of war crimes. Even today, we feel the repercussions. There is a straight line from the NATO bombing of Yugoslavia in '99 to Russia's annexation of Crimea in 2014. The new Cold War, they're calling it, with Russia and America mistrustful and antagonistic." He sighed, and I tried to look as if I knew what he was talking about.

"And the village?"

"Sergei learned that a rural area near the Polish border with Ukraine was camouflaging a Serb training camp— intelligence we realized later was faulty and perhaps even deliberately misleading. Sergei called an airstrike against an area that turned out to include a small hospital, a school, and some homes. I don't know who provided the information about the Serbian camp, but it was a catastrophic miscalculation. It broke Sergei. I have always felt his priestly vocation was some kind of expiation of his guilt."

He looked at me thoughtfully. "Have you ever considered what a former intelligence agent does in retirement?"

I shook my head; it wasn't an issue I realized had any bearing on my life until recently.

"With a few exceptions, we don't have families, and the only people who understand what our life has been like are others like ourselves. We have skills we can no longer practice, and in any event can't disclose, but we like to keep them honed."

I thought of all the anxiety I'd suffered, and tamped down a rush of anger. "Are you saying—are you saying you all followed me for the *practice*?"

"As I said, I owe your grandfather a great debt." He smiled again and showed some yellow teeth. All things considered, I preferred his frowns to his smiles. And I was almost sure he was lying.

CHAPTER TWENTY-EIGHT

Before Grandfather and Davie got even one step closer to disaster, I needed to find someone who benefited from Katrina's death. Even more difficult, the killer needed to be someone who benefited from the deaths of both Katrina and Sergei. Until I'd learned they were so closely connected, it had seemed unlikely that a single person would have motive to want such different people dead. Now it seemed a little more plausible that revenge was involved somehow. If Sergei's son—Pavel—were the killer, the motive would have to be revenge because St. Olga's got Katrina's money, and Sergei was a presumably penniless priest. I needed to find out more about the mysterious Pavel, but if the spies weren't going to help me—and it seemed pretty obvious they weren't going to—I had no idea how to go about it. I walked down to The Coffee to talk things through with Nat and Gavin, hoping they'd think of something that hadn't occurred to me.

Gavin made us hot drinks, and the three of us sat at a table, since the shop was empty. Finding a second body on our block had cut down on foot traffic considerably; Aromas didn't have any customers, either.

I pressed a notebook open on the table, prepared to take notes if we came up with something. I pulled out the envelope I'd used to write down my list of potential suspects. It looked very meager. Gavin sat up straight and folded his hands on the table, while Nat lay on the couch stuffing a couple of pillows behind his head and wriggling himself deeper into the couch cushions. Gavin bit back a smile.

"What?" Nat said to him. "I might as well get comfortable. Knowing Theo, this could take a while."

"Persistent, huh?" Gavin asked.

"You have no idea. Right." He stopped wriggling. "I'm all set like Jell-O; what're we talkin' about?"

"I'm trying to think of who might have wanted to kill both Katrina and Father Wolf," I said.

"Okay. Right," Gavin said, nodding. "Um—why? I mean, aren't the police working on it?"

"My grandfather is under suspicion, but he didn't do it, so I need to come up with a more plausible alternative so the police stop suspecting him."

"Your grandfather? Why would he kill Katrina? Did he even know her? Do the police think your grandfather killed Katrina because she was suing you?" He looked stricken. "God, I'm really sorry."

"Well, no, he's under suspicion for killing the priest they found in the vacant house down the block, but I was thinking the two deaths are related. Apparently, Katrina and Sergei knew each other very well in the past. *Very* well," I repeated. "And Sergei has a son who lives somewhere in Northern California."

Nat sat up. "Wait—are we sayin' he's Katrina and Sergei's son?"

"I don't know. It's possible. But all I have is a first name, Pavel, and a town, Willits. Haruto can't find anyone with that first name in Willits. He might have Americanized it by now, anyway." After Haruto had more-or-less thrown in the towel, I had told Lichlyter what little I knew, but since I couldn't tell her that my source of information was a former Soviet spy, I wasn't all that hopeful she'd find him, either.

Nat lay down again. "Katrina's lived here about fifteen years," he said slowly. "And she was—what? About fifty?"

"Fifty-two," Gavin said.

"So she moved here when she was thirty-seven, and there's been no husband or child since she moved here." He looked over at Gavin. "You've only known her for—what?— ten years?" Gavin nodded. "So if this Pavel kid is hers, and we assume she had him between the age of eighteen and thirty-seven, he could be any age between fifteen and thirty-four. Wow, that's a big range."

"I've been thinking of him as an adult," I said slowly. "I didn't think that he might still be a teenager."

"Or he could be a man in his twenties or thirties," Nat added.

"If he's on the younger end of that range, it means Katrina didn't raise him. He must have been fostered, or adopted." I tapped my pen on the table. "Until someone finds Pavel, we can't know anything for sure. Oh my God!"

Nat sat up and looked around, "What's wrong?"

I shook my head at him. I had just remembered that Valentina said Gavin's father had been a spy. And, as I knew only too well, spies sometimes ran in families. Gavin could be an intelligence agent. After all, we hardly knew him. I looked at him a little wildly.

"What?" he said, looking alarmed. I shook my head at him, too, and stared down at the table. And if Sergei Wolf was Pavel's father, because Sergei was an ex-spy, Pavel could be an intelligence agent, too, which meant we weren't likely to find him living quietly in Willits, or anywhere else, for that matter.

"Theo—what the hell?" Nat said.

"I can't tell you," I said. "Not my secret. But I've just remembered something else that gives me a whole new bunch of people who might hate Sergei." How could I have forgotten the village he had wiped off the map? This was getting ridiculous—Sergei's murder could have had a cast of dozens, a modern version of *Murder on the Orient Express*. But, again, how many of them would have hated Katrina, too?

"I need to narrow things down. St. Olga's keeps popping up; could the motive have something to do with the orphanage?" I turned to Gavin. "You probably know more about it than anyone."

He considered carefully before he answered. "There's not a lot of money. Katrina was generous, but the sisters made a point of keeping expenses as low as they could."

"But perhaps Katrina's will made a difference to the amount of money involved?"

"It will be a large amount when everything is settled," he agreed. "She had some investments, there were retirement accounts, and of course the building in Fabian Gardens. I mean, it adds up to maybe four million dollars or so?"

Nat whistled. "A nice little endowment. I wonder how come she didn't leave anything to this Pavel, if he was her kid?"

"I don't know he was hers," I said. "To be fair, I was told he was Sergei Wolf's son, and I drew a line from Sergei to Katrina because I knew they'd been involved back in the day."

Nat shook his head faintly. "Wait—this Pavel was a priest's kid?"

"From before he was a priest," I said. I hoped.

He shook his head. "So we don't know if he even had anything to do with Katrina?"

"I guess that's right," I said. "I just started to think of him as hers." I tossed down my pen. "I don't know much of anything for sure."

We sat in glum silence for a couple of minutes, sipping our hot drinks. "Gavin, did you know she was leaving everything to the orphanage?" Nat asked.

He smiled faintly. "I think she told me so I wouldn't have my feelings hurt, and she explained that I'd get an executor's fee. We were only very distant cousins. Our great-grandparents were brothers, I think. The link wasn't strong, but after my parents died, she and I gravitated toward each other a little, dinner or drinks after work a few times a year, stuff like that. And it was a godsend when she let me stay with her. She turned into a heavy-handed older sister," he said, rolling his eyes. "Always giving me career advice and telling me to set up a retirement account. I had to remind her I was a freelance journalist, not a lawyer with a 401(k). And then she asked me to help her organize the St. Olga's project. She wanted to pay me, but she was letting me live in that beautiful apartment of hers, basically for free, so I wouldn't accept anything. I was proud to take the lead on it for her, y'know?"

I nodded. "Why did you go over, this last time? Was there anything wrong?"

He shook his head. "It was a pretty typical trip. I know a bit of bookkeeping, so I looked through their accounts, checked into their expenses, and had a short meeting with the diocesan liaison. The house they lived in wasn't new, and they'd had to do some roof repairs, which had increased their spending a little for the previous quarter, but I told Katrina when I got back that everything checked out; the kids seemed happy and the place was in good repair." He rubbed at his temples. "God, I can't believe that was just before she was killed. It seems like months ago already."

"And there was nothing about the funding of the place that seemed, I don't know, odd in any way?"

He looked puzzled. "Like what?"

"I honestly don't know. It's just that I know this group of people, some of them from over there, who seem to have an interest in the place, and I can't figure out why."

Nat pricked up his ears. "Who are they? More priests?"

"Far from it! But it's not my—"

"Not your secret. Okay, I get it." He settled down with a disgruntled huff.

In an obvious effort to change the mood, Gavin chuckled. "I told her if there's anything I'd like to change, it's that the nuns have been pretty slow to adopt modern dress," he said. "Those long, black habits with wimples and veils down to their waists—pretty old school, but it's not my call."

"Wimples?"

"It's the white headdress thing they wear under their veils to cover their hair and neck."

He showed us one of the photos again, and Nat grimaced. "Yeah, that takes me back," he said. "Modern dress might make the kids more comfortable, I guess, but their order decides on the uniform."

"Huh. I don't know much about Catholic nuns," I said.

"Join the club. The trouble is," Gavin said after a minute

or two, "only St. Olga's benefits financially from Katerina's death, and it's kind of ridiculous to think a priest or a nun would come all the way from Ukraine to kill her. Unless there's some priest we don't know about."

"The body they found this week was a priest," I said slowly. "And he had connections to Ukraine."

He opened his mouth, then closed it again and seemed to be thinking. "Do you think he might have killed Katrina?"

"I suppose he could have," I said doubtfully. "But he didn't look like an assassin. He was sort of pudgy and his vision was poor."

"You knew him?" Gavin looked surprised.

"Not really. He came into Aromas looking for my grandfather."

Nat looked puzzled. "Why? Did they know each other?"

"I forgot to mention it. It's a long story," I sighed. "They knew each other years ago."

Gavin opened his mouth and then closed it again.

"What?"

"Nothing." He looked abashed.

"Out with it," Nat told him, resignedly. "I'm probably thinkin' the same thing."

"What's that?" I said.

He and Gavin exchanged a look, and Nat sat up. "Look, if your grandfather and this priest knew each other, who's to say they didn't have some old grudge goin', and your grandfather *did* kill him?"

"Nat! Of course he didn't. Sergei came looking for grandfather to get his help!"

"I'm not even gonna ask. Does Inspector Lichlyter know that?"

"I don't know," I said uncomfortably.

"Do they know any more about the—you know, the fingers?" Gavin nodded toward the empty space the microwave had briefly occupied.

"Could we not be talkin' about fingers?" Nat closed his eyes.

"They belonged to the priest, apparently," I said, ignoring him.

"But if he killed Katrina, then who killed him? And why cut off his fingers?" Gavin was looking as if he'd like to introduce another topic of conversation, too.

"I think the killer was trying to get the detectives to suspect South American gangs."

"Is that possible?"

"I'm beginning to think almost anything is possible," I said with a sigh.

Gavin looked at my list. "What about the legal cases Katrina was involved in? Maybe someone she'd beaten in a lawsuit or something? I don't know much about Katrina's day-to-day operations, but you don't get to be that successful without making enemies."

I wasn't ready to move on. "Was there ever any thought of the orphanage dealing in, I don't know, black market adoptions, or—"

He shook his head. "It isn't like one of the big state homes, with levels of administration and places where things could fall through the cracks or happen with nobody noticing. It's more like a group home. There are about a dozen children living there, and the population doesn't vary much; I'd have noticed if there was a sudden influx of new kids, or several of them were suddenly adopted or something. Did you know her law offices were broken into?" I nodded. "That makes it seem like it had something to do with one of her cases. I mean, why else would someone break in?"

Obviously, I didn't want to talk about that. "You said St. Olga's wasn't under the diocese but there was some kind of liaison?"

He nodded. "I sent quarterly reports to the Kiev diocesan office, although that was mostly just a courtesy because it wasn't really under their jurisdiction. The liaison was usually a priest in the Archbishop's office."

"It wasn't always the same one?"

He shrugged. "I guess they have turnover, like everywhere else." He leaned forward. "There *has* to be some other reason for Katrina to be killed. What about the woman who bought the buildings here for development? Katrina told me she was furious when the sale fell through. Then when Katrina made her an offer less than Noble's—well, I'd be mad, too. And don't forget—the dead guy was found in the buildings she owns."

That point hadn't escaped me, and she'd already made the list. So far I had 1. Pavel 2. St. Olga's 3. South American drug smugglers. I added: 4. Lawsuit Opponent. 5. Angela Lacerda. Mentally, I added: 6. Survivors and loved ones of bombed Ukrainian village, including, 7. Valentina Kompanichenko.

"Do you think the police are looking into her?" Gavin asked, and it took me a second to remember we hadn't been talking about Valentina.

"I hope so. I'm just afraid they feel they have the killer already in custody."

After we adjourned, I thought Gavin might be right about Angela Lacerda, and I hadn't paid her much attention beyond feeling sorry for her. She was fairly young, and as far as I knew, she was on her own in the apartment. I rang her doorbell, knowing I risked having the door slammed in my face, but she hesitated only for a few seconds before inviting me inside. She was still wearing the lemon yellow socks, but this time she had no shoes on.

"I'm sorry about before," she said. "It was a shock, and I lashed out at you for no reason. I felt as if things couldn't get any worse, but I guess I was wrong." She waved me into a chair. "I mean, who kills a priest? It's bad karma."

I untangled the religious implications of that. "You didn't know him, then?"

"No, and believe me, the police have been talking to everyone I ever met in my life to try and make a connection, but there's nothing to find. I mean, he wasn't even from around here. He came a long way just to screw up my life even more."

I looked around at her single girl's apartment, with its refurbished furniture and the few "nice" pieces she probably planned to take with her to her marriage. "Will you be staying on here, now?"

Her expression hardened. "It's a decent apartment, and I like the neighborhood well enough. I don't have to put up with Katrina Dermody as a neighbor, anyway. Can you believe it? One of the reasons I felt confident about the deal was because I thought a woman wouldn't screw another woman. Live and learn, I guess."

She waved me into a comfortable-looking chair. "It must have been a terrible shock when Noble withdrew from the project."

"I was furious—you knew she offered me about two-thirds of what Noble had agreed to pay before he reneged? I threw her out and told her I'd tell him." She dashed away a furious tear from her cheek with the flat of her hand. "I did tell Noble the day before she was killed. He was livid, and I heard she was fired. Serves her right," she added spitefully. "Anyway, even with everything that's happened, I've persuaded Jason—our engagement is unofficially back on—that the buildings are a good investment and that we can make a go of things, and his family is coming around. I did plenty of groveling. and his Mama is even feeling sorry for me, a young woman trying to make her way in the world, taken advantage of by the mean old property developer." Then she smiled. "I have really good survival instincts."

"Look, this is none of my business, but Katrina kept a record."

She went completely still. "What kind of a record?"

"A sort of dossier of people she wanted to—influence, I guess."

"You mean blackmail. People she wanted to blackmail."

"I thought it might be. Anyway," I said awkwardly, "you were included in it, because of what happened when you were in high school, and I just wondered if—"

"How much?"

"What?"

"Don't be shy; how much?"

"I don't understand."

"Sure you do," she said. "Unless you don't want money, is that it? Is there something else you want? Katrina was prepared to tell Jason's parents about my abortion, and I offered her money to keep it quiet. But it wasn't just money she wanted. She wanted me to accept her bid for the buildings. She said it would be impossible to accuse her of blackmail when I'd been paid three million dollars. I'd have been left with a two million dollar debt, and Jason's family would never have agreed to us getting married with that hanging over me."

Her expression hardened, the drab, rather colorless girl disappeared, and for the first time she looked like a formidable opponent. Katrina might very well have seen only the young woman with a lack of influence or connections, and underestimated her. "They're Catholic—I mean, *really* Catholic, like supporting the St. Francis of Assisi memorial nearly single-handed Catholic. They would never understand the desperation I felt when I was sixteen, and they control Jason's trust fund.

"I was raised in the projects" she said, her tone flat. "Marrying Jason, marrying into that family, is a dream come true. Nothing is getting in the way of that. Nothing. So I wouldn't get any ideas."

I gulped.

Angela smiled. "Lucky for me, Katrina died."

CHAPTER TWENTY-NINE

I was sweeping up the drift of paper from Aromas' entrance on Sunday morning for no reason, really, because we weren't open on Sundays, but I needed something to do besides think about Angela's rather eerie take on Katrina's murder, and what Grandfather and Davie were suffering in police custody. The little pile of flotsam reminded me of the neat pile of paper rubbish in the building where Sergei's body was found. The McDonald's wrappers were probably construction-worker lunches, and the coffee cups ditto, but I remembered something that didn't quite fit with the fast food and candy bar wrappers. It was crumpled, but small— I'd bent to look at it closely because of the glint of gold. It was a napkin from the Venus de Milo. I suppose one of the construction workers could have dropped it, but I'd swept up a Venus de Milo coaster at Aromas the day Sergei visited me. It wasn't much, but it might be a place to start reconstructing his movements in the days before he was killed, even if a priest walking into a strip club sounded like the beginning of a joke.

I had to do something. I took a cab to the landmark copper-clad flatiron building containing the Coppola Winery storefront in Little Italy. I dodged traffic on Green

Street heading toward the tall sign for San Francisco's most famous strip club, not far from its most famous bookstore, where the Beats hung out. The streets were full of tourists and the occasional homeless person shuffling along wrapped in a blanket or, in one case, pushing a shopping cart containing a small dog. On the cusp of Little Italy, Chinatown, and the Financial District, the air smelled like dim sum, spaghetti sauce, and diesel from the passing traffic. In other words, I was inhaling a fairly typical San Francisco mash-up.

I'd seen the inside of plenty of nightclubs, dance clubs, and what Nat called "joints." Most of them looked tawdry in daylight, like a theater between performances, so the Venus de Milo was a surprise. When I walked in there at two o'clock on Sunday, I was expecting a dusty, backstage smell and trompe l'oeil artificiality. Instead, I got an eyeful of old-fashioned glamour. The chrome poles at the front of the raised stage were gleaming, the floor glittered with some sort of imbedded sparkles as I walked across it, and the deep purple stage curtains looked new. The small tables were lit with individual lamps with fringed shades and pale pink bulbs. It looked oddly wholesome. The room was empty, so I went through an archway leading to a smaller room, and a smaller stage, where five musicians were hammering out "Satisfaction." A bank of wide open, ten-foot-high windows were keeping the air fresh, and opposite the stage, at the back of the bar, eye-popping carved mahogany panels of flowers, trees, and other innocent subjects rose to ceiling height. I paused to admire the carving as the band segued into "Ruby Tuesday."

"Like it?" The gravelly voice came out of thin air. When I turned, a man stepped down from a high table in a dark corner and waved a hand at the carvings. He was tall and big, not young, but not old enough for his full head of silver hair. He was all in black—jeans, shirt, belt, and motorcycle boots. A small, silver skull hung from a leather thong around his neck, and he was wearing a leather bracelet on one wrist and a Rolex on the other. "Rescued from the aught six fire."

"Half the buildings in the city seem to have that story."

"Came from a bawdy house up on Pacific, so that's different." He chuckled. "What can I do for you? Here to listen to the boys?" He tipped his head toward the musicians, who were intent on their instruments. The bass player looked up at me and winked. The band segued into "Waiting for a Lady" and I smiled. What can I say? My father was a Stones fan.

Mine host waved me to one of the stools at his table. "They play here for a couple of hours on Sunday afternoons; leave the windows open; pull in a few tourists. You don't look like a tourist."

"I don't?"

"Are you?"

"No."

"Well then. Like I said. Get you a drink?"

"Coke?"

He went around the bar and started fiddling with glasses. He slid the Coke over to me when he got back to the table. "Five bucks. You can leave it in the tip jar." He nodded at the coffee tin on a stool in front of the stage.

I leaned over to drop the bill in the jar. The bass player winked and smiled at me again. I sighed. A year ago I might have taken up the invitation in that smile; he had that thin grungy look, my favorite bad boy type not so long ago. I smiled back, minus the flirt, and he shrugged faintly. I turned back to my table companion.

I took a sip of my Coke, trying to decide if his hair was natural or if he'd had it colored. Nat would flirt with him and call him a silver fox. "I'm trying to fill in the blanks of a friend's visit here."

"Ask the friend."

"You'd think, but he's dead."

"My condolences," he said. "Not sure I can help. We get a lot of people through here."

"This one would be unusual. At least, I think so." Who knew what was unusual for a San Francisco strip club? "He was a priest."

He rubbed his chin. "That would make him stand out, all right. You mean a real priest or a guy in a costume? We get some cosplay folks. Barbarians, vicars and tarts, that kind of thing."

"I didn't know people did vicars and tarts over here. It's more of an English thing, isn't it?"

He shrugged. "Everything is international now and this is San Francisco. Any excuse to get into costume."

I couldn't argue with him there. On my way here I'd passed a pack of two dozen cross-dressing cyclists, led by someone with a fine handlebar moustache, wearing a pink sun dress. "Right. Well this was a real priest. Heavy accent, gold front tooth."

"Yeah, you don't see too many gold teeth nowadays. Was this an older guy?"

"Sixties, I'd guess. Looked older, though, so you might think he was early seventies. He had a—difficult life. That ages people, right?"

He sighed heavily. "Honey, you have no idea. Yeah, I saw

your friend. He was here one night a bit more than a week ago. Tuesday, maybe? He showed up in full dress uniform— you know, black suit, white collar, cross and chain. He caused a pause in the action, y'know? He marched in and picked a fight with a guy minding his own business at a back table. No idea what they were fighting about—you're right about that accent, honey—but whatever it was, it had the old boy exercised. Two of the bouncers escorted him outside. They're good boys," he added, as if to reassure me. "They didn't muscle him, just walked him out."

"Who was the other fellow—er, guy?"

"Don't know his name."

"Does he use a credit card? Maybe you could check?"

"This is a titty bar—a high class one, but still. He's gonna pay cash." He sighed when I didn't say anything. "Tell me why you wanna know. You're cute, and that accent works for you, honey, but I don't wanna be helping some woman get her jerk of a hubby into court."

"The priest was a good friend of my grandfather's. He's—well, he's really upset about his friend dying and wants to trace where he spent his last few days. He did a few things that were out of character, and his family lives in—Europe—so they can't find out much, and my grandfather feels an obligation to his old friend's family."

"Your grandfather, eh? Well, that's a new one. Was the old guy really a priest?"

"He was, yes," I said, and got a skeptical look.

He heaved himself off his stool. "Like I said, we deal in cash, mostly, but I'll see if any of the girls remember anything. They won't be in 'til later. You can come back or you can call."

"And maybe the doorman and bouncers?"

He sighed. "Yeah, okay."

"Do you have security cameras?"

He gave me a sardonic look and snorted. "Security cameras. My customers would freak. I wouldn't *have* any customers."

"I'll come back. What time do you think would be best?"

"Come at eight. I'll find out who was on for the first of that week."

I felt his eyes on me as I left.

Back at The Coffee, Nat was horrified. "The Venus! Why didn't you take me?"

"It was nice. Clean. No one there. I was fine. Strange fellow with a gray ponytail and sunglasses hanging out seemed to be in charge. He said he'd find out who argued with Father Segei. I'm going back tonight."

"Gray ponytail and—right, chickie. I'm comin' with." He held out a flat hand. "No arguments. What time?"

"He said about eight," I grumbled. "You know, it's not as if a strip club in the middle of the tourist trek is going to be dangerous. Did you know people go in costumes sometimes?"

"Furries?" Nat looked surprised.

"I don't know what furries are—"

"Lucky you."

"—but he mentioned cosplay. So Klingons, maybe?"

"*Qapla'!*" Nat said.

Nat wanted to take his gun and I asked him not to, so instead he took a sort of expanding baton thing in his Louis Vuitton messenger bag. We arrived in a cab just after eight thirty—Nat having made a last-minute wardrobe change after he decided to take the messenger bag—and I asked the man at the door for my friend from the afternoon.

There was a bit of hesitation, since I'd forgotten to get his name, but the ponytail and skull necklace description did the trick.

"Oh yeah, Zane told us to look out for you." He raised his arm and flicked a finger, and a young woman wearing heels, a glittery cami, and a micro-mini came tottering over to take charge of us.

"Zane?" I mouthed at Nat behind her back. He shrugged and gave me big eyes. She showed us to a booth against the back wall with a good view of a dancer, wearing not very much apart from Lucite shoes with six-inch platforms and a lot of glitter. She was fervently embracing the chrome poles at the edge of the stage in a variety of athletic positions. I'm not easily embarrassed, but it was still hard to know where to look. There weren't many people at the tables in the audience, except for one group of six or seven men in their thirties, who seemed determined to wring every ounce of entertainment out of the night. They were calling to the dancer and leaning over to tuck money into the strings of her thong. The music was almost painfully loud.

I looked at Nat a little helplessly and he grinned. "Too bad, the show's wasted on both of us," he shouted, and then he snorted and started to laugh so hard he bent over the table and his shoulders shook. I shoved him to get him to shut up, but his giggles were contagious and before long we were both convulsed. Every time one of us sobered even a little, we caught each other's eye and we started up again. He was banging his open hand on our table as Zane came over and snapped his fingers impatiently when neither of us noticed him. He turned away, and I hastily wriggled out of the booth to follow him. Nat grimaced at me behind his back as Zane led us up a flight of stairs into an office with a smoked glass window looking out over the club. He closed the door, which muffled the music instantly.

It turned out he was from Texas. He and Nat hit it off. They stared in each other's eyes in a way that straight men just don't, at least not if they want to keep their teeth, and after their handshake ended they kept their hands casually on the small conference table, fingers almost touching.

"How long have you been in the City, Zane?" Nat asked him.

"Since I was eighteen and figured out what my dick was for."

They grinned at each other, clearly equally pleased with the exchange.

I kept my peace for a few more minutes, but then I interrupted their conversation, which seemed to be mostly sly innuendo and double *entendres* filled in with the occasional hand gesture and sly allusions to the way things were done back home.

"So did you find out anything?" I asked Zane. Nat looked a little surprised, as if he'd forgotten I was there, and Zane blinked and looked over at me. I sighed. I guess it made a weird sort of sense for a gay man to be running a strip club. And Nat was single. But Zane was fifty if he was a day, which made the age difference considerable. And what the hell business was it of mine, anyway?

A waitress came in and put down paper coasters with the Venus de Milo in metallic gold, the same design I'd seen on the discarded napkin. "Get you something?"

Zane looked resigned and said to her, "Don't make me tell you again, Virginia."

"Sorry, boss." She regrouped, took a breath, and looked down at her hands, her lips moving like a child reading silently. She looked up at Nat with a dazzling smile. "Good evening. My name is Vanessa and I'll be at your service tonight. May I take your drinks order? I thought Vanessa was nice," she added to Zane in a confiding tone. "Better than Virginia, which is a shit name."

"Just keep to the same letter of the alphabet." She bit her lip and nodded. "Okay, honey, these people don't need drinks, they're here to ask you about the priest." He glanced at the view into the club downstairs and stood up. "I'll be back in a few minutes." He left us and Vanessa/Virginia looked at us both, wide-eyed. Her breasts were impossibly round, high, and immobile in her skimpy tank top. Nat smiled at her and she blinked and licked her lips. Good luck with that, kid, I thought.

"We're trying to find the man who got into an argument with the priest," I prompted, to get her attention. "Was it Tuesday, the week before last?"

She shook her head and flipped her hair back. "Oh, yeah; no, Wednesday. I remember because he left me a fifty-dollar tip. I bought these shoes the next day, which I know was Thursday because it was my night off." She lifted a leg, pointed a toe, and admired her shoe while I admired her ability to stand on one leg in four-inch stilettos.

"So, the customer," I prompted.

"Right. He comes in with a small group every now and then. Usually a weeknight. They pay cash, but that's not unusual. I thought maybe one of them got a thing for one of the dancers—but that's not unusual, either, a lot of the regulars have favorites. Wilma's real popular, and she was dancing that night. She dances as Wanda Love. That's her down there now."

Nat and I watched a few of the dancer's sinuous moves

in respectful silence. She was wearing a miniature thong, a gleaming coat of oil, and strategic patches of pink glitter almost covering her nipples. Both her bum cheeks were glittered, too, which we learned when she turned to swing them out over the edge of the stage. I think nude dancing is legal in San Francisco, but since this club was in an area mostly frequented by tourists, perhaps the thong was a sop to their finer feelings.

Vanessa was picking at her teeth with a highly decorated fingernail by the time Nat and I were able to tear our eyes away from Wanda Love. "Can you tell us anything about your customer? What does he look like? Do you know his name?"

"Not really. I mean, we're not supposed to notice anything, if you know what I mean. He's no kid, but well preserved. Sixty, maybe a bit older? Gray hair. Pretty blue eyes. English or Australian accent, maybe? He never told me his name and, like I said, he pays cash. He tips well, the girls like him, he never makes trouble. One of his friends got hammered this one time and told me they were secret agents." Ignoring my start of surprise, she rolled her eyes. "Anyhoo, the customers sometimes say things like that— they're astronauts or they're TV stars. Like we care, but we act all impressed and stuff." She sniffed. "A lotta the guys who come in here just wear casual, jeans or shorts even, but this customer always wears a sports coat—old school but sharp, y'know?" She shook her head at the enormity of the sartorial gaffe, while I told myself there were probably hundreds, maybe thousands, of gray-haired, older men with blue eyes and English accents within a mile of the club. And then gave up trying to imagine Grandfather sitting in a strip club even once, let alone more often.

By the end of the evening I had a splitting headache, and I'd decided all the (male) bartenders and bouncers were either gay or inhumanly blasé, because none of them spared a glance for the dancers. I was undecided whether the entertainment represented female empowerment or male exploitation, but either way, I found them really hard to ignore. We were waiting to talk to the bouncers. For his part, Nat kept turning his head to look at Zane, who sat at the bar facing the room with his legs spread wide, leaning back with both elbows resting on the bar.

The bouncers, the "good boys," were very fierce looking, with their tattoos and shaved heads, but rather sweet. They were both wearing dress slacks and lightweight windbreakers with the Venus de Milo name and logo. They finished each other's sentences and smiled agreeably every time I used their names.

They remembered the priest. "He was kind of whisper yelling at first," Roger said. "Then he got worked up and started yelling for reals, but like he didn't do it on the regular, y'know?"

His colleague, Stitch, nodded agreeably. "We got over there fast because the guy he was yelling at was a good customer, y'know. They even started to get into it a little bit—the priest made a move on him, and our customer grabbed back, broke a chain and cross from around the priest's neck, and pushed him away. We use conflict resolution techniques, took a class and everything," he said proudly, "so we got the Father to come with us and we took him outside. That took care of things, and the guy at the table left us fifty bucks each at the end of the night. Classy guy."

"Do you think they knew each other?"

"Yeah, they did. The Father's cross was on the floor under the table, and our customer picked it up and said he'd get it back to him."

"Roger. Stitch. Did you hear what the . . . er . . . Father was so angry about?"

"He was kind of hard to understand," Roger said apologetically. "But it was maybe about some girl, I think. Something like that. I mean, he had this weird accent. We get good at accents," he confided. "I mean we hafta, y'know? It wasn't Asian—they all sound different, but they sound kinda musical, except flat, and it wasn't Hindi or Tagalog, because they're real distinctive too." He looked at Stitch, who nodded, and took up the litany, frowning slightly in concentration. "It wasn't French or Italian or nothing like that. Mighta been Russian." He looked at Roger.

"Yeah," Roger said, "it coulda been Russian or one of those languages. We getta lotta Russians." He frowned. "I dunno, though; doesn't seem like it was Russian. I'm not sure I'd know if it was Turkish. We don't get many customers from Turkey or, y'know, the Middle East," he added. "They're mostly Muslim, and those guys don't drink. They like a titty show, though." He and Stitch shared a glance and a snigger.

Stitch took up the tale before I could stop him or steer the conversation in a more helpful direction. "But they mostly buy sodas. Our customer was drinking top shelf scotch. Twenty-five bucks a pop. Too expensive to get hammered; we keep an eye on the drinkers," he added, "y'know, in case of trouble."

"When you took the Father outside, what did he do?"

Stitch looked at Roger, who thought about it. "He just stood there for a coupla minutes, then he apologized, I think, and left. He crossed over Green, and we thought maybe he was headed to Peter and Paul's, it's just a block over that way, but he went into the pizza place across the street."

"Musta been hungry," Roger said.

CHAPTER THIRTY

A large meat lover's," Nat said at the counter as he sent me to commandeer a booth. The restaurant smelled deliciously of basil and tomato sauce and fresh baked bread. It was a busy place, with people picking up pizzas to go and cheerful groups taking up the tables and booths.

While I waited in my booth, and wondered with foreboding if a meat lover's was as bad as it sounded, a waitress took an order for a pitcher of beer.

Nat joined me. "Did you get beer?"

"Should be here in a minute. What's a meat lover's?"

"Cheese pizza with about four pounds of ground beef, salami, pepperoni, ham, chicken, and bacon."

"Mmmm."

He smiled at me. God, he was gorgeous. "C'mon, English; they have pizzas where you come from."

"With ham and sweet corn or artichoke and fresh tomato, not what sounds like half an abattoir."

"Next you'll be tellin' me McDonald's sells veggie burgers over there."

"Well—"

He shook his head. "No. Just, no. Besides, it's protein and I'm damn near hollow." He settled his Louis Vuitton messenger bag on the bench next to him and tugged at one shoulder of his lavender cashmere pullover because, apparently, it was microns out of true. I knew better than to interrupt. He finished rearranging himself and looked up. "What did you think of ol' Zane?"

"Seemed helpful. Nice enough fellow—guy. Weird name."

"Pretty common in Texas. Not short for anything; it's just Zane. I kinda liked him."

I rolled my eyes. "I gathered. A bit old for you."

"Maybe. Could be he's a daddy. Am I up for being ordered around and wearing a collar?" He seemed to consider it for a few seconds and then he grinned. "Nah, prob'ly not."

"He's pretty, though."

"Hmmm."

I hesitated. "Did that description Vanessa gave us sound familiar at all?"

"What, the guy? Not so's I noticed. D'you think I'd make a good Zane? I could have a professional name at The Coffee, like the waitress and the dancer."

"It would have to have the same initial, like Nicky or Noel. He *was* kind of bossy, now I think about it."

"Maybe in a good way," Nat said, with a campy little flutter of his eyelashes.

"Don't daddies want twinks? You're not a twink."

"Well, thanks for that," he said, and then scowled. "Twinks don't have to be blonde."

"Oh, please. Too tall. Why are we even talking about this? Nathaniel is a good name. And Nat is good—short and easy to remember. Come to think of it—your name is Nathaniel."

"Don't remind me."

"So why are you Nat and not Nate or Nathan?"

He shrugged, looking uncomfortable.

"Nat?"

"I was small and hyperactive as a kid," he said reluctantly. "Apparently, I was a real pest."

"Um, okay, but—small and hyper—" I stopped and my eyes flew open wide. "Oh my God! Your name is Gnat? Like a mosquito?" He grimaced and then nodded. "But that's a much better name for the coffee shop," I said gleefully. "Gnat's Coffee."

He looked around quickly and hissed, "Don't you tell another livin' soul, Theo."

Our order arrived just then, and as we each helped ourselves to a heaping pile of meat masquerading as a pizza, I decided to be merciful. I could always pick up the name thing another time. Often.

"Speaking of names, did you notice we didn't get a name?" I swallowed hurriedly, inhaled, and waved my hand around in front of my face in the universal sign for o-my-god-that-cheese-just-scorched-everything-it-touched.

"I did notice, yeah. Think they don't know it?"

I shrugged. "Could be."

He looked thoughtful. "I'm sorta surprised we got as far as we did. I mean, how come they talked to us at all?"

Our waitress seemed happy enough to pause by our table for a chat; the rush seemed to be settling down, and Nat had folded a twenty-dollar bill under the cheese shaker.

"We get priests pretty often because we're so close to Peter and Paul," she said. "Sometimes they don't wear their collars; I think they're embarrassed because of all the, you know, scandals, but we can tell they're priests. We know our regulars, anyway. They're good guys."

"This one came in Wednesday night a week ago. He was wearing a suit," I went on, "all in black with his collar."

She pursed her lips.

"And he had a gold tooth at the front and a very strong accent," I said.

"Yeah, okay, him. He ordered a soda and sat at that table by the window, nursing it for, like, two hours watching the street."

"He was alone? Did he talk to anyone?"

She thought for a minute and eyed the twenty-dollar bill. "Just after he came in, a guy sat down at the table with him. They talked for a couple of minutes."

"Was the second guy older, wearing a sports coat, with gray hair?"

"No, nothing like that. He was younger, in jeans and a hoodie. A guy I think, could've been a girl, hard to say; I had a full section and I was busy."

"What happened?"

"Nothing much. The young guy left; the priest stayed here and nursed his soda for about another hour, then he suddenly got up and left. Didn't leave a tip, and that's one of my best tables. I like to seat big parties there so people passing by can see what they're eating; it's good advertising, right?" She wrinkled her nose. "A priest by himself drinking a soda wasn't doing us any favors."

"Did you notice which way he went when he left?"

"Yeah, 'cause I was sort of pissed. Though I guess priests don't have much money. So I watched him and saw him cross the road."

"Toward the Venus?"

"Yeah, pretty funny, right, like one of those jokes, so I kept watching in case he went in, but he didn't. He picked up a guy who was leaving."

"What did the guy look like?"

"I couldn't really tell; I mean, it was across the street and all, and kind of dark."

"Did they argue?"

"No—just the opposite. They talked for a minute, then went off together. Then I stopped watching because I had a customer."

So Sergei had met with two men on the night he was killed. And I had no idea who they were.

The meat lover's was about as bad as I'd feared, but I was starved, so I finished my slice anyway.

CHAPTER THIRTY-ONE

Nat dropped me off, waiting to make sure I'd opened my front door and closed it behind me before making a merry little toot on his horn and heading toward home.

Lucy would usually waddle out to greet me and see if I'd been out buying Milk-Bones, but when I opened the door and switched on the hall light, she didn't appear. I checked her basket in the living room, but she wasn't there, either. Again, unusual. I checked to be sure the door to the back stairs was closed, then walked down the hall to my bedroom and pushed open the door. The light from the hall fell on her. She was curled up on my bed, fast asleep, tight against a man-sized lump in the duvet.

"Ben," I whispered. The duvet shifted, and he hauled himself up against the headboard and blinked at me. "Hey," he said, and then grunted when I landed on him. Lucy growled and jumped off the bed, which was good, because there wasn't room for three of us, and I wasn't leaving.

"You never call; you never write," I said, kissing him between every word.

He answered the thought rather than the words in between kisses.

"I flew stand-by at the last minute, and grabbed a cab as soon as we hit the ground at SFO. I sent you a text. God, it's good to be home. I missed you." His arms closed around me, strong and warm. He felt wonderful.

"How long have you been home? Did you get something to eat? There's some stuff in the fridge; I could make you a sandwich, or do you want coffee or a beer or—" I burst into tears.

"Hey, hey, is it that bad?"

"You don't know!" I sobbed. "Katrina's dead, Nat found fingers in his microwave, Sabina and I found a dead priest, and Davie and Grandfather have been arrested."

He pulled the duvet around us both while I grizzled and sniffed. Then he said quietly, with a sort of wonder, "Have I been gone longer than six weeks?"

An hour later he had calmed me down a little, and I was pulling a meal together—a recipe Sabina and I worked on after I told her about my pathetically limited range of menu items—when Ben dropped his own devastating piece of news.

"There's a lot going on, but after tonight there might not be time to talk so—I've decided to take the bar exam here."

I stopped sawing the bread into lopsided doorstops— slicing bread isn't as easy as YouTube makes it look—and glanced over at him in surprise. Ben wasn't looking at me, he was rummaging in a drawer for spoons as if he hadn't just walked into a minefield of atom bomb proportions.

"You are?"

He frowned. "What do you think we're doing here, Theo? I'm not just passing time; I'm all in." He sounded exasperated.

He'd been looking dissatisfied before he left this time, and I'd started to think he meant to break up with me. I'd even been trying to get used to the idea and deciding

I wouldn't like it. I'd be the first to admit I was difficult to get close to, and I was sure he'd tired of the effort. I was equally sure admitting how much of our life together was built on lies would be the tipping point, and he would leave me anyway.

I swallowed. "No, of course, I know that. I just—I mean, you haven't mentioned the bar exam before, and you took me by surprise, that's all. Um—when is it? Do you have to study?" Was that the right thing to say? Did I sound pleased and interested instead of terrified? I served up two bowls of cassoulet, forgetting that I'd already eaten two pounds of meat on my pizza.

He looked slightly mollified, although he was watching me carefully. "It's held twice a year; the next time is March."

"March, right," I said and hoped I didn't sound as relieved as I felt. March was months away; surely by then I'd have thought of a way to tell him who I was. I put the hot bowls on the forest green place mats Nat gave me to match some cooking pots he'd made me buy, and put out the basket of inexpertly cut bread. Ben poured olive oil into a shallow terra-cotta dish I didn't remember ever seeing before. It didn't seem like the right time to ask him where it came from.

"California doesn't have reciprocity with other states, so I have to take the exam here. I'll need to get up to speed on California law—"

I stopped staring at the terra-cotta dish. "Is the bar exam here difficult?" I stirred the cassoulet in my bowl and took a cautious mouthful.

"Yeah, it is. Maybe the toughest in the country." He tasted the cassoulet, too. "This is good, Theo."

I grinned at him. "Don't sound so surprised. So, um, do you think you can pass it? I mean, I'm sure you'll pass it," I said more robustly. "You've already passed it, right?"

"I've already passed two."

"Two?"

"New York and DC, and in case you were wondering, New York's was tough." Ben could be very dry.

"It's all one country; why don't they all have the same exam?" I found America puzzling in so many ways, and the culture shocks kept on coming. We might have shared a language, more or less, but things like this exposed the traps set for the unwary person trying to fit in.

"Maybe it has something to do with the piecemeal way we became a country."

"How do you mean?"

"It took, what—nearly two hundred years for us to get to fifty states?"

I hoped that was a rhetorical question, because I had no idea. English schools spend about half an hour on the American Revolution and no time at all on the American Civil War. I'd spent a lot of time memorizing the names and reigns of kings and queens. We have two thousand years of our own history to get through, and if there's any time left over to spend on foreign wars, we opt for those we fought against the French. I assume that's because they'd been entangled in our own history since the days of Alfred the Great and because, in spite of the grudging respect accorded Napoleon, we felt better about ourselves when we beat him.

He went on. "A lot of states joined up after they already had established legal systems." He looked thoughtfully at the bread before taking a chunk. "Louisiana's is based on Spanish and French law instead of English common law."

I didn't know what Louisiana had to do with anything, but there was apparently a link with France I'd missed somehow. I was already lost, but I nodded as if I knew what that meant. Being a university dropout had its downsides when it came to conversations about cultural mores, and when the culture was transatlantic, it was even harder to keep up.

After we cleared away our dinner things, I took Lucy downstairs for her late-night outing and followed her around as usual, while Ben built a fire upstairs. It was late, but he said he wasn't tired, and I was too wired to sleep. When I came back upstairs, he had the file from Katrina's office in front of him on the coffee table. My eyes went straight to it as I walked into the room.

He leaned toward me over the back of the couch. "Found it," he said, "under the pillows."

"Oh God—did you read it?"

"I glanced at it. Why do you have a dossier on our neighbors that looks like part of a law firm's filing system?"

I stared at him, horrified and embarrassed. Why, oh why, hadn't I burned the damn file, or handed it over to Nat, or not taken the blasted thing in the first place?

"I stole it from Katrina's office, but you can't ask me why." I was taking too many shallow breaths and talking too fast. I went over to sit on the coffee table before my legs gave out and snatched up the file.

Ben was silent for what felt like two hours. "Okay," he said slowly. "Can I ask what you're planning to do with it?"

"I haven't decided."

"Am I allowed to ask if you've read it?"

I shook my head so fast it made me dizzy. "No. I mean, yes, I've read it, but I felt guilty invading people's privacy."

He started to say something else, then closed his mouth and made a sort of huffing noise. He started to stand but then he bent forward, his shoulders shaking, and I realized he was trying not to laugh and losing the battle.

"It's not funny!" I hissed at him, and he looked up at me, straightening his face and clearing his throat.

"No, I can see that," he said and sat back on the couch. "So you have ethical concerns about privacy, but not about stealing. Good to know."

I blushed. "Katrina was gathering information about people as if—I don't know, as if she planned to blackmail them or something."

"And you knew about the file and so—what?—after she was killed you decided to steal it to save everyone some embarrassment?"

"No, I didn't know—" I faltered.

"So you didn't know about the file, but you broke into Katrina's office—I assume you broke in, yes?"

I nodded miserably.

"And you saw the file and decided to take it. Okay."

"Okay?"

"Well, not okay, really. You've just admitted to a crime. Give me a dollar."

"What? I—"

He put his hand out, palm up, and wiggled his fingers in a "gimme" motion. I dug into my jeans and pulled out a few dollar bills and some change. I picked out a dollar bill and gave it to him, and he folded it carefully and put it in his pocket. "Now I'm your attorney and our communications are privileged, and I don't have to turn you in to the cops. We'll ignore for the moment that I'm not licensed to practice in California. I knew taking the bar exam here was a good idea."

"Are you making fun of me?"

"No. Well, yeah, but only a little. Now, since our communications are privileged, you can tell me why you broke into Katrina's office in the first place."

Neatly trapped, I nevertheless shook my head. "I can't."

He was silent for a minute, then nodded, "Fair enough. So what do you want to do with this file?"

I looked over at the fire. "I suppose I should burn it. Except—"

"Except since you went to the trouble of stealing it in the first place it seems like a waste, and suppose there's something in there that sheds light on how Katrina was killed."

"Something like that."

"Privilege includes written communications."

"Other people's written communications?"

"It's a gray area. Do you want me to look it over? We can share a jail cell." I shook my head. "So what do you want to do with it?"

"I think it should go into the fire. I feel guilty knowing about these things."

"You're sure?"

I nodded ruefully and crumpled up the papers and fed them into the flames, thus ending my short, inglorious career as a cat burglar. As I watched them burn, I realized I hadn't told Ben about the intruder who'd shot at me, and I groaned.

"What?"

I pressed my hands against my forehead and into my

hair, holding it flat against my head. "All right, look," I said. "There was more to the story."

"Imagine my surprise," Ben said.

"When I was in Katrina's office, someone else broke in, and when they saw me they chased me and shot at me."

"They shot at you. With a gun."

He looked grim, so I knew not to make a joke. Instead, I nodded. "It was a man, but I was too busy running away to get a look at his face."

"Could he tell who you were? Did you have your hair covered?" He gave my red hair a flickering glance.

"I had on a green wig and a baseball cap."

"Don't—" He hesitated and then went on, "Please don't do anything else that puts you in the path of a homicidal maniac."

"Do you really think he's a maniac?"

"And of course that's your takeaway. Unless you think we have more than one killer in the neighborhood, someone has killed twice for reasons we can't fathom and who has a habit of chopping pieces off his victims."

"When you put it that way—"

"There's another way to put it?"

"No. You're right. Of course you're right. No more breaking and entering. Promise."

"That promise has an odd specificity. How about promising not to get involved any deeper in trying to find out who the neighborhood killer is?"

I shook my head. "I can't not try to help Grandfather and Davie."

"No," he said unhappily, "I can see that."

Neither of us was tired, and for the next hour, Ben worked on his laptop while I put together an order for Aromas and caught up on e-mails, but truthfully my attention was half-hearted at best. Mostly I worried about the bar exam and the level of commitment it implied on Ben's part, and whether I wanted him to move to California. We were never short of conversation, but maybe we weren't really communicating, because I'd had no idea he was considering it. How oblivious was I, anyway? I honestly hadn't seen it coming.

Ben flew out here from Washington, DC, twice a month. He stayed for several days, made at least one brief trip to LA or Las Vegas, and otherwise worked remotely for a national group of nonprofits serving mostly homeless and abused women.

I watched him as he concentrated on whatever he was working on. He wasn't handsome exactly, his profile was a little too rough for that, but he was funny, intelligent, decisive, and loyal. He had a sort of rugged, blue-collar charm in jeans and a leather jacket; in a suit he more closely resembled the lawyer he was. Both were good looks on him. His hair was almost black, with an occasional thread of silver. He was, in short, an attractive man in his early thirties, five or six years older than me. He looked up from his laptop, saw me staring at him, and raised an eyebrow.

"Nothing," I said. "Just thinking. Um—what time is it?"

He smiled and snapped his laptop closed. He had a great smile. "Time for bed," he said firmly and stood. Well, that was one area where we had no communication problems. At all.

CHAPTER THIRTY-TWO

Grandfather was released on bail late on Monday afternoon. He climbed into a cab outside the Hall of Justice after letting me kiss his cheek and telling me to watch over Davie. He looked up at me, holding the cab door open. "It might be a good idea, Theophania, for young Davie to stay with you for a few days."

"What about you? Would you like me to come with you?"

"No need, my dear." He seemed about to close the door, so I said hastily, "What did Adolphus Pratt say would happen next?"

"The police will be building their case. So far they have my fingerprint on the hoof pick and my blood type on Sergei's ring. It will take some time for DNA test results to confirm that it is my blood, but when that happens, I fear my bail will be revoked." He pulled thoughtfully on one ear and looked up at me. "Thank you, my dear, for speaking to Valentina."

He seemed about to leave, but I stopped him with a hand on his arm. "You said you and Sergei had a disagreement. Did you meet him at the Venus de Milo Club?"

He chuckled. "You are impressing me more and more, my dear. I feel sure my fellow members of the club are underestimating you. I am going home now, Theophania.

I'm a little tired; I may take a nap." That scenario was so unlikely that I was still watching in astonishment as he pulled the door closed, and his cab drew away into traffic.

Ben and I went to collect Mr. Rillera and took him to get Davie out of custody.

Davie and Ben exchanged fist bumps as he and his father came down the front steps. "Good to see you, man," Ben said, and Davie said something equally manly and unemotional, while I sniffled into a tissue. Remembering Grandfather's suggestion (another parliamentary writ), I suggested Davie might want to stay the night at my place.

"Sounds good. You okay with that, Davie?" Mr. Rillera said quickly. "I've got stuff to do; you'll be fine with her, eh? Closer to school, too."

Davie said, "Sure, Dad," and looked desolate.

At Davie's request, we had pizza for an early dinner, and then he, Nat, and Ben went to a Giants game. I telephoned Grandfather, who said he was visiting a friend for a couple of days and ignored my queries about who he was staying with and where.

"It hasn't escaped my notice that neither you nor Davie are at home in your own beds," I said sharply.

"Just a precaution, my dear. Probably quite unnecessary."

"Only probably?"

"Likely, then. Don't worry, my dear. Good night." He hung up.

I made up the futon in the second bedroom for Davie. He had school the next day, which meant he'd need to be on his way by seven. He went to Lowell, out near Lake Merced, near where Valentina lived, and which, as Davie once told me proudly, was the alma mater of Rube Goldberg. I had to look him up. Eccentric alumni aside, Lowell was a public magnet school. Their standards were high, and the workload was heavy. Even on days when he wasn't on the schedule to work at Aromas, Davie frequently did his homework here rather than at home.

I made a quick visit to Mr. Lee's grocery store to pick up some food suitable for feeding two male appetites. Mr. Lee's fortune-teller advises him to arrange his products according to some sort of incomprehensible system that places toilet paper next to the Hamburger Helper, while paper towels and boxes of cereal (except for the Grape-Nuts) are with the peanut butter and window cleaner. His small deli area, under the iron control of his daughter-in-law, is immaculate and logical, but chaos reigns everywhere else. Tinned peaches and light bulbs surround Mr. Lee at his cash desk, where he usually sits reading a Chinese-language newspaper or an out-of-date copy of *People* magazine. None of this seems unusual anymore, and when I find myself in a regular grocery store it seems wrong not to find Swiffer refills next to the cranberry juice, and jars of salsa with the baby wipes.

I made Davie a couple of thick roast beef sandwiches to take the next day for his lunch. I felt better about the roast beef after I piled on some lettuce. Even if he scraped it off, I'd done my best. I added two candy bars, a couple of apples, a banana, some string cheese, a bottle of water, and two orange sodas. I looked at what seemed like enough food to feed a family of four and transferred everything to a larger paper sack, then added a cheese sandwich, a bag of carrot sticks, a couple of rice pudding cups, and two bags of chipotle chips. Half an hour later, I added a box of cookies in case he wanted a snack some time before or after lunch. Then I put a five-dollar bill in there in case I'd forgotten anything.

When Ben and Davie got in it was nearly eleven. They'd eaten a second dinner at the ballpark and agreed that the game was good, but not great, since one of the stars was on something called the IL, which, Davie was careful to explain, used to be the DL. Since I'd never heard of either, I just let it go. They relived for my benefit a bases-loaded situation, which was apparently a highlight.

"That sounds amazing, Davo; so did the Giants win?"

"Nah, but it was a good game."

"Oh." Sympathy didn't seem to be required. "Well, it sounds very exciting." Ben winked at me from behind Davie's back.

"Where am I gonna sleep?" Davie looked around as if he expected to find a pallet on the kitchen floor.

"You're in here," I said, leading him down the hallway. "That's a clean T-shirt and track pants of Ben's to sleep in. You know where the bathroom is; I've left a toothbrush and a fresh bar of soap for you." He dropped his backpack on the floor by the bed. "I've made a lunch for you to take tomorrow; it's in a bag in the fridge, so don't eat it if you get up in the night and want a snack. There's some leftover pizza if you're hungry."

He blinked at me. "You made me a lunch?"

I hesitated. "Wasn't that the right thing? I didn't know if you took a lunch or not . . ."

"Nah. That's good, Theo." He frowned down at the clean towels on the bed and then turned away.

"If you drop your stuff in the bathroom I'll run everything through the washer and dryer for you before I go to bed, okay?"

"Yeah." He cleared his throat. "Sounds good."

When I woke up it was only about four a.m. I wasn't sure I could get out of bed without waking Ben, since our legs were more or less braided together. He had pulled his pillow over his head in the night as he often did. For some reason I found it endearing. I was on my stomach; one of my arms was tucked under my own pillow, and the other was resting across his chest, with my hand caught up in his. That was pretty endearing, too.

I thought about Davie—I *had* to start thinking of him as Davo, since that's what he wanted—and that led me to thinking about my grandfather. The judge had taken his passport and set his bail at an eye-watering two million dollars. Lichlyter hadn't looked happy when Honest Eddie had come up trumps, and Grandfather was released. His arraignment had made the news. I could only hope the little local news story didn't break out into the wider world and reach the eyes and ears of our family.

The blot on the family escutcheon was poor repayment for moving here to help me. Like me, he'd been grieving; he just didn't show it. His generation believed feelings were embarrassing, so they tried not to have any.

His two older brothers—including the current Earl—were kind enough, but the cause of genteel eye rolls in the family whenever their names came up. My two great-aunts were content to roll their eyes and return to their mah-jongg cronies (in Great Aunt Kitty's case) and a London penthouse (in Great Aunt Georgie's). The sisters took Grandfather's recommendations to their stockbroker and managed to double their inheritances, which hadn't been as large as their brothers', because that's the way it was then. He was the youngest of his siblings, but I always believed he was the only one with any real brains. Great Uncle James had three interests—breeding, racing, and betting on Thoroughbred racehorses. Great Uncle Teddy was the Earl, and he struggled to find the resources to support the leaky and decrepit family manor he'd inherited. He'd lately brought in a herd of bison to encourage visitors and opened a farm shop to sell things like meat butchered on the estate, cheese made at the home farm, and baskets woven from reeds from the estate waterways. My cousin Frederick, who was always in need of a job because he was basically unemployable, had been Uncle Teddy's first choice to run it. Grandfather had persuaded him to hire a competent manager instead, so it was doing well.

When life wasn't filled with drama, Grandfather and I met every two weeks for tea, which his cook/housekeeper presented on Royal Crown Derby china, Arthur Price sterling, and starched Irish linen. Our topics of conversation ranged from the weather, Aromas, and either Davie's latest escapade or their most recent outing. Sometimes I asked him to play a piece on the piano, and we finished off the visit with a final thought about the weather before he allowed me to kiss his cheek and I left. Approaching him with more questions about a strip club wasn't even remotely possible.

"What do you think?" I asked Ben later that morning. "How likely is it that my grandfather—and you know him, Ben—would spend an evening at the Venus de Milo and then get into a physical fight with a priest in said club while naked women gyrate to Nickelback and the Arctic Monkeys." I shook my head. "I can hear myself saying it and I can't believe I'm even thinking about it."

Ben rinsed his coffee mug and stuck it in the dishwasher.

"The Venus doesn't sound like somewhere he'd go for entertainment; but if I was a seventy-year-old British aristocrat with an impeccable reputation for sobriety I might choose a strip club to meet someone because it was the least likely place for people to look for me."

And I thought I was doing well to dye my hair and wear a pair of unnecessary glasses.

Two mornings later I waited with Ben for an Uber driver to take him to SFO and said goodbye—again—as he left for his flight to DC. He hesitated as he tossed his bag into the trunk and turned back to me.

"I have to go," he said, answering an objection I hadn't made. "I'll deal with things as quickly as I can and be back, probably four or five days." I nodded. We'd already been over this. He looked away for a few seconds, then turned back to me, his jaw set. "Look, think about telling me why you needed to get into Katrina's office. Whatever it is, we'll deal with it, okay? You can trust me; I'm a lawyer. And if you go anywhere else off the beaten track, make sure you take Nat with you. I love you." I stood, unmoving, struck dumb. He touched my cheek with his hand before kissing me lightly on the lips, and then he was gone.

CHAPTER THIRTY-THREE

I hadn't been able to think of why someone would have killed both Katrina and Sergei. It hadn't been easy to imagine who could have wanted the deaths of a priest *and* a cutthroat attorney. Looking at the two people they had been in the past gave me more to work with, but I still hadn't found anyone besides Valentina who knew both of them.

Grandfather knew Sergei, but as far as I knew he had never met Katrina, and Davo had never met either one. Amos Noble, the D'Allessios, and Kurt Talbot knew Katrina but, as far as I knew, they had never met Sergei. Gavin was close to Katrina, but hadn't met Sergei. My gopher-killing spy friend, Jacob, knew Sergei, but not Katrina. Valentina said she knew Katrina and Sergei, and she had reason to hate and perhaps even kill Sergei, although she didn't have any obvious reason to kill Katrina. So was Valentina my chief suspect? Twenty years was a long time to wait for her revenge, but maybe she wanted Katrina and Sergei together before she killed them? But they weren't killed together. Maybe she wanted to kill Katrina first, in such a way that Sergei, her ex-lover, would suffer and know that he was next? Maybe she had somehow engineered Sergei's visit to San Francisco by killing his priest friend in Kiev?

Huh. That was actually kind of plausible. But then why had she given Grandfather an alibi for the nights of both deaths if she was going to set him up as the fall guy for Sergei's murder? It would make more sense to have him suspected of both killings, because otherwise she would need a second fall guy. And then it hit me. She did have a second fall guy. Davo was a suspect, too.

I needed to speak to the other person with a strong connection to Katrina through the condo development. Maybe he knew Sergei, too. Or knew someone who knew him.

While I waited in his outer office to speak to Amos Noble, I wondered if someone who needed a pit bull like Katrina on his team was a nice guy who couldn't, or didn't want to, do his own dirty work. Or maybe he was someone with a similar barbed wire personality who needed someone he could relate to. I wasn't in any doubt for long. I knew him slightly, but every time we'd met in the past he'd been insulated by layers of attorneys and advisors.

His company's offices were in a modern high-rise in the Mission District. When I made my way through the frosted glass doors from the elevator, the young woman at the reception desk was handling a call long enough for me to take a look around. The waiting area was expensively furnished, with pale couches, metal tables, and color renderings of various Noble properties. One wall was given over to plaques and framed citations awarded to him for various reasons, including a framed photo of the children I had seen in Katrina's office, with a little brass plate at the bottom that said *Top Donor*.

The receptionist, wearing a multicolored wrap-around dress held in place, a little too low, by a sparkly brooch about to pop loose under the strain, finished her call. One of the things I'd found surprising about the city was its almost complete lack of a dress code. Even in downtown law firms the staff often looked as if they were dressed to go clubbing—or hiking.

She was briskly efficient and gave me a prospectus to read while I waited. It was mostly more color renderings of contemporary, multi-use buildings, all much larger than the one he had planned for the Gardens. I looked more closely at the drawings; they all had the same rather dreamlike quality, with pastel colors, cloudless skies, and lots of street trees. One was supposed to be in the Tenderloin, a neighborhood more nightmarish than dreamy. Maybe they were future projects and not completed ones. It could explain why he'd been interested in a relatively small project at Fabian Gardens—something quick and inexpensive to keep the business ticking over while he got permits for his larger projects. Or maybe his intention was always to force nearby property owners to sell so the project could be enlarged. I was escorted through the suite to Noble's office. Everything was quieter than I'd expect for a busy and successful firm. Where were all the admin staff buzzing around, and why was there no one in the glass conference rooms or in the offices we passed?

Noble's chair was turned toward the huge window behind his desk, and as I came into the room a cloud of blue smoke rose up from behind it. There was a faint haze in the room, and until I saw the overflowing ashtray on his desk I thought we should be heading for the nearest fire escape. I don't smoke but I know cigars, and the one he puffed throughout our conversation was definitely of the corner bodega variety. He was middle-aged and paunchy, and in a city where every second person was a devotee of raw food or tai chi, or some other brand of healthy living, he clearly didn't give a damn. His color was high with either high blood pressure or suppressed anger.

"If you're here to harass me, you're behind on the news, Ms. Bogart," he growled. "We've decided to move on to other projects."

I raised an eyebrow to express my astonishment. "Did Katrina's unfortunate death have anything to do with that?"

"I know everyone thought Katrina was a huge pain in the ass, but she was our pain in the ass, and she was brilliant." He waved the cigar. "She found something wrong with the title to one of those properties, and she told us it would be been an expensive battle on top of what we were already paying to fight the city and you Fabian Gardens Nazis. Frankly, I'd already lost interest; I have other fish to fry. So we pulled out of the deal. It was disappointing in one way, I guess, but I was grateful to her. Katrina saved us millions."

"I heard something about her proposing to buy the buildings herself; it didn't sound very above board."

His face darkened further. "I heard something about that, but it made no difference to me if she was willing to get into it. Like I said, I'd already moved on." He looked at me shrewdly. "If you're looking for someone who hated her, try Angie Lacerda. She persuaded those property owners to sell for a pretty penny, and bought the properties, intending to sell them on to us for development. Us nixing the sale cost her several million."

"I—er—understood that she was buying them on your behalf."

He held up his cigar and examined the ash before he

brushed it gently on the rim of an overflowing ashtray, and it fell silently onto the ghosts of his earlier cigars.

"Ms. Lacerda misunderstood the level of our interest. It was just business."

"Did you happen to know a priest, Father Sergei Wolf? He was the man they found dead in one of those properties."

"Interesting, but fortunately not my problem." I showed him the photo Grandfather had shared with me of Sergei with the Coit Tower murals. He shook his head. "No, I didn't know him. A priest you say? A local?"

"He was visiting from South America. But he seems to have had an interest in the Kiev orphanage Katrina was supporting."

Noble snorted. "Katrina was proud of that place. She was pretty discreet about it, but she lobbied her clients for donations. She was hard to resist; believe me, I know."

"So you donated, too?"

"I gave her twenty-five grand last year." He narrowed his eyes. "It was tax deductible against the business."

"Did Katrina ever mention someone called Pavel? Maybe someone involved with the orphanage," I improvised, "or someone she knew here in San Francisco?"

"I've never heard the name. Sounds—what? Russian?"

"I think it means '*little*' in Russian," I agreed, having looked it up. He shrugged.

He didn't get up to see me out, just waved his cigar at me as I said my goodbyes. As I was passing the receptionist's desk, she rose and smiled. "Let me show you how to work the elevator."

Maybe she was tasked with making sure Noble's visitors actually left. She walked me to the elevator and as we waited, watching the lights above it indicating its progress, the way you do, she said quietly, "He was seriously pissed about the Fabian Gardens deal falling through. I hear a lot, you know? He's way overextended; he's had to let people go in admin, sales, and even construction. The offices are practically empty. He was counting on that deal to keep the company afloat. He and Ms. Dermody had a scream-ing fight about her putting in a bid to buy the buildings after he"—she tossed her head in the direction of her boss's office—"pulled out. He fired her."

"When did this happen?"

"A day or two before she was killed. She was a piece of work, that lady." She hesitated. "My aunt and uncle live in Fabian Gardens."

"Who?" I whispered, and she giggled.

"The D'Allessios. Uncle Guillermo was super relieved when everything fell apart." She winked and glided back through the frosted glass doors.

That evening, I told Nat what I'd learned.

"So let me get this straight. Katrina told Noble the problem with the title would mean another long, costly le-gal battle, which Angela Lacerda said was a lie because it amounted to nothin' but a clerical error. Noble said he was happy with Katrina's efforts on his behalf and didn't care about her tryin' to buy the buildings, and didn't mention that he'd fired her when he found out."

"Right," I said. "So Katrina lied and Noble lied. At least Angela was up front about hating Katrina," I added. "And is it weird that the neighborhood association had a vested interest in preventing Noble from getting hold of the build-ings? Because from the outside it looked as if they and Katrina were on opposite sides, but they were actually working toward the same end."

"It's a rattler's den. No tellin' where one snake ends and another one starts."

"So Noble could have killed her because he felt she cheated him in the business deal, or Angela might have killed her for the same reason, or for some other reason."

"Yeah, but I don't get it. All the decisions had already been made before she died. Noble had pulled out, and Angie was reconciled to holding on to the buildings. If everyone's telling the truth, why'd they kill her?"

CHAPTER THIRTY-FOUR

Faye-Bella waved me in to Bonbons Chocolat as I walked past.

"Hi, Bella, what's up?" I was talking to her, but I was looking at the coconut chocolates in the big glass case. She used tongs to pick one up without asking me, dropped it into a little pleated paper cup, and put it on the top of the case. Yep, I was probably here too often. My own customers at Aromas were either less habit-driven, or I wasn't paying enough attention to them. Although, now that I came to think of it, I guess a lot of them did just come in for refills of the same shampoo or lotions. That made me feel better, for some reason; maybe I wasn't so inattentive after all. I pulled some change from the front pocket of my jeans and put it on the case, then picked up the sweet and nibbled it.

She said, "Matthew was asking about you this morning; he seemed anxious to talk to you."

"Matthew always seems anxious," I said, and then sighed. It wasn't Matthew's fault that every conversation with him was an effort. It was hard to know what was best. Was he better off on the streets or in some sort of permanent living situation with rules about showers and clean clothes, where he would get decent meals and help with his medications? I was still aghast that a city as rich as this one, in a country as rich as this one, was comfortable letting people live on the streets—hungry, filthy, and often in need of help. My grandfather told me once that it was possible to ignore the poverty in the streets of Mumbai or Delhi, that fairly quickly one simply stopped seeing the poverty and the lives it held in thrall. I didn't ever want to be like that, but the enormity of changing even a small thing about people's lives was daunting. I admired Ben's ability to keep soldiering on in the face of indifference and outright hostility to his work with abused and homeless women.

"True," she said ruefully. "And I wouldn't have known for sure what he wanted, but he kept saying 'black; no sugar,' and I know you're his favorite barista." She smiled at me. "I suppose I'm guessing it was you he wanted."

I looked out onto the street. "Does anyone know where he goes when he's not here?"

"Apparently he has a place near the Panhandle, up past Weller. In some sort of derelict building. Some days he goes down to the cable car turn-round at Powell to pick up a few dollars from the tourists."

"It's not much of a life."

"He doesn't have a lot of coping skills. And you hear these terrible stories about homeless people being beaten up. A few years ago someone doused one poor guy with gasoline and set him on fire." Her eyes were wide with horror. "Anyway, I was worried too, so I asked around."

I hadn't done anything to find out Matthew's story, if he had any sort of comforts in his life, if he was safe, or if he had family. "That was really nice of you, Bella."

Her cheeks turned pink. "I think it was because I started to look after his comforter for him," she said.

"He's lucky to have you," I said, still feeling guilty.

"It's all of us, really," she said. "Father Martin makes sure he gets a shower occasionally; you get him his morning coffee and a pastry; Julie up at the sandwich shop gives him lunch some days, and Jonnie at the pizza place gives him a slice and a soda on other days. Marge from the drugstore gives him a toothbrush and toothpaste and a comb every now and then. It really does take a village sometimes. We have to look out for each other." Tears lingered on her lashes; she pressed her lips together and nodded. "Anyway, you can ask Matthew tomorrow what he wanted; although maybe he'll have forgotten by then."

But Matthew wasn't in his doorway the next morning, or the next, and I forgot about what Bella had said until three days later, when Nat and I were trying to think of how Sergei had been lured to the empty building, or his body transported there in the small hours. There was no guarantee some local wouldn't roll out of Coconut Harry's, or step off a late-night bus up on California, at an inopportune time. Even in our famously *laissez faire* city, I couldn't imagine anyone seeing a dead body being carried through the streets without at least taking a selfie. How had that been done?

"San Francisco isn't like London, with CCTV cameras on every corner," I said. "They're intrusive, but one of them would come in handy now."

"Matthew might've seen something that night," Nat said, and I thought of Matthew's shopping cart. If there was one thing almost no one would remember or think was important, it was a homeless man pushing a shopping cart. It wouldn't take the killer much more effort than wrapping a blanket around his shoulders and tossing another blanket over the body.

"We should try and find him," I said. "I haven't seen him for a few days."

"How we gonna do that?"

"Bella said he lives in a derelict building near the Panhandle. Maybe we could find it. Or maybe Father Martin knows something."

"I'm trying to remember what I know," Father Martin said when I called. "I think someone here said he has a place in an old—police station, maybe? Something like that."

"Do you think you could find out?"

"What's going on?"

"Nothing. He just hasn't been around, and I was wondering if he's okay."

"Let me ask around this evening and see what I can find out."

He called me early the next morning, more helpful than I expected given our oddly abrasive first meeting. One of their volunteers thought Matthew lived in the semi-basement of a decrepit former firehouse near the Panhandle of Golden Gate Park.

"Do you want me to come with you?"

"I'll call you if we find him," I said instead.

Nat and I drove over to the Panhandle and scoped out several blocks on either side before we found it. It was very obviously a squat, since no sane person would have allowed the place to be occupied legally. Not by human beings, at least. The front of the building was sealed with plywood and two-by-fours over the windows and doors, and it was surrounded by a formidable chain-link fence. The narrow vacant lot next door must have been too small for the city to approve a building permit; it was overgrown with eucalyptus trees, shedding their bark in long, ragged ribbons. For some reason I was reminded of the dancers at the Venus. We made our way back along the fence, the ground under our feet slippery with years, perhaps decades, of fallen eucalyptus leaves, seedpods, and strips of bark. Both the firehouse and the vacant lot backed onto a ten-foot retaining wall topped with wooden palings, so there was no way in there. But near the wall, the fence had been pushed and flattened until it was possible, if not easy, to climb over onto a strategically placed, upturned crate in the firehouse yard. Nat went first and helped me across, grumbling when he caught the sleeve of his sweater on a stray wire. We approached the back of the firehouse, and I went down three uneven stone steps to a door, hanging on one hinge and sheltered by the second-story overhang. When I couldn't get the door open, Nat came down to lean his weight against it. It screeched and scraped until it was more or less open.

Matthew's crib was an education in the variety of pungent smells caused by moldy newspapers, cats, old fast-food containers, and a nonfunctioning toilet. The atmosphere was like a physical barricade. We both stopped on the threshold and looked into the room as far as we could, which wasn't very far. Canyon walls of unstable piles of cartons, papers, pallets, and random pieces of plywood and lumber reaching almost to the ceiling loomed over a narrow walkway leading into the apartment. A cat ran at us, back low, ears flat—and as we stood there exchanging an appalled look, a carton slithered off one of the towers and took one of the smaller stacks down. It landed with a thump more or less at our feet, missing the cat by inches and raising a miasma of dust and another appalling stink. The cat made its escape. Nat coughed and pulled his sweater up at the waist to hold it around his mouth and nose.

"Doesn't help," he said, and dropped the sweater again. He looked into the apartment and then back at me. "I'm not steppin' one foot in there," he said loudly, as if I'd suggested it. When I turned my head, took a deep breath, and started to go through the door, he grabbed my arm and said hastily, "And you, either. God knows what kinda germs are floatin' around." He had a point. Even if I wanted to go in—and I really, really didn't—I wasn't sure I could inhale more than once without throwing up. "Matthew!" I shouted from the doorway. The silence was broken only by some loudly buzzing flies making a dash for the open door. We both ducked reflexively. Ugh.

"He's not here; let's go," Nat said.

"Wait a minute," I said.

He raised a fist and cupped it in his other hand. "Rock, paper, scissors?" he said hopefully. "Two outa three?"

I rolled my eyes and held my hands around my mouth. "Matthew! Are you home?"

This time I did hear something. It was coming from somewhere in the depths of the room.

"Probably another cat or somethin'," Nat said cautiously. "Smells as if the place might have one or two. Or three."

The noise, this time obviously a low groan, came again. That was no cat. I sidled to the center of the labyrinth as quickly as I could without knocking against anything or slipping on something foul, and gagged at the smell. The only light came from a couple of ground-level windows, grimy and barely translucent, but I could still see more than I really wanted to, as I grabbed at a pile on the floor of disintegrating newspapers and trash covered in maggots.

I uncovered an ankle with a foot at an odd angle, wearing a tattered sport shoe. "Nat! Come and help!"

"Dear God, do I hafta?" But he came around the corner quickly enough, saw what I was trying to do, and bent to help. I knew it was Matthew under there, but I found myself hoping it was someone else, some stranger I didn't need to feel responsible for. Another moan came from the pile of trash. It was wispy, weaker than the first, and contained a small squeak that didn't seem to bode well for his lungs. And then I uncovered Matthew's face. His eyes wandered until they settled on mine. "Call 911," I gasped at Nat as I tried to smile at Matthew. "He's still alive. You'll be okay, Matthew. You're nearly out of there." He closed his eyes and started to mumble. "Coffee, black. Coffee, black."

I was crying now and barely managed to choke out, "That's right, Matthew, coffee, black. Hang on, okay?"

I kept digging, flinging things off him at random, and Nat finished the call and bent down again to help at first, but then stood to lean back against a wavering tower that seemed in danger of falling and flattening us all.

By the time the fire truck and the EMTs arrived, I had managed to uncover Matthew's chest, so at least he was able to breathe, but he had lapsed into unconsciousness. He was looking terrible. His face was badly scraped up, he'd bled heavily from a head wound, one of his hands was crushed, and one of his legs looked broken. And heaven knew what kind of internal injuries one of those toppling mountains had caused. The wheezy breaths continued, but they scarcely moved his chest at all, and I was afraid that each one would be his last. The EMTs pushed their way to us, hauling their cases and pulling on latex gloves, moving sideways so their shoulders wouldn't catch on anything. I got out of the way, which wasn't easy since there was so little room to maneuver, and slipped and stumbled back to the door. The EMTs made it clear they needed Nat to stay, and as I brushed past him he was resolutely holding back the slanting, unstable tower, looking anywhere but at Matthew's bloody wounds or at his own torn and bleeding hands. Mine were no better; they were scratched and filthy, and my nails were ragged.

When Matthew was stabilized enough to move, they brought him out on a sort of clamshell stretcher, closely followed by Nat. As they reached the door, the teetering tower they'd just left behind crash-landed, making a horrible noise and producing clouds of stinking dust that reached me standing just outside the door, and made all of us cough.

The firefighters had used bolt cutters to remove a section of the fence and roll it aside. The EMTs were in a hurry, and I had to shout at their backs, "Where are you taking him?"

"St. Mary's!" one of them yelled back.

His partner yelled over her shoulder as they transferred Matthew into the ambulance. "You need tetanus shots, and you might have inhaled something toxic. There's another unit on the way. Wait here." They stepped up into the ambulance, I got one more glimpse of Matthew looking small and pale, the doors closed, and with hardly a second's delay they drove off with a splashy display of synchronized lights and sirens. Their speed was heartening; they'd only hurry like that if Matthew were still alive.

I leaned back against Nat's Jaguar, shaking from the adrenaline. I said to him as he joined me, "Come on, Nat; let's go to the hospital."

He had cobwebs in his hair and smears of black and

green stuff on his sweater. I supposed I looked much the same and brushed my hands down my jeans. "Ow," I said. My hands stung.

He gave me an exasperated look and made a futile effort to brush himself off. "The gal said to wait."

I opened the passenger door and talked to him over the roof of the car. "I know, but we can get checked out at St. Mary's. And I should call Father Martin." I got in, pulling out my phone. He climbed in behind the steering wheel with a resigned sigh.

Father Martin arrived at the hospital, flustered and demanding news. He was wearing a thin purple brocade scarf around his neck and carrying a small zippered pouch. I joined him at the reception desk, and we spoke briefly before he was allowed back into the emergency medical bays.

Nat and I sat in the waiting room surrounded by misery and anxiety. People were quietly bleeding or holding crying babies, and in all it wasn't a restful place to wait. Nat and I were obviously low on the priority list, but we were eventually given tetanus and antibiotic shots and antibacterial salve and gauze for the cuts on our hands. I mentioned the toxic air in Matthew's place, but since we weren't coughing or turning blue, the doctor told us to check back with our own doctors and mention inhaling possible particulates to see if we were at risk for what he called chemical pneumonia. If we started to get short of breath, began a fever, chest pain, or swelling of our eyes or tongue, we should get ourselves back to an ER.

I could see Nat running his tongue around inside his mouth. The doctor smiled at us both. "I think you'll be fine," he said. "The injuries to your hands shouldn't get infected."

Nat stopped feeling his neck glands and looked closely at his hands. "How are we gonna know if they're infected?"

The doctor's lips twitched, but he answered seriously enough. "The scratches will get red and swollen. But I've pumped you full of antibiotics, and I want you to get these filled and take them for ten days." He tore off two prescription sheets, handed one to each of us, and returned the pad to the pocket of his white coat.

I managed to get Nat back to the waiting room, where he kept clearing his throat and asking me every five minutes if I thought his eyes looked red.

"What was in Father Martin's little bag thing, do you think?" I asked in an attempt to distract him. "And why was he wearing that scarf?"

"The scarf is called a stole, and it's what they wear when they administer the sacraments."

"Sacraments? Is he saying Mass back there?"

"He'll be givin' Matthew the anointin' for the sick—it used to be a sort of final blessin' if you looked as if you were checkin' out."

I gulped. "Does that mean that Matthew—"

He patted my hand. "Nah. Now priests can give it to you if you're just sick, even if you might be recoverin'. That's what he had in that little pouch prob'ly—it includes a blessing with holy oil."

"Huh. How do you know so much about it, anyway?"

Nat just shrugged. "Early trainin'. It never goes away."

"Are you Catholic?" I was surprised because I knew the Catholic Church didn't exactly embrace gay men and women. Or anyone, really, who wasn't heteronormative. Say what you will about the Church of England, and God knows I've said a lot, they're an accepting bunch.

"I wanted to be. But they don't want me, so . . ." He shrugged again.

"Do you go to church? Why don't I know this about you?"

"You don't know everythin' about me, English," he said, but now he was smiling. "I go sometimes. I don't know this Father Martin too well; I can tell you this much—there are people on both sides of the aisle who wouldn't mind him crossing over; know what I mean?"

"You think you're being subtle, but yes, I get it." I rolled my eyes. "Is he gay?" I added after a brief pause.

"Dunno."

I frowned. "But—"

"It's actin' on it that's the problem for them," he said. He was putting on a careless front, but I decided the Catholic Church could bite me. I held his hand gently in mine, avoiding the sore spots on both our hands. We sat quietly for a while.

Time stopped meaning very much in that weird way it does in hospitals. Eventually, Father Martin came out through the double doors. We stood up and waited for him to get to us. "Matthew's still with us," he said quietly, gesturing for us both to sit. "I gave him the sacrament, but he hasn't regained consciousness. They said it could be hours yet. You two look as if you could use a shower and some rest. I'll stay for a while and let you know if there's any change."

CHAPTER THIRTY-FIVE

I telephoned Inspector Lichlyter as soon as I got home and, while I didn't think she would help me, stranger things have happened. I got the information I wanted, but I can't say the conversation was a complete success.

"I was wondering if you could put me in touch with Katrina Dermody's office assistant. Her name is Janine something; I met her at Katrina's memorial."

"You want to contact her?"

"Yes. I . . . er . . . wanted to call her, or maybe send her a note. She seemed so upset at the memorial, and I thought of writing to her. A note. Of condolence."

"I can't release her address or phone number." She sounded very firm. "But her last name is Ryan." After another brief pause she added, "Her husband is Liam."

"Is the investigation doing well?" I gave myself a mental bitch slap. "I mean, do you have any more suspects?"

"We don't usually need more than one when the evidence is compelling. If that's all, Ms. . . . Bogart, no doubt you'll let me know if there are any other condolence notes you want to write."

I thought Janine was probably the only person who knew about the day-to-day running of Katrina's law practice. Her paralegal had recently resigned, and Gavin only went to the office occasionally. I was clutching at straws, but I hoped she could give me some new information, some new leads to follow. She might also be the only person to know if Katrina were the mother of Sergei's son, Pavel, and if he'd ever visited her at her offices. With Haruto's help, I found Janine and Liam Ryan in Montara that afternoon. I telephoned her and left a message. That evening I heard back from her husband.

"I'm just returning your call because you haven't heard the news, and I wasn't sure . . ." His voice faded.

"What news?"

He cleared his throat. "Janine is in the hospital; she was in an accident ten days ago."

My heart sank. "I'm so very sorry. A car accident?"

"Yeah, she liked that she had to be in the office so early because she missed most of the early morning traffic. Janine"—his voice broke—"doesn't remember, and so no one's sure what happened. She might have taken a curve too fast. She went over the cliff on one of those bends along there. The police are still investigating."

Suddenly feeling that Janine's information was much more important than I realized, but unable to talk to her, I wasn't sure where to take the conversation. I'd thought she and I could just chat casually in case she knew something helpful. Liam was waiting, and I said the first thing that occurred to me. "We met at Katrina Dermody's memorial, and it was obvious that Katrina relied on her quite a bit."

"She loved her job because she was given so much responsibility." I thought cynically that Katrina probably loaded her up with too much work.

"So she was more than an assistant," I said, still finding

my way. "Janine told me about taking responsibility for a report or something, was that right?"

"Janine realized some report was overdue, so she pulled it together, cleared it with Ms. Dermody, and sent it off. Janine felt her contribution was valued, you know?"

"So she was in Katrina's confidence; she probably knew a lot about St. Olga's orphanage. That was a surprise to most of us," I said.

"She did. The report she wrote was something to do with the orphanage. She thought of Ms. Dermody as a role model." I swallowed a snort as he cut himself off. "Look, I have to go; I'm heading back to the hospital. I appreciate your call and I'll let Janine know."

"Please tell her I hope she's back on her feet very soon."

I finished the call, convinced someone had tried to silence the only person to shed a tear over Katrina's death. But why?

CHAPTER THIRTY-SIX

I heard the doorbell ring in the rectory and stood on the wide steps behind St. Christopher's, waiting for Father Martin to answer the door, thinking that I'd been foolish to come alone. Maybe he'd want another priest to hear his confession; wasn't that what Catholics did?

The door flung open and he appeared, handsome and scowling, dressed this time in a dignified black suit.

He led the way to his office and waved me to a chair, but I stayed standing in case I needed to make a quick getaway. Remembering his impatience on my first visit, I said quickly, "I know you stole the photograph of Katrina, and I think you took the doll, too. It was the one with the teacup, the one in the photograph. Am I right?"

He was probably in his fifties, and I wondered for the first time if priests retired on a pension and what they did after they retired. After a few seconds of stony silence, he turned to open a drawer in the small table next to the beaten-up leather chair and scrabbled for a second before pulling out the *matryoshka*. He held it so tightly his knuckles were white. He waved me to the hard-backed chair again, and this time I sat down. He leaned over to open and close a drawer in the desk, then turned and abruptly shoved the stolen photo of Katrina at me. It was the one of her with the young man. I realized with a mild shock I was sitting across from the same man, with the addition of three decades and a clerical collar. He threw himself into the chair and held the doll in his hand for another moment, his expression bleak, then he pushed that into my hands, too. I put the photo and the doll on the table next to him.

"It was an impulse. I don't know what I was thinking," he said dismally. "I bought Katrina that *matryoshka* thirty years ago." He looked down at his folded hands. "Have you ever read a priest's obituary?"

"Not that I remember, why?"

"There are never any survivors; no wife, no children, no grandchildren, often no siblings left alive. Katrina and I had a history. I liked knowing that there would be someone to care; someone to come to my funeral. Instead I went to hers."

He sounded remarkably like Jacob, the spy. I barely resisted promising him I'd attend his funeral.

"How did you know each other?"

The impulse to explain was stronger than his impatience. "We were girlfriend and boyfriend when we were just kids." He scowled at me. "I resisted my vocation for a long time because I wanted to be with her." He clenched his hands into fists, and I pressed against the back of my chair to put as much distance between us as I could.

"Katrina didn't take it well when I entered the seminary, and by the time I was ordained she had moved away. We wrote occasionally, so I knew when she married, when she moved to this country, when she divorced. I've lived in America myself for years now, mostly in the Midwest. When I was told six months ago I'd be posted here I contacted her. I wasn't sure she'd want to see me, but we were gradually able to repair our friendship. Of course she'd changed," he faltered. "But then so have I."

I thought of the laughing young couple in the photo album and then of the somber middle-aged people they'd become. "What kinds of things did you talk about? Did she tell you about her son?"

He paled. "No. She never mentioned that she had a son. How old was he, do you know?" I could see him rapidly doing some arithmetic.

"He could be anywhere from a teenager to a grown man. No one seems to know anything about him."

"She didn't include him in her estate plan? That doesn't sound like Katrina."

"You said she'd changed a lot. Gavin says she left everything to St. Olga's, the orphanage she supported in Kiev."

"Gavin? Do you mean Gavin Melnik?" He looked startled.

"Yes, Gavin is her cousin. He doesn't inherit anything, but he's her executor."

"I had no idea. He never mentioned—well, why would he? He didn't know that Katrina and I knew each other. When he started to volunteer here last month, I think I was away on retreat. Our clients like him. He seemed to have a special connection with Matthew." He ran a hand through his hair. "I suppose I should break the news about Matthew's accident to him."

"You were right about the fingers belonging to a priest," I said. "Did you know him, the priest who was killed? He was from South America. His name was Sergei Viktor Wolf."

"He doesn't sound very South American," he said brusquely.

"No, but he lived in Kiev for a time. Like Katrina. Like you."

"All roads lead to Rome, is that it?" he said wearily. "No, I didn't know him. But I knew Katrina had a lover called Sergei, back in the day. She was beside herself with rage when he entered the priesthood. She was angry with God, and I feared for her soul." I always find talk of souls a little disconcerting, but he did it without any self-consciousness. "Years later, she told me she'd given the two men she loved to the Church, that she was giving them nothing else. But she wanted to do something for children without parents. I thought she was referring to herself, but now you tell me she had a child—"

"Is that where the idea for St. Olga's came from?"

"She was proud of St. Olga's as an alternative to the huge state orphanage she'd experienced. More like a home, really. She refused to allow the local diocese any oversight, but she said she had a sort of bagman running interference, and he was able to finesse things so that they provided a small group of sisters to run the home. She said it was being run by a small group of Olivetans." He huffed in what was almost a laugh. "She didn't know anything about them, and said they sounded like an Italian soccer team. I told her they're a teaching order, and some of them are nurses, part of the Benedictines, so they're ideal for working with children. A bit unworldly, but kind-hearted women and very hard-working."

"So if I have a question about the orphanage, I should ask Gavin." My heart sank a little. I wasn't sure he could be objective.

He shrugged. "Katrina just referred to her cousin; I didn't realize she meant Gavin. I know she trusted him and, truthfully, she didn't have any time to do anything except work. I don't think she ever took a weekend off." He frowned. "She'd heard from a priest in Kiev about some kind of problem, and since Gavin was already over there, she was getting him to sort it out."

"Do you remember the name of the priest who wrote to her?"

"I probably still have the e-mail; is it important?"

"I think it is."

He opened a laptop on the desk and spent a couple of minutes scrolling through. "Here it is. It was a Father Ponomarenko."

"Did Katrina say what the problem was?"

"Just that the priest must be fairly junior, because he wasn't aware of St. Olga's. She responded to him eventually, but he didn't get back to her."

I nodded and tried to think of another way around to what I needed to know. In the meantime, he was looking impatient, so I asked the first thing that came into my head. "I'm not Catholic myself," I said. "And I've always felt those long black outfits with the—you know, wimples"—I felt proud for remembering—"were sort of severe, scary for kids."

He frowned. "Most orders wear modern dress now, and anyway, the Olivetan Sisters wear white habits; always have."

"What do you mean? Gavin showed photos of the nuns at Katrina's memorial, and they were wearing black."

He frowned. "I must have left by then. But anyway, Olivetans wear white habits. If the women in the photos were in black, they weren't Olivetans, and they weren't at St. Olga's."

As he closed the door behind me and I walked down the front steps, I felt I'd learned more than I expected.

I left the photo and the doll with Father Martin. What he did with them was up to him.

CHAPTER THIRTY-SEVEN

I raised a hand to Haruto as I walked past the doorway to Aromas and kept going until I got to The Coffee. Without asking, Nat made me an Earl Grey latte (which, with the addition of almond syrup, he'd named the San Francisco Fog on his menu board), and I said, "I might have wanted something different."

He shrugged. "Do you?"

"Well, no."

He snorted. "One thing I've already noticed, people like ridin' on familiar trails. I don't know all the names yet, but I can tell you their coffee order. Maybe it's mostly too early in the mornin' for them to be thinkin' of options." He nodded at a woman walking past the front window carrying a yoga mat. "She's a vanilla latte, low fat; she comes in with a guy who's an Americano, triple shot—which I'd know anyway from his shakin' fingers."

He handed me my tea and smiled at a woman approaching the counter. "House blend, large, room for cream?"

She smiled and nodded at him, looking pleased.

He winked at me. It reminded me of Faye-Bella putting out my favorite chocolate. He was right, people really did prefer to ride familiar trails. My smile faded. What else did that remind me of?

I walked slowly back to Aromas. The street was still quieter than usual on a midweek afternoon, and Nat was probably right, people were finding two corpses a little hard to ignore. I sat in my office and tried to add together the few random facts at my disposal. Grandfather and Davo were still in Lichlyter's sights, and I hadn't found anything to help them get out from under the weight of her suspicions. I hadn't found the mysterious Pavel. Was the orphanage an elaborate charade, existing only on paper and for the brief moments of Gavin's visits? He'd said he didn't know much about Catholic nuns, so he wouldn't know they were wearing the wrong outfits. Katrina had been uncharacteristically reticent about trumpeting her philanthropic efforts, but, if Amos Noble were typical, she had solicited significant donations. Haruto said $200,000 a year moved through St. Olga's. Had Katrina laundered those donations through the phony orphanage? Did Sergei discover the fraud through his priest friend in Kiev and come here to confront Katrina, only to find that she'd been killed? But if the orphanage was an elaborate charade, it had to be built by someone with the technical expertise to set up the web-based shadow accounts, and the contacts to have a priest killed in Kiev.

I looked at my list of suspects and crossed off the South American drug smugglers. I had no way of finding out if they were involved, and Lichlyter was welcome to them. People Katrina had bested, in court or out, were obviously still possibilities, and that included Amos Noble. I reluctantly crossed off Angela Lacerda, who seemed to use her lawyers to fight her battles rather than taking direct action.

I started a new list with Amos Noble at the top, well aware that I wanted him to be guilty so the others on my list were off the hook. He'd lied when he said the loss of the

Fabian Gardens project was unimportant; he needed that project to keep his company afloat. And he'd lied about not being angry with Katrina over her defection, because as soon as he found out, he fired her over it. What if Katrina had backed away from his company because she'd discovered he was involved in something illicit? That would explain the "criminal fraud" accusation she was hurling during the phone call I overheard the day before she was killed. But he didn't have a motive to kill Sergei, unless Sergei was a witness to Katrina's murder. If Sergei was hanging around Polk Street waiting for me to lead him to my grandfather, maybe he was nearby when Katrina was killed. And Matthew might simply have been in the wrong place at the wrong time, seen something he wasn't supposed to, and paid the price. No, that practically required stadium seating for the crowd observing Katrina's murder. I had no idea if Noble was involved in anything crooked, or how to find out, although the lies I knew about were real enough. I had to leave him to Lichlyter, too. I'd tell her what I knew about the end of his relationship with Katrina, but investigating his business took resources I didn't have.

Unhappily, because I had liked her, I was back to Valentina and I reluctantly put her down next. If she wasn't a computer expert herself, she must surely know of at least one in the shadowy world she had inhabited. Still inhabited, if I was any judge. With an expert on tap, she could have organized the building of the online presence and financial background of the nonexistent orphanage. It was easy to see her reacting quickly to kill Katrina once the lawyer discovered the scam that had cost her hundreds of thousands of dollars. Sergei's sudden appearance on Polk Street twenty years after the death of her husband and child must have been a terrible shock and then an opportunity too good to be missed. It explained why his body was found nearby. It had nothing to do with Fabian Gardens; he just happened to be here when she killed him. It even explained the grisly fingers in Nat's microwave. She as good as told me he should never have been accepted into the priesthood after his bloody and murderous past; they were the symbolic removal of his ordination.

Even if I stopped assuming a theoretical computer hacker on her payroll, it still seemed all too possible. For all I knew, she had an advanced degree in computer programming. But could Grandfather be so wrong about her? He was aware of her past, and it hadn't apparently occurred to him that she might be guilty. Or maybe it had, and he hadn't shared that with me. Or he was investigating her. Or he was more attached than I realized and simply couldn't see her guilt. In which case, exposing her was likely to cause him some genuine pain, and I'd do almost anything to avoid that. Anything except let her get away with murder.

I tried Kurt (and Sabina, I supposed) on for size, but I didn't want either of them to be guilty, either. Kurt's deal with Katrina might not pass an ethics test—not that I was throwing stones, considering my visit to Katrina's offices—but nothing I knew about it made me think he would benefit by killing her. Although he had come out the other side of their partnership on his feet—or at least he seemed content to let things lie. And I could think of no possible reason for him to kill Sergei or Matthew except for the stadium-seating thing. I put his name at the bottom of my list.

I could also build a strong case against someone else I'd come to like. Gavin had the best opportunity to set up St. Olga's as a scam. The only thing mitigating that was his lack of computer knowledge—he could barely cope with his laptop presentation at Katrina's memorial—and Haruto said it would take serious hacker-level skills to do what had been done to hide St. Olga's finances. Otherwise, Gavin fit the frame nicely. Katrina had somehow discovered what he'd done; she'd threatened him, and so he'd killed her. Sergei's murder could be explained by two possible scenarios: Sergei was a witness to Katrina's murder, and/or he had found out about the orphanage scam. That fit. Weighing against that was the fact that he wasn't living above his means. *Somebody* was siphoning off $200,000 a year from the orphanage accounts, which would seem capable of providing a better lifestyle than a studio apartment and a job as a barista. He was also kind and seemed too gentle, somehow, to be a cold-blooded killer. I'd seen him with Matthew that day, and he'd been sensitive to Matthew's foibles and brought him coffee. "Black, no sugar," as Matthew would say to me. I smiled. Actually, that's what he said to everyone. Except, I thought, still trying to make everything fit, he *didn't* say that to everyone. Not *everyone*. Maybe that's what Nat's "familiar trails" had been trying to remind me of.

Feeling suddenly chilled, I thought of something else, picked up my phone, and texted Ben. We talked every night but had mostly stayed away from discussing the murders. His response came within a couple of minutes. ETH stood for *Eidgenössische Technische Hochschule*. I looked it up on line. ETH produced some of the world's best computer scientists, programmers, and engineers. And I knew someone in our little group who had earned a degree there.

CHAPTER THIRTY-EIGHT

I walked back over to The Coffee, where Gavin made me a San Francisco Fog, and I asked him to join me at a table. Nat had gone out somewhere, and I was the only customer, so we headed over to a table in the window. I remembered the pizza restaurant waitress who used her window table to advertise, and I thought we should do the same for The Coffee. Besides, I wanted to be where we could be seen. Not that there were many people on the street these days.

"Where's Nat?" I said, picking off the cover and blowing on my tea. It was too hot to drink.

He smiled. He really was a sweet, good-looking guy, with his dark eyes and multi-shades of blonde hair. "He'll be back soon. I should really stay behind the counter while he's not here."

"I've been thinking about everything we talked about the other day, and I have a couple of questions you can help me with," I said. "Sit down. Make yourself comfortable. It must be tough being on your feet all day."

"Sure. What do you want to know?"

Well, that was the question, wasn't it? I felt about as certain as I could be that he wasn't the innocent he appeared, but was he just an embezzler or was he a murderer, too? Katrina had been shot late at night, and it would only have taken a few minutes to shoot her, rifle her briefcase, and then dodge fifty yards to get off Polk Street and into the alley to make his escape. Say five minutes total. Sergei, however, had been stabbed after a struggle, and his hands mutilated, which took time and privacy. It hadn't happened in the vacant building where he was found, or in Katrina's apartment.

I took my time taking the cover off my drink, setting it on the table, and picking up a couple of napkins to wipe up the resulting spot of tea as if it were my life's work. "You heard the news about Matthew?"

"Father Martin told me. I know you were fond of him." His expression was suitably grave, but I caught an unpleasant, malicious gleam in his eyes. It was the first break in his good-guy persona, and now I knew what to ask.

"Did Katrina have a wine cellar built in her garage?"

He frowned slightly and then chuckled. "Wow, that came out of left field. Why do you ask?"

"I just wondered where she was storing all her wine."

"Oh"—he huffed out a breath—"it went to an expert for valuation and sale. I don't know anything about wine."

I took a sip of my drink. Still too hot. "Like you don't know anything about computers," I said pleasantly. "Did you know that Olivetan nuns wear white habits?"

He looked puzzled. "No, I'm sorry. I told you I don't know anything about Catholic nuns."

"What do you know about?"

"What do you mean?"

"Well," I said playfully, "you don't know anything about wine, computers, or Catholic nuns."

"I guess I do sound like an idiot," he said ruefully. "But in some circles I'm considered quite intelligent." He chuckled again. "I'm writing an article now about San Francisco's coffee culture. See? I've learned a lot working here, and a writer uses every one of life's opportunities. I have you to thank for that idea, by the way."

I waved my coffee cup at him. "Consider it a freebie. I suppose there really is a coffee culture here; I never thought of it that way." I fiddled with my cup. "Even the homeless fellows on the street are particular about their coffee. Did I ever tell you about the first cup of coffee I gave Matthew?"

He leaned forward, his eyes bright, almost too attentive. "What happened?"

"It had cream and sugar in it, and he turned it down! That was the first time I heard him say—what was his little catch phrase? Oh, right—black, no sugar."

He smiled and took the kitchen cloth off his shoulder. "I should get back to the counter. Nat likes the mugs to be stacked when they come out of the dishwasher. Your drink seems too hot to enjoy. Let me add a splash of cold milk."

He took my cup behind the counter while I stared out over the café curtains Nat had agonized over. I wished he were here; for some reason this conversation felt as if it could go off the rails any minute. When he slid my cup over to me, I tried it again, feeling like Goldilocks, and then drank half of it down. I was thirsty, I needed the caffeine, and I hadn't eaten all day. "It's just right now. You're a good barista."

He walked back behind the counter and began stacking the mugs. "Nat likes to use these unless the customer wants a go-cup."

He took his time, building his mug pyramid slowly, aligning them carefully before adding the next layer. I watched him, a little cynically, recalling how clumsy and shy he had seemed when he first walked into Aromas, and wondered if that had been just another piece of theater.

He was taking too long. I stood up to go, and then sat down again heavily. I was much more tired than I realized. "One more thing, though." I tried to get up again and somehow couldn't. I wasn't sure what I wanted to ask him.

He sat down and took a set of keys from his pocket, held one of them up, and laid them on the table. "This is the key to the garage, if you want to check it out." He got up and walked over to the front door, turned the dead bolt, and flipped the door sign to *Closed*, then went to the espresso machine and poured milk into a metal jug. "We have a regular customer who comes in around this time and likes his drink to be ready," he said.

I frowned, trying to understand why the door was locked if a customer was expected. Had he locked the door or not? I listened to the milk hissing and bubbling and wondered how hot steamed milk was—as I said, science wasn't my best subject in school. I had to walk past him to leave, and I wanted to leave. I moved slowly, feeling as if I suddenly weighed a thousand pounds, fussing with the lid of my drink, and then dropping it, counting the seven steps I still had to walk before I got to the door.

As I drew abreast, he turned and threw the boiling milk at my head. I flinched instinctively and threw up a protective arm. Most of it missed of my face, but the milk soaked into my sleeve and hot, stinging burns traveled down my arm and neck. I screamed and struggled out of my T-shirt, and threw it in a soggy heap on the floor, then my feet got tangled in it and I clutched the edge of the counter to stay upright.

"How clumsy of me," he said, in a parody of concern. "I

should get something to put on that for you. Here, let me help you."

He came around the counter and put an arm like steel around my waist. I needed to run, but I couldn't remember why. I slumped against him and closed my eyes.

The next time I opened them I was sitting on a hard chair, and I could hear the trickle of water somewhere nearby. My hands seemed to be stuck to my legs, which was uncomfortable, and I couldn't move. The chair rocked when I tried and nearly tipped over. My feet were wet. I had a bad headache, and one of my arms was stinging, as if it had been burned. I couldn't make sense of anything and I didn't remember much of anything, either. I thought backward, but the last thing I remembered clearly was sitting in my office. I'd had an Earl Grey latte; or was that earlier? I had no idea.

"Feeling better?" Gavin's quiet voice reached me out of the gloom.

"Not really, to be honest. Where are we? Are we prisoners?" I was slurring my words, and even as I said it, I realized it didn't make sense, but nothing did.

"Well, *you* are, anyway," he said, sounding amused. "But don't worry; it won't be for long. I just need some of the roofie to leave your system. The autopsy will find it, but you take it to help you sleep, so it won't be unexpected." He splashed through the water and bent over me. I tried to focus on him, but I couldn't really make out the details of his face. It sounded like Gavin, but I couldn't be sure. He tugged on whatever was holding me to the chair, apparently satisfied.

"I don't take anything to help me sleep." I frowned. "Autopsy?"

"You have insomnia, so you take it to help you sleep. You can get it in England for that."

"I can?" I thought about it. I wasn't sleeping well, but I didn't remember taking anything, so I shook my head, which might have been a mistake since it made me very dizzy. "I don't take anything." I thought for another minute. "Autopsy?"

"It's too bad, but the city's a dangerous place at night. I have to get back to The Coffee to finish my shift. But I'll be back later."

"M'okay." I closed my eyes and went back to sleep.

He was there again when I woke up. My head was a little clearer, but not much, and the headache was a lot worse. I had no idea how much time had passed. I was still tied to the chair, but not with cord. I was wrapped heavily from neck to ankles, like a mummy. It felt hot and unpleasant, and my arm was hurting. It stung, like burns. I stared at it and then lifted my head. He was standing a few feet in front of me.

"Where are we?"

"The wine racks didn't give you a clue?" He still sounded amused, and as gentle and pleasant as ever, but his face was sharp and tight with tension.

I turned my head, painfully. LED lights glowed from the edges of tall wine racks full of bottles.

I looked down at myself. "Is this—am I wrapped in bubble wrap?" It seemed all of a piece with the surreal nature of my evening. I assumed it was evening.

He chuckled. "I had plenty of it from packing up Katrina's things. Bubble wrap and duct tape. It's true what they say—duct tape is good for everything. Couldn't risk rope burns and bruises being found at the—"

"Autopsy," I said hollowly.

"Exactly. Smart girl."

I squinted at the wall next to me. "Is that blood?"

"This is where I killed the priest and cut off his fingers. Pretty gross, right?" He actually wrinkled his nose, as if it was distasteful. "Lucky he wanted to see Katrina's wine collection."

I closed my eyes and felt my head pounding. "What time is it?"

"It's about two in the morning. Nat was pissed you weren't answering your phone earlier. I explained you'd come in for your usual afternoon tea and then left." He bent over and fished around near his feet. He picked up my dripping phone, then held it out to me. "Oops." He made a mock regretful face. "He'll start to worry tomorrow probably, but by then you'll have met with an unfortunate accident, or possibly a mugging gone wrong. I'll think of something."

I shifted to ease some of the pressure on my arm and looked up at him. He really was a sweet, good-looking guy if you ignored the fact that he was a stone-cold killer. "You've done pretty well so far."

He looked delighted. "I know, right? It's all been improvisation and so far, so good." He held up his hand with crossed fingers and grinned at me, his eyes glittering. I shivered, even though I was sweating in my plastic cocoon. How could I not have noticed that he was completely insane?

"You fooled everyone," I croaked.

"Not you though, right?" He hitched his own chair closer and he looked . . . excited. "So what was it? What gave you your first clue?"

If he wanted to talk, I was willing to indulge him. At least while we were talking, he wasn't killing me.

"I think it was when I found Matthew so badly injured and he said, 'coffee, black.' That's what he said to you that morning you brought him his coffee, remember?"

His face was screwed up in concentration. He started to shake his head, then stopped, his eyes wide. "Oh, I remember. But how did that help you?" He looked annoyed. "Don't lie to me."

"It was just the first tiny thing," I said hastily. "To everyone else, he always said 'black, no sugar.' It probably doesn't sound like much, but—"

"No, no, it's your story, and that was really smart." He beamed at me. "What else?"

Oh god, he looked like a kid waiting for the next chapter in a bedtime story. "Well, there were the nuns' habits." I decided to keep Father Martin out of it; God knew if he'd be in danger, too. "I don't know much about nuns, but I heard somewhere that they were Olivetans. I was curious, so I looked them up online, and it said they wore white habits, not black."

He tipped his head to one side and inspected me through narrowed eyes. "That's not true. You saw the photos plenty of times, and they were wearing black. Who told you?"

He grabbed hold of my chair and shook it fiercely back and forth, leaning into me, his face inches from mine, his breath hot and his expression enraged. My head flopped from side to side. I was afraid my neck would break. Then he suddenly stopped, stepped back, and resumed his friendly, conversational tone. He sat down again and looked reflectively up at the ceiling. "Never mind; we'll come back to that. What else?"

I cleared my throat. "I'm thirsty; can I have a drink of water?"

He unscrewed the cap of a bottle of water from the shelf next to my head. "You should have said something sooner. Here." He tipped it slowly into my mouth, and I took several large gulps. "There. Better?" he said kindly. I nodded. "Now, what else?"

My stomach lurched. I wasn't sure I could keep the water down and talk to that weirdly pleasant face at the same time. "Can you tell me your part of the story? I'm really interested."

He preened slightly, which was terrifying to watch. "I'll tell you my part, and then you can tell me more, okay?" I nodded. "Where shall I start?"

"Tell me about Katrina."

"Good. Good. That's the start, I guess. She asked me to set up the kids' home for her. I made sure I was the go-between with the diocese over there. It was pretty simple to tell them she was still considering the project, and telling Katrina it was all moving ahead. It took organization, but I'm careful, and you can get just about anything done in Kiev if you know the right people and you have a little money to spend. She was always telling me I was wasting my education, so I decided to show her." He giggled. "She paid quarterly into an account I set up, and the money came out gradually over the course of the year, apparently for things to maintain the house, feed and clothe the poor little orphans. Photos were simple—just some local kids and women who dressed up and posed for photos for the equivalent of twenty bucks. It was easy. Katrina left all the details to me, and I gave her copies of the same reports I was supposedly sending to the diocese—with spreadsheets and everything." He giggled again, which was just—unsettling.

"What went wrong?"

"That stupid new assistant sent a report about St. Olga's to the archdiocese for real; used her initiative, Katrina said. Some priest read it and left a message for Katrina that there was no St. Olga's. I always kept track of everything going in and out of Katrina's e-mail accounts, so I had his name and I was able to find him and kill him. Hit-and-run that time. After that, I figured it was best to make them all different, you know? So it would take anyone who was looking longer to put everything together." His gentle face looked almost dreamy.

"When I got back from Kiev, Katrina was suspicious because the priest hadn't followed up, and then she found out he'd died. She made some phone calls and whatever she found out, she realized things weren't right. She was a smart cookie, you know? She should have trusted me." He shook a gentle, admonishing finger in my face. "I got in the car so she could scream at me, but it didn't last long. She hated leaving that car on the street—God, she was so pissed when her contractor broke through into some buried creek or something, and the wine cellar flooded." He giggled again. It was chilling.

"What happened with the priest who came here?"

He shifted forward in his seat and said, as if to reassure me, "He wasn't suspicious of me. He was just looking for answers, and my name was in Katrina's obituary, as her survivor. We met at some pizza place in North Beach and I invited him to come up to Katrina's place for a drink. He told me how his priest friend in Kiev had told him the odd story of the nonexistent orphanage. Then when he was run over and killed, I guess this priest got suspicious. I played it puzzled and then outraged, and said we needed to get to the bottom of it. And then I asked if he wanted to see

Katrina's wine collection." He gave another of those little giggles.

"For an old guy he was pretty tough, but with the roofie and him not being in the best shape, I snatched his key ring, and it had this handy little point, so I jammed it in his neck. Then I chopped off his fingers, too." He actually shuddered. "He said he was from South America, and I read once about these South American gangs who did that, and I thought it might point the cops away from the reason he was here."

I was having real difficulty keeping my eyes open. I drifted off then jerked awake, terrified he'd killed me. I tried to think of something to keep him talking. "Why didn't you leave him down here? Why did you take him over to the vacant building?"

He explained, patiently, as if I should have thought of it myself. "He'd started to smell, and with it being Katrina's building, I mean, nobody knew this place was here except me, and I had all her keys, and with the blood and everything it would point the finger right at me. Point the finger!" He giggled again. "That's funny. Anyway, I left him down here for a couple of days, while I figured something out. Then I remembered the empty buildings. There was an old shopping cart across the street, and I grabbed it. That guy, Matthew, saw me returning it, and he got upset, kept mumbling and muttering, 'thief, thief, thief.' You know how he was. I got him settled down. I told him I'd found it down the block and I was bringing it back to him. You know the funny part?"

He looked at me brightly, waiting for a response, so I forced out, "No, what was funny?"

"That guy, the guy everyone calls Matthew? His name

is Pavel Matthew. He was her *son,* can you believe it?" He
burst into loud, genuine laughter. "I know, right? You look
so shocked! He was in line to inherit everything. She had
the trust set up and everything, so her estate didn't have to
go through probate. She made me swear not to tell anyone.
Her will said if he died first everything went to St. Olga's,
so that was a no-brainer. Easy to find his dump of a place
and push one of those piles of crap onto him. All I have to
do now is wait for him to die because he's kind of sickly
anyway, or help him along if he gets out of the hospital. I'll
produce a DNA sample to prove the relationship, get everything transferred over to St. Olga's. Easy-peasy, lemon
squeezy. Okay, your turn."

My mind was no clearer; the nausea was getting worse.
Matthew, Pavel—living in the gutter where his mother
parked her $100,000 automobile. Gavin's eyes narrowed.
"Why are you crying? Stop crying! Stop it! Stop it!"

My head rolled forward, and I tried to think of something, anything, that would turn me back into an apprecia-
tive audience. He snatched at my hair and pulled back my
head. I blurted out, "Did you break into Katrina's office?"

He drew in a breath and said admiringly, "That was
you? Oh, wow, you really had me going. I had to see if there
was anything to point the finger at me. Get it? So come on,
your turn now. What else gave me away?"

"You said you didn't know anything about computers,
and for a while I thought it would stop you from doing all
the sophisticated financial setup for the orphanage. But
then I found out you went to a Swiss university which is the
equivalent of MIT, where you earned a degree in computer
science."

He sat back. "That's amazing. And that was all?"

"Basically, yes," I said. Added to the nuns' outfits and Matthew's—Pavel's—coffee habits, I guess it wasn't much, and I'd had little more than suspicion when I'd gone to talk to him. He'd confirmed everything else.

"Well, I'm impressed." He sat back in his chair and inspected me shrewdly. "The way I see it, you only figured it out while we were talking today. I mean, that's why I roofie'd you, so I don't guess you shared this with anyone. I'm sorry, but I have to leave you again. I'll be back later, and then we'll see. Do you want another drink of water before I go?"

My mouth and throat felt parched. "Yes, please."

He picked up the bottle again and held it to my mouth while I took two gulps. "There's a little sleeping magic in that one," he said. "You rest. I have to go now. I have some arrangements to make," he said apologetically, as if I were going to miss his company. "I may be a while, but I'll see you later," he added, before he climbed up the stairs, opened a trapdoor on some sort of hydraulic lift, and disappeared.

I tried to wriggle out of my bubble wrap and duct tape shroud, but it was hideously effective, and I was in real danger of knocking the chair over. With me completely immobilized, the six inches of water on the ground was probably enough to drown in. I shook my head every few minutes for a while to stave off sleep, but I could feel my eyes getting heavy and I finally closed them, thankful for the oblivion that awaited.

CHAPTER THIRTY-NINE

Hours or days later, something was banging, loudly, overhead. The noise reverberated through the wine cellar, and I thought my head would split open. I'd heard of sound waves killing dolphins; is that what was happening?

"Hey!" I yelled, or at least tried to. It came out as a barely audible whisper. I coughed and tried again. "Hey, down here!" After one final bang, the noise stopped. A large square of light appeared above my head.

"She's down here!" I squinted against the light and heard an excited babble of voices.

"Jesus Christ!" That sounded like Ben.

"Ben?" I croaked. I couldn't see anything except the light.

"It's okay, I've got you."

I leaned into him. He smelled like Ben. "Be careful. He'll be back," I whispered. "He's insane."

"Theophania, my dear. Hold still."

"Grandfather?"

I could feel something being done to the bubble wrap locking me to the chair at the back, and then I felt it loosen and I fell forward into Ben's arms. He pulled me free of the chair and, when my legs wouldn't support me, bent down to pick me up instead. He carried me up into the garage, where he laid me down on the floor next to a sledgehammer and the battered remains of the trapdoor. It felt blissful to stretch out after hours of being cramped rigid on that bloody chair. The garage door was open, the air smelled fresh, and since the sky was faintly gray in the east, the night had passed and a new day was upon us.

"We've got medics coming," Ben said to me.

I nodded. "Okay," I whispered and struggled to sit up. "I'm really glad to see you. Will you help me to stand up?" I put my arms around his neck and let him pull me to my feet.

"Okay?" he said before he relaxed his hold, and I nodded. My mind felt weird and everything hurt, but I felt better standing, even on trembling legs. I couldn't talk above a whisper.

And then, with no warning, came an outraged scream, "No! No! No! No!", and Gavin reappeared, crashing into one of the people who'd created a protective phalanx around me. It wasn't until he screamed again and flew through the air to land on his back, more or less at my feet, that I recognized Valentina and a classic jujitsu, over-the-shoulder throw. She knelt on his chest, but he wasn't struggling. In fact, he was completely still, and I looked with some alarm at the growing blood pool on the ground around his head.

"Head wounds bleed," Valentina said to me, coolly efficient, as she tied his hands together with—were those zip ties? Who carried zip ties around? And then I remembered why I shouldn't be so surprised. She half-turned and zip-tied his ankles together, too. "He'll probably be fine when he wakes up."

"That was—very impressive," I croaked. She shrugged.

From the corner of my eye I caught a glimpse of another familiar face, and I turned to look. Jacob made me an odd little salute and a rubber-faced smile Grandfather was standing there, too, speaking on his phone, looking pale and resolute.

"How did you all find me?"

"Apparently, you've had a sort of honor guard keeping an eye on you, thanks to your grandfather's friends," Ben said.

I tottered over to Gavin, who was starting to come around, and kicked him, hard, in the ribs. It probably would have hurt him more if I hadn't been barefoot. As it was I dislocated my baby toe, and an EMT had to put it back in place, but I didn't care.

Valentina shrugged out of her jacket. I thought she meant to use it under Gavin's head, and she was holding it out to me before I realized I was in my bra. Not a sports bra, either, but a frothy little confection of purple satin and lace. I refused to be embarrassed. I was part of a grand tradition of fierce women in underwear: Me, Wonder Woman, and Brandi Chastain.

"What's goin' on?" I heard Nat's voice before he pushed his way through. "Have you found her? What are you doin' out here in your scanties?" he added, catching sight of me and sounding slightly scandalized. He frowned. "Is it Mardi Gras?" Before I could answer, he looked down at Gavin, still flat-out and bleeding. I knew what was coming next. Nat's eyes fluttered, and he went down like a house of cards, falling against Grandfather, who put out an arm to hold him up until he and Jacob eased him to the floor and propped him gently against the wall.

"He's been frantic," Ben said quietly to me, looking over at Grandfather and Nat. "Both of them," he added.

I started to pull on the jacket, but the sleeve scraped

painfully against the burns on my arm. I pulled it around my shoulders instead.

Ben had a supportive arm at my back. He nuzzled my ear. "Nice bra," he whispered.

Gavin was taken to St. Francis by the EMTs, who arrived more or less at the same time as Inspector Lichlyter. I was afraid she wouldn't take me seriously when I explained why he would need a heavy police guard—less for his own protection than for everyone else's. I wasn't sure exactly what was required to get someone called a serial killer, but I felt three murders (nearly four, if we counted the attempt on Janine's life) and a kidnapping qualified him for special handling. Somewhat to my surprise, she agreed. She even said, as the EMTs were treating my burned arm, that I was probably in shock, and she could wait a day to interview me. She and Grandfather exchanged nods as she was leaving.

The guest room door burst open as Ben and I reached the top of my apartment stairs, and Davo thundered down the hallway and snatched me off my feet in a painful bear hug. "Jeez, Theo, where the hell were you? We had half the fuc—flaming neighborhood hunting for you. Your granddad told me to go to bed a couple of hours ago; I got exams today or I'd have kept looking. Damn, I'm glad you're okay. You know you smell really weird, right? You should get a shower."

He wasn't wrong. Ben wrapped my bandaged arm in a plastic bag so I could stand under blissfully hot water and sluice off the last eighteen hours. We found a note from Nat written a few hours earlier, saying he'd walked and fed Lucy and I had better CALL ASAP!!!

Lucy woke up, stayed in the bathroom with me, and

licked the water off my lower legs when I got out of the shower.

I was two steps into the bedroom, wrapped in a bathrobe and looking forward to falling face down on my bed, when Ben followed me in and said, "Okay, there's good news and bad news."

"Oh God, really?"

"Well, no. It's the same news. I guess it depends how you look at it. Nat called. Everyone's at The Coffee, and they all want to know how you're doing, and Nat says if you go there now and let them see you, it will probably save you a hundred separate conversations later. Your call."

I dropped my head against his chest. "I have to go, don't I?"

"Afraid so."

"You coming?"

"I won't move from your side."

"Okay, then."

It was only when I got there and saw everyone making coffee and heating up croissants and taking up seats at the tables that I realized how many rescuers I had. They were all in the middle of a chatty debrief, moving from table to table and sharing bits of the story they might have missed, and I got the feeling that they were ready to do the search and rescue all over again.

I got a round of applause as we arrived, and while I was still laughing through my surprise and taking a bow, I saw Grandfather with Valentina and went over to them. Someone handed me a chocolate croissant.

Grandfather looked almost gray with weariness. "How are you feeling, my dear?"

"Surprisingly well," I said, chewing happily on my croissant. "I probably have about twenty minutes before I fall asleep standing up, and until that happens"—I leaned over and put my arms around him—"thank you for taking such good care of me."

He gave my back a few stiff little pats and then suddenly pulled me close into a real hug. Chairs at a nearby table magically emptied. He guided me into one of them and Valentina into another, before he and Ben took seats themselves.

"Sergei's visit alarmed me, Theophania. At first I thought he had exposed you to danger from unknown sources, and I asked the members"—he hesitated—"my friends to keep watch to see if they saw any signs of interest in you. When Sergei was killed, and the threat was more localized, more personal, if you will, they were kind enough to continue their vigil."

"Grandfather—it was you and Sergei at the Venus de Milo, right?" He pursed his lips and reluctantly nodded. "Do you know who he met in the pizza place across from the club?"

"At the time he said only that he was meeting the young relative of a friend to discuss—wine, I think." He shook his head slightly. "I paid too little attention; I thought he was planning a trip to the wine country." He snorted. "It seems fairly clear now that it was Melnik. I—"

"We are very sorry to have fallen down on the job at a critical juncture," Valentina interrupted as he struggled. I liked her for it. "We saw you go into the coffee shop, but he took you out through the rear door. We thought you were in no danger in broad daylight. We didn't plan for that eventuality."

Jacob came over and took up the story, which had gathered a fascinated audience. "We thought he must have brought you to where we eventually found you. We searched through the building and even looked in the garage, but it seemed empty."

Valentina added, "We didn't see the special trapdoor. It was covered in boxes and the same color as the floor—ach." She waved an irritable hand. "We should have noticed, but we did not."

Jacob went on, "Then we searched the two empty buildings, because of course we knew he had made use of them before. Your friends Dr. and Mrs. Talbot helped us to search, and they were as tireless as one could hope."

"Professor D'Allessio organized the Garden Gnomes—is that right? Garden Gnomes?" He looked around for confirmation, and two of the nearby Gnomes cheerfully waved mugs of coffee at him. "Yes, and they searched the gardens and the toolshed and small areas behind the buildings, and a lot of garages."

"We were sure, you see, that you had to be somewhere close by, because he couldn't have carried you very far without attracting notice."

"And then Nathaniel insisted that we search everywhere again, and in particular he thought we should look for a wine cellar. When we came back to search again we were able to see that there was, indeed, a sort of trapdoor set flush into the floor. We had to get heavy tools to break our way in. And here you are!"

Father Martin showed up and, embarrassingly, led a prayer for my safe delivery. Then he told me that Matthew was awake and insisting that he had to leave the hospital before someone stole his stuff. "I've invited him to stay at the rectory for the time being; I can't let him go back to that horrific squat." I thought—but didn't say—that Matthew would soon be able to buy a whole lot of better stuff. He was going to need a protector and some advisors, and I wondered what happened to an estate whose executor was very likely criminally insane. Matthew's inheritance could be eroded completely by expensive legal fees. Evidently understanding some of the cause of my agitation, Ben squeezed my hand. "Huh," as Davo would say. Matthew could be in luck; I knew a lawyer who might work pro *bono*.

Angela Lacerda, still wearing her lemon-colored socks, introduced me to "My fiancé, Jason." He was incredibly good-looking in an old-fashioned, movie-star way, with dark hair, broad shoulders, a smile for everyone, and a rather doe-like expression. His arm was around her. She was wearing her engagement ring again. "Jason and I are setting up a new business." She beamed at me as Jason smiled happily and squeezed her shoulder. "Lacerda Property Management."

"You've got a great start," I said.

"Angie's a great businesswoman," Jason said proudly. "Latte, Angie?" he said.

"Please hon, that would be great." He set off toward the counter.

"OMG, he's gorgeous," I whispered to her

Her eyes went wide. "I know, right?" she whispered back. "Lucky I'm smart enough for us both." And she snorted.

We both watched him go in a sort of trance. After a few seconds Ben cleared his throat. "His family is okay with—everything?" I asked her hurriedly.

She narrowed her eyes at me and flicked a glance at Ben. "Jason and I have no secrets now. We decided his family doesn't need to know everything. And we're moving up the wedding." She said her goodbyes to Ben and me and followed Jason to the counter, where two girls from the neighborhood were flirting with him. He looked clueless, but she extracted him efficiently and ordered their coffee drinks in go-cups.

The impromptu party continued, but gradually people left, either to get some sleep or to get ready for work. Haruto spent an hour helping Nat behind the counter, and I could see another part-time job in the offing. Davo stopped by on his way to school and said, since I hadn't left him a lunch, he needed a ten-dollar advance on his wages. He hugged me so hard I thought my bones would break.

No one left without giving me a hug or a kiss. Sabina and Kurt appeared. Sabina burst into tears and wouldn't stop hugging me. Kurt mumbled something about being glad to see me safe and was eventually able to persuade Sabina that I could be safely left with Ben and my grandfather, and the two dozen other people still hanging around.

Grandfather, Valentina, and Jacob were chatting quietly—with Zane, I was astonished to see—and I assumed that the two strangers who joined them were fellow members of their exclusive little club. Zane, still wearing his skull necklace, broke off his conversation with them to raise a mug in my direction. I looked over to where Nat was making his umpteenth pot of coffee, and I gave him wide eyes and lifted eyebrows as I tipped my head in Zane's direction. Nat winked at me, and I decided it was a conversation for another day. I went over to him. "Is that coffee fair trade, organic, and cruelty-free? And are these napkins a hundred percent post-consumer recycled, renewable—"

"Don't joke," he said, turning to face me with a teary laugh. "This has been the worst night of my life." I went around the counter and walked into a hug.

"I hear it was your idea to look for a wine cellar."

"Yeah, well, it was a dumb idea until it wasn't."

"You know you gave me one of my big clues to catch that miserable bastard, with how good you were at remembering everyone's coffee orders?"

"I did? Too bad he caught you first."

"Look, I made you a new logo." I handed him a paper napkin on which I'd drawn a huge mosquito and printed *GNAT'S JAVA HOUSE.*

"Not gonna happen, English, and I told you dire consequences will ensue."

"Can I tell Ben?"

"No!"

"I love you. Thanks for saving me. Again."

"I love you, too. Is Ben gonna take you home now so I can get some peace and quiet?"

Ben came over, having left us to our moment, and wordlessly stuck out his hand. Nat shook it, and that was that. Men.

When Ben and I got home, we were, as the saying goes, alone at last, and while I eventually got to sleep, it wasn't our first thought as we walked in the door. Later, I asked him sleepily when he had to leave.

"I'm taking some vacation time," he said.

I opened one eye. "How long?"

"A month. I'm not letting you out of my sight. We can even go away if you want. Rome? London? Sonoma?"

"Not London."

"I thought you might say that. Or we can stay here. We'll have time to talk, time to get to know each other without the Army or work or random police investigations."

"It sounds . . . wonderful." It did sound wonderful. I snuggled deeper under our duvet and felt myself drifting to sleep, so I almost missed Ben getting the last word.

"We can talk about London, too."

ACKNOWLEDGMENTS

To the cat burglar who stole my manuscript and who embroiled me in my very own mystery novel.

To the anonymous DNA technician who proved conclusively that burglars are burglars because they're not smart enough to do anything else.

To Detectives Danielle Whitefield and Evelyn Gorfido.

To my editor, Kelley Ragland, who gave me the time and space to rewrite the novel from scratch.

To McGarvey Black, who read parts of the novel while it was being rebuilt, and who said encouraging things and made helpful suggestions.

To the many friends who said, often in so many words, "You can do this."

Thank you.